The Second
VIRAGO BOOK
of FAIRY TALES

The Second
VIRAGO BOOK
of FAIRY TALES

edited by
ANGELA CARTER

illustrated by CORINNA SARGOOD

Published by VIRAGO PRESS Limited 1992
20–23 Mandela Street, Camden Town, London NW1 0HQ

Reprinted 1992

A CIP catalogue record for this book is available from the British Library

Typeset by Goodfellow & Egan
Printed and bound in Great Britain by
Mackays of Chatham PLC, Chatham, Kent

Designed by Lone Morton

Contents

4. MOTHERS AND DAUGHTERS

5. MARRIED WOMEN

6. USEFUL STORIES

Acknowledgements

Permission to reproduce these fairy tales is gratefully acknowledged to the following: Pantheon Books, a division of Random House, Inc. for 'The Old Woman Against the Stream' from *Norwegian Folktales* by Christen Asbjornsen and Jorgen Moe and 'A Fable of a Bird and Her Chicks' from *Yiddish Folktales* by Beatrice Silverman Wienreich; Constable Publishers for 'The Werefox' and 'The Mirror' from *Chinese Ghouls and Goblins* by G. Willoughby-Mead, copyright © 1924; The American Folklore Society for 'Old Foster', from *Journal of American Folklore* XXXVIII (1925) and 'The Untrue Wife's Song from *Journal of American Folklore* XLVII (1934); The University Press of Kentucky for 'The Telltale Lilac Bush' from *The Telltale Lilac Bush and Other West Virginian Ghost Tales* by Ruth Ann Musick, copyright © 1965; University of Chicago Press for 'Pretty Maid Ibronka', 'The Witches' Piper, 'The Midwife and the Frog' and 'A Stroke of Luck' from *Folktales of Hungary* by Degh © 1956 by University of Chicago; 'The Greenish Bird' from *Folktales of Mexico* by Paredes © 1970 by University of Chicago; 'Resaon to Beat your Wife' from *Folktales of Egypt* by El Shamy © 1980 by University of Chicago; 'The Witchball', 'Father and Mother Both "Fast" ' and 'The Beans in the Quart Jar' from *Buying the Wind* by Dorson © 1964 by University of Chicago; Jonathan Cape and Basic Books for 'The Height of Purple Passion' from *The Rationale of Dirty Jokes*; Stanford University Press for 'The Three Lovers'; Columbia University Press, New York, for 'The Sleeping Prince', 'The Letter Trick' and 'Spreading the Fingers' from *Suriname Folklore*, by Melville J. Herskovits and Frances S. Herskovits, © 1936 and C. W. Daniel Company for 'Vasilissa the Fair', 'Enchanter and Enchantress', 'The Little Old Woman with Five Cows', 'Story of a Bird Woman', 'The Crafty Woman', 'The Dog's Snout People' from *Siberian and Other Folktales: Primitive Literature of the Empire of the Tsars*, collected and translated by C. Fillingham Coxwell © 1925; University of Calfornia Press for 'Šāhīn', 'Tănjur, Tănjur', 'The Woman Who Married Her Son' and 'The Seven Leavenings' from *Speak Bird, Speak Again: Palestinian Arab Folktales* collected and edited by Ibrahim Muhawi and Sharif Kanann, copyright © 1988 The Regents of the University of California; Oxford University Press for 'The Frog Maiden' from *Burmese Folktales* by Maun Htin Aung, Calcutta, 1948; Holmes and Meier publishers for 'Diirawic and her Incestuous Brother', 'Achol and her Wild Mother', 'Achol and her Adoptive Lioness-Mother', 'Duang and his Wild Wife' from *Dinka Folktales, African Stories from Sudan* by Francis Mading Deng, (New York, Africana publishing Company, a division of Holmes & Meier, 1974), copyright © 1974 by Francis Mading Deng; Pantheon Books, a division of Random House, Inc. for 'Salt, Sauce and Spice, Onion Leaves, Pepper and Drippings' and 'Tale of an Old Woman, from *African Folktales* by Roger D. Abrahams copyright © 1983 Roger D. Abrahams; Popular Publications for 'The Orphan' from *Tales of Old Malawi*, edited by E. Singano & A.A. Roscoe, 1977, 1986.

Every effort has been made to trace the copyright holders in all copyright material in this book. The publisher regrets if there has been any oversight and suggests that Virago be contacted in any such event.

Introduction

Italo Calvino, the Italian writer and fabulist and collector of fairy tales believed strongly in the connection between fantasy and reality: 'I am accustomed to consider literature a search for knowledge,' he wrote. 'Faced with [the] precarious existence of tribal life, the shaman responded by ridding his body of weight and flying to another world, another level of perception, where he could find the strength to change the face of reality.'[1] Angela Carter wouldn't have made the same wish with quite such a straight face, but her combination of fantasy and revolutionary longings corresponds to the flight of Calvino's shaman. She possessed the enchanter's lightness of mind and wit – it's interesting that she explored, in her last two novels, images of winged women. Fevvers, her aërialiste heroine of *Nights at the Circus*, may have hatched like a bird, and in *Wise Children*, the twin Chance sisters play various fairies or feathered creatures, from their first foot on the stage as child stars to their dalliance in Hollywood for a spectacular extravaganza of *A Midsummer Night's Dream*.

Fairy tales also offered her a means of flying – of finding and telling an alternative story, of shifting something in the mind, just as so many fairy tale characters shift something in their shape. She wrote her own – the dazzling, erotic variations on Perrault's Mother Goose Tales and other familiar stories in *The Bloody Chamber* – where she lifted Beauty and Red Riding Hood and Bluebeard's last wife out of the pastel nursery into the labyrinth of female desire. She had always read very widely in folklore from all over the world, and compiled her first collection, *The Virago Book of Fairy Tales*, two years ago; this second volume is being published after her death, in February 1992, from cancer.

She found the stories in sources ranging from Siberia to Suriname, and she arranged them into sections in a sequence that runs from one tale of female heroic endeavour to another about generosity rewarded. There are few fairies, in the sense of sprites, but the stories move in fairyland, not the prettified, kitschified, Victorians' elfland, but the darker, dream realm of spirits and tricks, magical, talking animals, riddles and spells. In 'The Twelve Wild Ducks', the opening tale, the heroine vows not to speak or to laugh or to cry until she has rescued her brothers from their enchanted animal forms. The issue of women's speech, of women's noise, of their/our clamour and laughter and weeping and shouting and hooting runs through all Angela Carter's writings, and informed her love of the folk tale. In *The Magic Toyshop* the lovely Aunt Margaret cannot speak because she is strangled by the silver torque which the malign puppetmaster her husband has made her as a bridal gift. Folklore, on the other hand, speaks volumes about women's experience, and women are often the storytellers, as in one of the dashingly comic and highly Carteresque tales in this collection ('Reason to Beat Your Wife').

Angela Carter's partisan feeling for women, which burns in all her work, never led her to any conventional form of feminism; but she continues here one of her original and effective strategies, snatching out of the jaws of misogyny itself, 'useful stories' for women. Her essay 'The Sadeian Woman' (1979) found in Sade a liberating teacher of the male–female status quo and made him illuminate the far reaches of women's polymorphous desires; here she turns topsy-turvy some cautionary folk tales and shakes out the fear and dislike of women they once expressed to create a new set of values, about strong, outspoken, zestful, sexual women who can't be kept down (see 'The Old Woman Against the Stream'; 'The Letter Trick'). In *Wise Children*, she created a heroine, Dora Chance, who's a showgirl, a soubrette, a vaudeville dancer, one of the low, the despised, the invisible poor, an old woman who's illegitimate and never married (born the wrong side of the blanket, the wrong side of the tracks), and each of these stigmas is taken up with exuberant relish and scattered in the air like so much wedding confetti.

The last story here, 'Spreading the Fingers', a tough morality tale from Suriname about sharing what one has been given with others, also discloses the high value Angela Carter placed on generosity. She gave herself – her ideas, her wit, her incisive, no-bullshit mind – with open but never sentimental prodigality. Her favourite fairy tale in the first *Virago Book* was a Russian riddle story 'The Wise Little Girl', in which the tsar asks her heroine for the impossible, and she delivers it without batting an eyelid. Angela liked it because it was as satisfying as 'The Emperor's New Clothes', but 'no one was humiliated and everybody gets the prizes'. The story comes in the section called 'Clever Women, Resourceful Girls and Desperate Stratagems', and its heroine is an essential Carter figure, never abashed, nothing daunted, sharp-eared as a vixen and possessed of dry good sense. It's entirely characteristic of Angela's spirit that she should delight in the tsar's confounding, and yet not want him to be humiliated.

She did not have the strength, before she died, to write the introduction she had planned to this volume, but she left four cryptic notes among her papers:

'every real story contains something useful, says Walter Benjamin

the *unperplexedness* of the story

"No one dies so poor that he does not leave something behind," said Pascal.

fairy tales – cunning and high spirits'.

Fragmentary as they are, these phrases convey the Carter philosophy. She was scathing about the contempt the 'educated' can show, when two-thirds of the literature of the world – perhaps more – has been created by the illiterate. She liked the solid common sense of folk tales, the straightforward aims of their protagonists, the simple moral distinctions, and the wily stratagems they suggest. They're tales of the underdog, about cunning and high spirits winning through in the end; they're practical, and they're not high-flown. For a fantasist with wings, Angela kept her eyes on the ground, with reality firmly in her sights. She once remarked, 'A fairy tale is a story where one king goes to another king to borrow a cup of sugar.'

Feminist critics of the genre – especially in the 1970s – jibbed at the socially conventional 'happy endings' of so many stories (for example, 'When she grew up he married her and she became the tsarina'). But Angela knew about satisfaction and pleasure; and at the same time she believed that the goal of fairy tales wasn't 'a conservative one, but a utopian one, indeed a form of heroic optimism – as if to say: One day, we might be happy, even if it won't last.' Her own heroic optimism never failed her – like the spirited heroine of one of her tales, she was resourceful and brave and even funny during the illness which brought about her death. Few writers possess the best qualities of their work; she did, in spades.

Her imagination was dazzling, and through her daring, vertiginous plots, her precise yet wild imagery, her gallery of wonderful bad-good girls, beasts, rogues and other creatures, she causes readers to hold their breath as a mood of heroic optimism forms against the odds. She had the true writer's gift of remaking the world for her readers.

She was a wise child herself, with a mobile face, a mouth which sometimes pursed with irony, and, behind the glasses, a wryness, at times a twinkle, at times a certain dreaminess; with her long, silvery hair and ethereal delivery, she had something of the Faerie Queene about her, except that she was never wispy or fey. And though the narcissism of youth was one of the great themes in her early fiction, she was herself exceptionally un-narcissistic. Her voice was soft, with a storyteller's confidingness, and lively with humour; she spoke with a certain syncopation, as she stopped to think – her thoughts made her the most exhilarating companion, a wonderful talker, who wore her learning and wide reading with lightness, who could express a mischievous insight or a tough judgement with scalpel precision and produce new ideas by the dozen without effort, weaving allusion, quotation, parody and original invention, in a way that echoed her prose style. 'I've got a theory that . . .' she'd say, self-deprecatorily, and then would follow something that no one else had thought of, some sally, some rich paradox that would encapsulate a trend, a moment. She could be Wildean in her quickness and the glancing drollery of her wit. And then she would pass on, sometimes leaving her listeners astonished and stumbling.

Angela Carter was born in May 1940, the daughter of Hugh Stalker, a journalist for the Press Association, who was a Highlander by birth, had served the whole term of the First World War, and had come south to Balham to work. He used to take her to the cinema, to the Tooting Granada, where the glamour of the building (Alhambra-style) and of the movie stars (Jean Simmons in *The Blue Lagoon*) made an impression which lasted – she has written some of the most gaudy, stylish, sexy passages about seduction and female beauty on record; 'snappy' and 'glamorous' are key words of pleasure and praise in her vocabulary. Her mother was from South Yorkshire, on her own mother's side; this grandmother was tremendously important to Angela: 'every word and gesture of hers displayed a natural dominance, a native savagery, and I am very grateful for all that, now, though the core of steel was a bit inconvenient when I was looking for boyfriends in the South'. Angela's mother was a scholarship girl, and 'liked things to be nice'; she worked as a cashier in Selfridge's in the 1920s, and had passed exams and wanted the same for her daughter. Angela went to Streatham grammar school, and for a time entertained a fancy of becoming an Egyptologist, but left school to take up an apprenticeship on the *Croydon Advertiser* arranged by her father.

As a reporter on the news desk, she had trouble with her imagination (she used to like the Russian storyteller's formula, 'The story is over, I can't lie any more') and switched to writing a record column as well as features. She got married for the first time when she was twenty-one, to a chemistry teacher at Bristol technical college, and began studying English at Bristol University in the same year, choosing to concentrate on medieval literature, which was then definitely uncanonical. Its forms – from allegory to tales – as well as its heterogeneity of tone – from bawdy to romance – can be found everywhere in her own *oeuvre*; Chaucer and Boccaccio remained among her favourite writers. She also remembered those days, in a recent interview with her great friend Susannah Clapp, for the talking in cafés 'to situationists and anarchists . . . It was the Sixties . . . I was very very unhappy but I was perfectly happy at the same time.'

During this period, she first began developing her interest in folklore, discovering with her husband the folk and jazz music scenes of the 1960s. (At a more recent, staid, meeting of the Folklore Society, she fondly recalled those counter-cultural days when a member would attend with a pet raven on one shoulder.) She began writing fiction: in her twenties she published four novels (*Shadow Dance*, 1966; *The Magic Toyshop*, 1967; *Several Perceptions*, 1968; *Heroes and Villains*, 1969; as well as a story for children, *Miss Z, the Dark Young Lady*, 1970). She was heaped with praise and prizes; one of them – the Somerset Maugham – stipulated travel, and she obeyed, using the money to run away from her husband ('I think Maugham would have approved'). She chose Japan, because she revered the films of Kurosawa.

Japan marks an important transition; she stayed for two years, from 1971. Her fiction till then, including the ferocious, taut elegy *Love* (1971; revised 1987), showed her baroque powers of invention, and her fearless confrontation of erotic violence, of female as well as male sexuality: she marked out her territory early, and men and women clash on it, often bloodily, and the humour is mostly of the gallows variety. From the beginning, her prose was magnificently rich, intoxicated with words – a vivid and sensual lexicon of bodily attributes, minerals, flora and fauna – and she dealt in strangeness. But Japan gave her a way of looking at her own culture which intensified her capacity to conjure strangeness out of the familiar. She also deepened her contact with the Surrealist movement at this time, through French exiles from *les évènements* of '68 who had fetched up in Japan. On her return, she examined various English sacred cows as well as the style of the times (from scarlet lipstick to stockings in D.H. Lawrence) in her wonderfully pungent series of articles for *New Society* (collected as *Nothing Sacred* in 1982).

Two novels arose from her time in Japan, though they do not deal with Japan directly: *The Infernal Desire Machines of Doctor Hoffman* (1972) and *The Passion of New Eve* (1977), in which contemporary conflicts are transmuted into bizarre, multiple, picaresque allegories. Though she never won the bestseller fortunes of some of her contemporaries (she would reflect ruefully that it was still a Boys' Club out there, and did not really mind much), and was never selected for one of the major prizes, she enjoyed greater international esteem: her name tells from Denmark to Australia, and she was repeatedly invited to teach – accepting invitations from Sheffield (1976–78), Brown University, Providence (1980–81), the University of Adelaide (1984), and the University of East Anglia (1984–87). She helped change the course of postwar writing in English – her influence reaches from Salman Rushdie to Jeanette Winterson to American fabulists like Robert Coover.

Distance from England helped her lay bare women's collusion with their own subjection. In the new collection of her criticism, *Expletives Deleted*, she remembers, 'I spent a good many years being told what I ought to think, and how I ought to behave . . . because I was a woman . . . but then I stopped listening to them [men] and . . . I started answering back.'[2] Angela was never someone to offer an easy answer, and in her frankness she was important to the feminist movement: she liked to quote, semi-ironically, 'Dirty work – but someone has to do it' when talking about facing hard truths, and she would say of someone, in a spirit of approval 's/he doesn't temper the wind to the new-shorn lamb'. Her publisher and friend Carmen Callil published her in Virago and her presence here since the start of the house helped establish a woman's voice in literature as special, as *parti pris*, as a crucial instrument in the forging of an identity for post-imperial, hypocritical, fossilised Britain. For in spite of her keen-eyed, even cynical grasp of reality, Angela Carter has always believed in change: she'd refer to her 'naive leftie-ism', but she never let go of it.

The American critic Susan Suleiman has celebrated Angela Carter's fiction as truly breaking new ground for women by occupying the male voice of narrative authority and at the same time impersonating it to the point of parody, so that the rules are changed and the dreams become unruly, transformed, open to 'the multiplication of narrative possibilities', themselves a promise of a possibly different future; the novels also 'expand our notions of what it is possible to dream in the domain of sexuality, criticizing all dreams that are too narrow'.[3] Angela's favourite icon of the feminine was Lulu, in Wedekind's play, and her favourite star was Louise Brooks who played her in *Pandora's Box*; Louise/Lulu was hardly someone who rejected traditional femaleness, but rather took it to such extremes that its nature was transformed. 'Lulu's character is very attractive to me,' she would say dryly, and she borrowed from it to create her wanton, ribald and feisty heroines of the boards in *Wise Children*. Lulu never ingratiated herself, never sought fame, or fortune, and suffered neither guilt nor remorse. According to Angela, 'her particular quality is, she makes being polymorphously perverse look like the only way to be'. If she had had a daughter, she once said, she would have called her Lulu.

She liked to refer to her opinions as 'classic GLC' but in spite of these demurrals she was an original and committed political thinker too. *Wise Children* (1989) was born out of her democratic and socialist utopianism, her affirmation of 'low' culture, of the rude health of popular language and humour as a long-lasting, effective means of survival: her Shakespeare (the novel contains almost all his characters and their plots in one form or another) isn't a poet for the élite, but an imagination springing out of folklore, with energy and know-how.

She found happiness with Mark Pearce, who was training to become a primary schoolteacher when she became ill. She often spoke of the radiance of children, their unutterable beauty and their love; their son Alexander was born in 1983.

Sometimes, in the case of a great writer, it's easy to lose sight of the pleasure they give, as critics search for meaning and value, influence and importance; Angela Carter loved cinema and vaudeville and songs and the circus, and she herself could entertain like no other. She included a story from Kenya in *The Virago Book of Fairy Tales* about a sultana who is withering away while a poor man's wife is kept happy because her husband feeds her 'meat of the tongue' – stories, jokes, ballads. These are what make women thrive, the story says; they are also what Angela Carter gave so generously to make others thrive. *Wise Children* ends with the words, 'What a joy it is to dance and sing!' That she should not have thrived herself is sad beyond words.

Since her death, tributes have filled the papers and the airwaves. She would have been astonished by the attention, and pleased. It did not come to her in her lifetime, not with such whole-heartedness. It's partly a tribute to her potency that while she was alive people felt discomfited by her, that her wit and witchiness and subversiveness made her hard to handle, like some wonderful beast of the kind she enjoyed in fairy tales. Her friends were lucky knowing her, and her readers too. We have been left a feast and she laid it out with 'spread fingers' for us to share.

Marina Warner, 1992

1. Italo Calvino, *Six Memos for the Next Millennium*, trans. William Weaver (London, 1992), p. 26.
2. Angela Carter, *Expletives Deleted* (London, 1992), p. 5.
3. Susan Rubin Suleiman, *Subversive Intent: Gender, Politics and the Avant-Garde* (Harvard, 1990), pp. 136–40.

This introduction contains material from Marina Warner's obituary of Angela Carter which appeared in the Independent *18 February 1992.*

Part One

STRONG MINDS AND LOW CUNNING

The Twelve Wild Ducks

(Norwegian)

ONCE on a time there was a queen who was out driving, when there had been a new fall of snow in the winter; but when she had gone a little way, she began to bleed at the nose, and had to get out of her sledge. And so, as she stood there, leaning against the fence, and saw the red blood on the white snow, she fell a-thinking how she had twelve sons and no daughter, and she said to herself –

'If I only had a daughter as white as snow and as red as blood, I shouldn't care what became of all my sons.'

But the words were scarce out of her mouth before an old witch of the Trolls came up to her.

'A daughter you shall have,' she said, 'and she shall be as white as snow, and as red as blood; and your sons shall be mine, but you may keep them till the babe is christened.'

So when the time came the queen had a daughter, and she was as white as snow, and as red as blood, just as the Troll had promised, and so they called her 'Snow-white and Rosy-red'. Well, there was great joy at the king's court, and the queen was as glad as glad could be; but when what she had promised to the old witch came into her mind, she sent for a silversmith, and bade him make twelve silver spoons, one for each prince, and after that she bade him make one more, and that she gave to Snow-white and Rosy-red. But as soon as ever the princess was christened, the princes were turned into twelve wild ducks, and flew away. They never saw them again – away they went, and away they stayed.

So the princess grew up, and she was both tall and fair, but she was often so strange and sorrowful, and no one could understand what it was that ailed her. But one evening the queen was

3

also sorrowful, for she had many strange thoughts when she thought of her sons. She said to Snow-white and Rosy-red, 'Why are you so sorrowful, my daughter? Is there anything you want? If so, only say the word, and you shall have it.'

'Oh, it seems so dull and lonely here,' said Snow-white and Rosy-red; 'everyone else has brothers and sisters, but I am all alone; I have none; and that's why I'm so sorrowful.'

'But you *had* brothers, my daughter,' said the queen; 'I had twelve sons who were your brothers, but I gave them all away to get you'; and so she told her the whole story.

So when the princess heard that, she had no rest; for, in spite of all the queen could say or do, and all she wept and prayed, the lassie would set off to seek her brothers, for she thought it was all her fault; and at last she got leave to go away from the palace. On and on she walked into the wide world, so far, you would never have thought a young lady could have strength to walk so far.

So, once, when she was walking through a great, great wood, one day she felt tired, and sat down on a mossy tuft and fell asleep. Then she dreamt that she went deeper and deeper into the wood, till she came to a little wooden hut, and there she found her brothers. Just then she woke, and straight before her she saw a worn path in the green moss, and this path went deeper into the wood; so she followed it, and after a long time she came to just such a little wooden house as that she had seen in her dream.

Now, when she went into the room there was no one at home, but there stood twelve beds, and twelve chairs, and twelve spoons – a dozen of everything, in short. So when she saw that she was so glad, she hadn't been so glad for many a long year, for she could guess at once that her brothers lived here, and that they owned the beds, and chairs and spoons. So she began to make up the fire, and sweep the room, and make the beds, and cook the dinner, and to make the house as tidy as she could; and when she had done all the cooking and work, she ate her own dinner, and crept under her youngest brother's bed, and lay down there, but she forgot her spoon upon the table.

So she had scarcely laid herself down before she heard

4

something flapping and whirring in the air, and so all the twelve wild ducks came sweeping in; but as soon as ever they crossed the threshold they became princes.

'Oh, how nice and warm it is in here,' they said. 'Heaven bless him who made up the fire, and cooked such a good dinner for us.'

And so each took up his silver spoon and was going to eat. But when each had taken his own, there was one still left lying on the table, and it was so like the rest that they couldn't tell it from them.

'This is our sister's spoon,' they said; 'and if her spoon be here, she can't be very far off herself.'

'If this be our sister's spoon, and she be here,' said the eldest, 'she shall be killed, for she is to blame for all the ill we suffer.'

And this she lay under the bed and listened to.

'No,' said the youngest, ''twere a shame to kill her for that. She has nothing to do with our suffering ill; for if anyone's to blame, it's our own mother.'

So they set to work hunting for her both high and low, and at last they looked under all the beds, and so when they came to the youngest prince's bed, they found her, and dragged her out. Then the eldest prince wished again to have her killed, but she begged and prayed so prettily for herself.

'Oh! gracious goodness! don't kill me, for I've gone about seeking you these three years, and if I could only set you free, I'd willingly lose my life.'

'Well!' said they, 'if you will set us free, you may keep your life; for you can if you choose.'

'Yes; only tell me,' said the princess, 'how it can be done, and I'll do it, whatever it be.'

'You must pick thistledown,' said the princes, 'and you must card it, and spin it and weave it; and after you have done that, you must cut out and make twelve coats, and twelve shirts and twelve neckerchiefs, one for each of us, and while you do that, you must neither talk, nor laugh nor weep. If you can do that, we are free.'

'But where shall I ever get thistledown enough for so many

neckerchiefs, and shirts, and coats?' asked Snow-white and Rosy-red.

'We'll soon show you,' said the princes; and so they took her with them to a great wide moor, where there stood such a crop of thistles, all nodding and nodding in the breeze, and the down all floating and glistening like gossamers through the air in the sunbeams. The princess had never seen such a quantity of thistledown in her life, and she began to pluck and gather it as fast and as well as she could; and when she got home at night she set to work carding and spinning yarn from the down. So she went on a long long time, picking, and carding and spinning, and all the while keeping the princes' house, cooking, and making their beds. At evening home they came, flapping and whirring like wild ducks, and all night they were princes, but in the morning off they flew again, and were wild ducks the whole day.

But now it happened once, when she was out on the moor to pick thistledown – and if I don't mistake, it was the very last time she was to go thither – it happened that the young king who ruled that land was out hunting, and came riding across the moor, and saw her. So he stopped there and wondered who the lovely lady could be that walked along the moor picking thistledown, and he asked her her name, and when he could get no answer he was still more astonished; and at last he liked her so much, that nothing would do but he must take her home to his castle and marry her. So he ordered his servants to take her and put her up on his horse. Snow-white and Rosy-red wrung her hands, and made signs to them, and pointed to the bags in which her work was, and when the king saw she wished to have them with her, he told his men to take up the bags behind them. When they had done that the princess came to herself, little by little, for the king was both a wise man and a handsome man too, and he was as soft and kind to her as a doctor. But when they got home to the palace, and the old queen, who was his stepmother, set eyes on Snow-white and Rosy-red, she got so cross and jealous of her because she was so lovely, that she said to the king, 'Can't you see now, that this thing whom you have picked up, and whom

6

you are going to marry, is a witch? Why, she can't either talk, or laugh or weep!'

But the king didn't care a pin for what she said, but held on with the wedding, and married Snow-white and Rosy-red, and they lived in great joy and glory; but she didn't forget to go on sewing at her shirts.

So when the year was almost out, Snow-white and Rosy-red brought a prince into the world, and then the old queen was more spiteful and jealous than ever. At dead of night she stole in to Snow-white and Rosy-red, while she slept, and took away her babe, and threw it into a pit full of snakes. After that she cut Snow-white and Rosy-red in her finger, and smeared the blood over her mouth, and went straight to the king.

'Now come and see,' she said, 'what sort of a thing you have taken for your queen; here she has eaten up her own babe.'

Then the king was so downcast, he almost burst into tears, and said, 'Yes, it must be true, since I see it with my own eyes; but she'll not do it again, I'm sure, and so this time I'll spare her life.'

So before the next year was out she had another son, and the same thing happened. The king's stepmother got more and more jealous and spiteful. She stole in to the young queen at night while she slept, took away the babe, and threw it into a pit full of snakes, cut the young queen's finger, and smeared the blood over her mouth, and then went and told the king she had eaten up her own child. Then the king was so sorrowful, you can't think how sorry he was, and he said, 'Yes, it must be true, since I see it with my own eyes, but she'll not do it again, I'm sure, and so this time too I'll spare her life.'

Well, before the next year was out, Snow-white and Rosy-red brought a daughter into the world, and her, too, the old queen took and threw into the pit full of snakes, while the young queen slept. Then she cut her finger, smeared the blood over her mouth, and went again to the king and said, 'Now you may come and see if it isn't as I say; she's a wicked, wicked witch, for here she has gone and eaten up her third babe too.'

Then the king was so sad, there was no end to it, for now he couldn't spare her any longer but had to order her to be burnt alive on a pile of wood. But just when the pile was all ablaze, and they were going to put her on it, she made signs to them to take twelve boards and lay them round the pile, and on these she laid the neckerchiefs, and the shirts and the coats for her brothers, but the youngest brother's shirt wanted its left arm, for she hadn't had time to finish it. And as soon as ever she had done that, they heard such a flapping and whirring in the air, and down came twelve wild ducks flying over the forest, and each of them snapped up his clothes in his bill and flew off with them.

'See now!' said the old queen to the king, 'wasn't I right when I told you she was a witch; but make haste and burn her before the pile burns low.'

'Oh!' said the king, 'we've wood enough and to spare, and so I'll wait a bit, for I have a mind to see what the end of all this will be.'

As he spoke, up came the twelve princes riding along as handsome well-grown lads as you'd wish to see; but the youngest prince had a wild duck's wing instead of his left arm.

'What's all this about?' asked the princes.

'My queen is to be burnt,' said the king, 'because she's a witch, and because she has eaten up her own babes.'

'She hasn't eaten them at all,' said the princes. 'Speak now, sister; you have set us free and saved us, now save yourself.'

Then Snow-white and Rosy-red spoke, and told the whole story; how every time she was brought to bed, the old queen, the king's stepmother, had stolen in to her at night, had taken her babes away, and cut her little finger, and smeared the blood over her mouth; and then the princes took the king, and showed him the snake-pit where three babes lay playing with adders and toads, and lovelier children you never saw.

So the king had them taken out at once, and went to his stepmother, and asked her what punishment she thought that woman deserved who could find it in her heart to betray a guiltless queen and three such blessed little babes.

'She deserves to be fast bound between twelve unbroken steeds, so that each may take his share of her,' said the old queen.

'You have spoken your own doom,' said the king, 'and you

shall suffer it at once.'

So the wicked old queen was fast bound between twelve unbroken steeds, and each got his share of her. But the king took Snow-white and Rosy-red, and their three children, and the twelve princes, and so they all went home to their father and mother and told all that had befallen them, and there was joy and gladness over the whole kingdom, because the princess was saved and set free, and because she had set free her twelve brothers.

Old Foster

(*Hillbilly, USA*)

HEY use to be an old man, he lived way over in the forest by hisself, and all he lived on was he caught women and boiled 'em in front of the fire and eat 'em. Now the way my mother told me, he'd go into the villages and tell 'em this and that and get 'em to come out and catch 'em and jest boil they breasts. That's what she told me, and then I've heard hit that he jest eat 'em. Well, they was a beautiful stout woman, he liked 'em the best (he'd a been right atter me un your mother) so every day he'd come over to this woman's house and he'd tell her to please come over to see his house. 'Why, Mr Foster, I can't find the way.' 'Yes, you can. I'll take a spool of red silk thread out of my pocket and I'll start windin' hit on the bushes and it'll carry ye straight to my house.' So she promised him one day she'd come.

So she got her dinner over one day and she started. So she follered the red silk thread and went on over to his house. When she got there, there was a poor little old boy sittin' over the fire a boilin' meat. And he says, 'Laws, Aunt' – she was his aunt – 'what er you doin' here? Foster kills every woman that comes here. You leave here jest as quick as you can.'

She started to jump out the door and she saw Foster a comin' with two young women, one under each arm. So she run back and says, 'Jack, honey, what'll I do, I see him a comin'?' 'Jump in that old closet under the stair and I'll lock you in,' says Jack.

So she jumped in and Jack locked her in. So Foster come in and he was jest talkin' and a laughin' with those two girls and tellin' the most tales, and he was goin' to taken 'em over to a corn shuckin' next day. Foster says, 'Come on in and have supper with me.' So Jack put up some boiled meat and water. That's all they had. As soon as the girls stepped in and seed the circumstance

10

and seed their time had come their countenance fell. Foster says, 'You better come in and eat, maybe the last chanct you'll ever have.' Girls both jumped up and started to run. Foster jumps up and ketched 'em, and gets his tomihawk and starts upstairs with 'em. Stairs was shackly and rattly, and as they went up one of the girls retched her hand back and caught hold of a step and Foster jest tuck his tomihawk and hacked her hand off. It drapped into whar my mother was. She laid on in there until next day atter Foster went, then Jack let her out.

She jest bird worked over to where the corn shuckin' was. When she got there Foster was there. She didn't know how to git Foster destroyed. The people thought these people got out in the forest and the wild animals ud ketch 'em. So she says, 'I dreamt an awful dream last night. I dreamed I lived close to Foster's house and he was always a-wantin' me to come to his house.'

Foster says, 'Well, that ain't so, and it shan't be so, and God forbid it ever should be so.'

She went right on, 'And I dreamt he put out a red thread and I follered hit to his house and there uz Jack broilin' women's breasts in front of the fire.'

Foster says, 'Well, that ain't so, and it shan't be so, and God forbid it ever should be so.'

She went right on, 'And he says, "What er you doin' here! Foster kills every woman uz comes here." '

Foster says, 'Well, that ain't so, and it shan't be so, and God forbid it ever should be so.'

She went right on, 'And I seed Foster a-comin' with two girls. And when they git thar the girls their hearts failed 'em and Foster ketched 'em and gets his tomihawk and starts up stairs with 'em.'

Foster says, 'Well, that ain't so, and it shan't be so, and God forbid it ever should be so.'

She went right on, 'The stairs was shackly and rattly and as they went up, one of the girls retched her hand back and caught hold of a step and Foster jest tuk his tomihawk and hacked her hand off.'

Foster says, 'Well, that ain't so, and it shan't be so, and God forbid it ever should be so.'

11

She says, 'Hit is so, and it shall be so and here I've got the hand to show.'

And they knowed the two girls was missin' and they knowed it was so, so they lynched Foster and then they went and got Jack and bound him out.

Šāhīn

(Palestinian Arab)

NCE there was a king (and there is no king-ship except that which belongs to Allah, may He be praised and exalted!) and he had an only daughter. He had no other children, and he was proud of her. One day, as she was lounging about, the daughter of the vizier came to visit her. They sat together, feeling bored.

'We're sitting around here feeling bored,' said the daughter of the vizier. 'What do you say to going out and having a good time?'

'Yes,' said the other.

Sending for the daughters of the ministers and dignitaries of state, the king's daughter gathered them all together, and they went into her father's orchard to take the air, each going her own way.

As the vizier's daughter was sauntering about, she stepped on an iron ring. Taking hold of it, she pulled, and behold! it opened the door to an underground hallway, and she descended into it. The other girls, meanwhile, were distracted, amusing themselves. Going into the hallway, the vizier's daughter came upon a young man with his sleeves rolled up. And what! there were deer, partridges, and rabbits in front of him, and he was busy plucking and skinning.

Before he was aware of it, she had already saluted him. 'Peace to you!'

'And to you, peace!' he responded, taken aback. 'What do you happen to be, sister, human or jinn?'

'Human,' she answered, 'and the choicest of the race. What are you doing here?'

'By Allah,' he said, 'we are forty young men, all brothers.

13

Every day my brothers go out to hunt in the morning and come home toward evening. I stay home and prepare their food.'

'That's fine,' she chimed in. 'You're forty young men, and we're forty young ladies. I'll be your wife, the king's daughter is for your eldest brother, and all the other girls are for all your other brothers.' She matched the girls with the men.

Oh! How delighted he was to hear this!

'What's your name?'

'Šāhīn,' he answered.

'Welcome, Šāhīn.'

He went and fetched a chair, and set it in front of her. She sat next to him, and they started chatting. He roasted some meat, gave it to her, and she ate. She kept him busy until the food he was cooking was ready.

'Šāhīn,' she said when the food was ready, 'you don't happen to have some seeds and nuts in the house, do you?'

'Yes, by Allah, we do.'

'Why don't you get us some. It'll help pass away the time.'

In their house, the seeds and nuts were stored on a high shelf. He got up, brought a ladder, and climbed up to the shelf. Having filled his handkerchief with seeds and nuts, he was about to come down when she said, 'Here, let me take it from you. Hand it over!' Taking the handkerchief from him, she pulled the ladder away and threw it to the ground, leaving him stranded on the shelf.

She then brought out large bowls, prepared a huge platter, piled all the food on it, and headed straight out of there, taking the food with her and closing the door of the tunnel behind her. Putting the food under a tree, she called to the girls, 'Come eat, girls!'

'Eh! Where did this come from?' they asked, gathering around.

'Just eat and be quiet,' she replied. 'What more do you want? Just eat!'

The food was prepared for forty lads, and here were forty lasses. They set to and ate it all.

'Go on along now!' commanded the vizier's daughter. 'Each one back where she came from. Disperse!'

She dispersed them, and they went their way. Waiting until

14

they were all busy, she took the platter back, placing it where it was before and coming back out again. In time the girls all went home.

Now we go back. To whom? To Šāhīn. When his brothers came home in the evening, they could not find him.

'Oh Šāhīn,' they called. 'Šāhīn!'

And behold! he answered them from the shelf.

'Hey! What are you doing up there?' asked the eldest brother.

'By Allah, brother,' Šāhīn answered, 'I set up the ladder after the food was ready and came to get some seeds and nuts for passing away the time. The ladder slipped, and I was stranded up here.'

'Very well,' they said, and set up the ladder for him. When he came down, the eldest brother said, 'Now, go bring the food so we can have dinner.' Gathering up the game they had hunted that day, they put it all in one place and sat down.

Šāhīn went to fetch the food from the kitchen, but he could not find a single bite.

'Brother,' he said, coming back, 'the cats must have eaten it.'

'All right,' said the eldest. 'Come, prepare us whatever you can.'

Taking the organs of the hunted animals, from this and that he made dinner and they ate. Then they laid their heads down and went to sleep.

The next morning they woke up and set out for the hunt. 'Now brother,' they mocked him, 'be sure to let us go without dinner another evening. Let the cats eat it all!'

'No, brothers,' he said. 'Don't worry.'

No sooner did they leave than he rolled up his sleeves and set to skinning and plucking the gazelles, rabbits and partridges. On time, the vizier's daughter showed up. Having gone to the king's daughter and gathered all the other girls, she waited till they were amusing themselves with something and then dropped in on him.

'Salaam!'

'And to you, peace!' he answered. 'Welcome to the one who took the food and left me stranded on the shelf, making me look ridiculous to my brothers!'

'What you say is true,' she responded. 'And yet I'm likely to do

15

even more than that to the one I love.'

'And as for me,' he murmured, 'your deeds are sweeter than honey.'

Fetching a chair, he set it down for her, and then he brought some seeds and nuts. They sat down to entertain themselves, and she kept him amused until she realised the food was ready.

'Šāhīn,' she said, 'isn't there a bathroom in your house?'

'Yes, there is,' he replied.

'I'm pressed, and must go to the bathroom. Where is it?'

'It's over there,' he answered.

'Well, come and show it to me.'

'This is it, here,' he said, showing it to her.

She went in and, so the story goes, made as if she did not know how to use it.

'Come and show me how to use this thing,' she called.

I don't know what else she said, but he came to show her, you might say, how to sit on the toilet. Taking hold of him, she pushed him inside like this, and he ended up with his head down and his feet up. She closed the door on him and left. Going into the kitchen, she served up the food on to a platter and headed out of there. She put the food under a tree and called to her friends, 'Come eat!'

'And where did you get all this?'

'All you have to do is eat,' she answered.

They ate and scattered, each going her way. And she stole away and returned the platter.

At the end of the day the brothers came home, and there was no sign of their brother. 'Šāhīn, Šāhīn!' they called out. 'O Šāhīn!' But no answer came. They searched the shelf, they searched here, and they searched there. But it was no use.

'You know,' said the eldest, 'I say there's something odd about Šāhīn's behaviour. I suspect he has a girlfriend. Anyway, some of you go into the kitchen, find the food, and bring it so we can eat. I'm sure Šāhīn will show up any moment.'

Going into the kitchen, they found nothing. 'There's no food,' they reported. 'It's all gone! We're now sure that Šāhīn has a girlfriend, and he gives her all the food. Let's go ahead and fix whatever there is at hand so we can eat.'

Having prepared a quick meal, they ate dinner and were

content. They prepared for sleep, but one of them (All respect to the listeners!) was pressed and needed to relieve himself. He went to the bathroom, and lo! there was Šāhīn, upside down.

'Hey, brothers!' he shouted. 'Here's Šāhīn, and he's fallen into the toilet!'

They rushed over and lifted him out. What a condition he was in! They gave him a bath.

'Tell me,' said the eldest, 'what's going on?'

'By Allah, brother,' replied Šāhīn, 'after I cooked dinner I went to relieve myself, and I slipped.'

'Very well,' returned the eldest. 'But the food, where is it?'

'By Allah, as far as I know it's in the kitchen, but how should I know if the cats haven't eaten it?'

'Well, all right!' they said, and went back to sleep.

The next morning, as they were setting out, they mocked him again. 'Why don't you leave us without dinner another night?'

'No, brothers!' he said. 'Don't worry.'

Pulling themselves together, they departed. Now, on time, the daughter of the vizier came to see the king's daughter, gathered the others, and they came down to the orchard and spread out. Waiting until they were all caught up with something, she slipped away to him, and listen, brothers! she found him at home.

'Salaam!'

'And to you, peace!' he retorted. 'Welcome! On the shelf the first day, and you made away with the food; and the second day you threw me into the toilet and stole the food, blackening my face in front of my brothers!'

'As for me,' she said, 'I'll do even more than that to the one I love.'

'And to me, it's sweeter than honey,' he responded, bringing her a chair. She sat down, he brought seeds and nuts, and they passed away the time entertaining themselves. She kept chatting with him, until she knew the food was ready.

'Šāhīn,' she said.

'Yes.'

'Don't you have some drinks for us to enjoy ourselves? There's meat here, and seeds and nuts. We could eat and have something to drink.'

'Yes,' he replied, 'we do.'

'Why don't you bring some out, then?' she urged him.

Bringing a bottle, he set it in front of her. She poured drinks and handed them to him. 'This one's to my health,' she egged him on, 'and this one's also for my sake,' until he fell over, as if no one were there. She then went and took some sugar, put it on to boil, and made a preparation for removing body hair. She used it on him to perfection, and, brother, she made him look like the most beautiful of girls. Bringing a woman's dress, she put it on him. Then, bringing a scarf, she wrapped it around his head and laid him down to sleep in bed. She powdered his face, wrapped the scarf well around his head, put the bed covers over him, and left. Then into the kitchen she went, loaded the food, and departed. The girls ate, and the platter was replaced.

When the brothers returned in the evening, they did not find Šāhīn at home.

'O Šāhīn! Šāhīn! Šāhīn!'

No answer. 'Let's search the bathroom,' they said among themselves. But they did not find him there. They searched the shelf, and still no sign of him.

'Didn't I tell you Šāhīn has a girlfriend?' the eldest declared. 'I'd say Šāhīn has a girlfriend and goes out with her. Some of you, go and see if the food's still there.' They did, and found nothing.

Again they resorted to a quick meal of organ meat. When it was time to sleep, each went to his bed. In his bed, the eldest found our well-contented friend stretched out in it. Back to his brothers he ran. 'I told you Šāhīn has a girlfriend, but you didn't believe me. Come and take a look! Here's Šāhīn's bride! Come and see! Come and see!'

He called his brothers, and they all came, clamouring, 'Šāhīn's bride!' Removing his scarf, they looked at him carefully. Eh! A man's features are hard to miss. They recognised him. 'Eh! This is Šāhīn!' they shouted. Bringing water, they splashed his face till he woke up. Looking himself over, what did he find? They fetched a mirror. He looked at himself, and what a sight he was – all rouged, powdered and beautified.

'And now,' they asked him, 'what do you have to say for yourself?'

'By Allah, brother,' answered Šāhīn, 'listen and I'll tell you the truth. Every day, around noon, a girl with such and such features comes to see me. She says, "We're forty young ladies. The king's daughter is for your eldest brother, I am yours, and all the other girls are for all your other brothers." She's the one who's been doing these things to me every day.'

'Is that so?'

'Yes, it is.'

'Fine. All of you go to the hunt tomorrow,' suggested the eldest, 'and I'll stay behind with Šāhīn. I'll take care of her!'

Pulling out his sword (so the story goes), he sat waiting in readiness. By Allah, brothers, in due time she came. She had gathered the girls as usual, and they had come down to the orchard. Waiting until their attention was caught, she slipped away to him. Before he was even aware of her, she had already saluted him.

'Salaam!'

'And to you, peace!' he answered. 'The first item on the shelf, and I said all right; the second time in the bathroom, and I said all right; but the third time you put make-up on me and turned me into a bride!'

'And yet I'm likely to do even more than that to the one I love.'

No sooner had she said that than up rose the eldest brother and rushed over to her, his sword at the ready.

'Listen,' she reasoned with him. 'You are forty, and we are forty. The king's daughter is to be your wife, and I, Šāhīn's; and so and so among us is for so and so among you, and so on.' She calmed him down.

'Is it true, what you're saying?' he asked.

'Of course it's true,' she replied.

'And who can speak for these girls?'

'I can.'

'You're the one who can speak for them?'

'Yes.'

(Šāhīn, meanwhile, was listening, and since he was already experienced, he mused to himself that his brother had been taken in already.)

'Agreed,' said the eldest brother. 'Come over here and let me pay you the bridewealth for the forty girls. Where are we to meet you?'

'First pay me the bridewealth,' she answered, 'and tomorrow, go and reserve a certain public bath for us at your expense. Stand guard at the gate, and as we go in you yourself can count us one by one – all forty of us. We'll go into the baths and bathe, and after we come out each of you will take his bride home by the hand.'

'Just like that?' he wondered.

'Of course,' she assured him.

He brought out a blanket, she spread it, and – count, count, count – he counted one hundred Ottoman gold coins for each girl. When he had finished counting out the money, she took it and went straight out. Calling her friends over, she said, 'Sit here! Sit under this tree! Each of you open your hand and receive your bridewealth.'

'Eh!' they protested, 'You so and so! Did you ruin your reputation?'

'No one's to say anything,' she responded. 'Each of you will take her bridewealth without making a sound.' Giving each of them her money, she said, 'Come. Let's go home.'

After she had left their place, Šāhīn said to his brother, 'Brother, she tricked me and took only the food. But she tricked you and got away with our money.'

'Who, me?' the brother declared, 'Trick me? Tomorrow you'll see.'

The next day the brothers stayed at home. They went and reserved the baths at their own expense, and the eldest stood watch at the door, waiting for the girls to arrive. Meanwhile, the vizier's daughter had got up the next day, gathered all the girls, the king's daughter among them, and, leading them in front of her, headed for the bath with them. And behold! there was our *effendi* guarding the door. As they were going in, he counted them one by one. Count, count, he counted them all – exactly forty.

Going into the baths, the girls bathed and enjoyed themselves. But after they had finished bathing and put on their clothes, she, the clever one, gave them this advice: 'Each of you is to shit in the tub she has bathed in, and let's line the tubs up all in a row.' Each of them shat in her tub, and they arranged them neatly in a row, all forty of them. Now, the baths had another door, away from the entrance. 'Follow me this way,' urged the vizier's daughter, and they all hurried out.

The eldest brother waited an hour, two, three, then four, but the girls did not emerge. 'Eh!' he said. 'They're taking a long time about it.'

'Brother,' said Šāhīn, 'they're gone.'

'But listen!' he replied, 'where could she have gone? They all went inside the bath-house together.'

'All right,' said Šāhīn, 'let's go in and see.'

Going into the bath-house, brother, they found the owner inside.

'Where did the girls who came into the bath-house go?'

'O uncle!' replied the owner, 'they've been gone a long time.'

'And how could they have left?' asked the eldest brother.

'They left by that door,' he replied.

Now, Šāhīn, who was experienced, looked in the bathing place and saw the tubs all lined up.

'Brother!' he called out.

'Yes. What is it?'

'Come here and take a look,' he answered. 'Here are the forty! Take a good look! See how she had them arranged so neatly?'

Finally the brothers went back home, wondering to themselves, 'And now, what are we going to do?'

'Leave them to me!' volunteered Šāhīn. 'I'll take care of them.'

The next day Šāhīn disguised himself as an old lady. Wearing an old woman's dress, he put a beaded rosary around his neck and headed for the city. The daughter of the vizier, meanwhile, had gathered the girls, and she was sitting with them in a room above the street. As he was coming from afar, she saw and recognised him. She winked to her friends, saying, 'I'll go call him, and you chime in with, "Here's our aunt! Welcome to our aunt!" ' As soon as she saw him draw near, she opened the door and came out running. 'Welcome, welcome, welcome to our aunty! Welcome, aunty!' And, taking him by the hand, she pulled him inside to where they were. 'Welcome to our aunty!' they clamoured, locking the door. 'Welcome to our aunty!'

'Now, girls, take off your clothes,' urged the vizier's daughter. 'Take off your clothes. It's been a long time since we've had our

21

clothes washed by our aunty's own hands. Let her wash our
clothes!'

'By Allah, I'm tired,' protested Šāhīn. 'By Allah, I can't do it.'

'By Allah, you must do it, aunty,' they insisted. 'It's been such a
long time since we've had our clothes washed by our aunty's
hands.'

She made all forty girls take off their clothes, each of them
leaving on only enough to cover her modesty, and she handed
the clothes to him. He washed clothes till noon.

'Come girls,' said the vizier's daughter. 'By Allah, it's been such
a long time since our aunty has bathed us with her own hands.
Let her bathe us!'

Each of them put on a wrap and sat down, and he went
around bathing them in turn. By the time he had finished
bathing them all, what a condition he was in! He was exhausted.

When he had finished with one, she would get up and put on
her clothes. The vizier's daughter would then wink at her and
whisper that she should take the wrap she was wearing, fold it
over, twist it, and tie a knot at one end so that it was like a whip.

When all forty girls had finished bathing, the leader spoke out,
'Eh, aunty! Hey girls, she has just bathed us, and we must bathe
her in return.'

'No, niece!' he protested. 'I don't need a bath! For the sake
of . . .'

'Impossible, aunty!' insisted the vizier's daughter. 'By Allah,
this can't be. Eh! You bathe and bathe all of us, and we don't
even bathe you in return. Come, girls!'

At a wink from her, they set on him against his will. They were
forty. What could he do? They took hold of him and removed
his clothes, and lo and behold! he was a man.

'Eh!' they exclaimed. 'This isn't our aunty. It's a man! Have at
him, girls!'

And with their whips, each of them having braided her robe
and tied knots in it, they put Šāhīn in the middle and descended
on his naked body. Hit him from here, turn him around there,
and beat him again on the other side! All the while he was
jumping among them and shouting at the top of his voice. When
she thought he had had enough, she winked at them to clear a
path. As soon as he saw his way open, he opened the door and

dashed out running, wearing only the skin the Lord had given him.

His brothers were at home, and before they were even aware of it, he showed up, naked. And what a condition he was in! Up they sprang, as if possessed. 'Hey! What happened to you?' they asked. 'Come! Come! What hit you?'

'Wait a minute,' he answered. 'Such and such happened to me.'

'And now,' they asked among themselves, 'what can we do?'

'Now, by Allah,' answered Šāhīn, 'we have no recourse but for each of us to ask for the hand of his bride from her father. As for me, I'm going to ask for her hand. But as soon as she arrives here, I'm going to kill her. No other punishment will do. I'll show her!'

They all agreed, each going to ask for his bride's hand from her father, and the fathers gave their consent.

Now, the daughter of the minister was something of a devil. She asked her father, if anyone should come asking for her hand, not to give his consent before letting her know. When Šāhīn came to propose, the father said, 'Not until I consult with my daughter first.' The father went to consult with his daughter, and she said, 'All right, give your consent, but on condition that there be a waiting period of one month so that the bridegroom can have enough time to buy the wedding clothes and take care of all the other details.'

After the asking for her hand was completed, the minister's daughter waited until her father had left the house. She then went and put on one of his suits, wrapped a scarf around the lower part of her face, and, taking a whip with her, headed for the carpenter's workshop.

'Carpenter!'

'Yes, Your Excellency!'

'In a while I'll be sending you a concubine. You will observe her height and make a box to fit her. I want it ready by tomorrow. Otherwise, I'll have your head cut off. And don't hold her here for two hours!'

'No, sir. I won't.'

She lashed him twice and left, going directly – where? To the halva maker's shop.

'Halva maker!'

'Yes.'

'I'm going to be sending you a concubine momentarily. You will observe her. See her shape and her height. You must make me a halva doll that looks exactly like her. And don't you keep her here for a couple of hours or I'll shorten your life!'

'Your order, O minister,' said the man, 'will be obeyed.'

She lashed him twice with the whip and left. She went and changed, putting on her ordinary clothes, then went to the carpenter's shop and stayed a while. After that she went and stood by the halva maker's shop for a while. Then she went straight home. Changing back into her father's suit, she took the whip with her and went to the carpenter.

'Carpenter!'

'Yes, my lord minister!'

'An ostrich shorten your life!' responded the girl. 'I send you the concubine, and you hold her here for two hours!'

She descended on him with the whip, beating him all over.

'Please, sir!' he pleaded, 'it was only because I wanted to make sure the box was an exact fit.'

Leaving him alone, she headed for the halva maker's. Him too, she whipped several times, and then she returned home.

The next day she sent for her slave and said to him, 'Go bring the wooden box from the carpenter's shop to the halva maker's. Put the halva doll in it, lock it, and bring it to me here.'

'Yes, I'll do it,' he answered.

When the box was brought, she took it in and said to her mother, 'Listen, mother! I'm going to leave this box with you in trust. When the time comes to take me out of the house and to load up and bring along my trousseau, you must have this box brought with the trousseau and placed in the same room where I will be.'

'But, dear daughter!' protested the mother, 'what will people say? The minister's daughter is bringing a wooden box with her trousseau! You will become a laughing-stock.' I don't know what else she said but it was no use.

'This is not your concern,' insisted the daughter. 'That's how I want it.'

When the bridegroom's family came to take the bride out of

her father's house, she was made ready, and the wooden box was brought along with her trousseau. They took the wooden box and, as she had told them, placed it in the same room where she was to be. As soon as she came into the room and the box was brought in, she threw out all the women. 'Go away!' she said. 'Each of you must go home now.'

After she had made everyone leave, she locked the door. Then, dear ones, she took the doll out of the box. Taking off her clothes, she put them on the doll, and she placed her gold around its neck. She then set the doll in her own place on the bridal seat, tied a string around its neck, and went and hid under the bed, having first unlocked the door.

Her husband, meanwhile, was taking his time. He stayed away an hour or two before he came in. What kind of mood do you think he was in when he arrived? He was in a foul humour, his sword in hand, ready to kill her, as if he did not want to marry her in the first place. As soon as he passed over the doorstep, he looked in and saw her on the bridal seat.

'Yes, yes!' he reproached her. 'The first time you abandoned me on the shelf and took the food, I said to myself it was all right. The second time you threw me into the toilet and took the food, and I said all right. The third time you removed my body hair and made me look like a bride, taking the food with you, and even then I said to myself it was all right. After all that, you still weren't satisfied. You tricked us all and took the bridewealth for the forty girls, leaving each of us a turd in the washtub.'

Meanwhile, as he finished each accusation, she would pull the string and nod the doll's head.

'As if all that weren't enough for you,' he went on, 'you had to top it all with your aunty act. "Welcome, welcome, aunty! It's been a long time since we've seen our aunty. It's been such a long time since aunty has washed our clothes!" And you kept me washing clothes all day. And after all that, you insisted, "We must bathe aunty." By Allah, I'm going to burn the hearts of all your paternal and maternal aunties!'

Seeing her nod her head in agreement, he yelled, 'You mean you're not afraid? And you're not going to apologise?' Taking hold of his sword, he struck her a blow that made her head roll. A piece of halva (if the teller is not lying!) flew into his mouth.

25

Turning it around in his mouth, he found it sweet.

'Alas, cousin!' he cried out. 'If in death you're so sweet, what would it have been like if you were still alive?'

As soon as she heard this, she jumped up from under the bed and rushed over to him, hugging him from behind.

'O cousin! Here I am!' she exclaimed. 'I'm alive!'

They consummated their marriage, and lived together happily.

This is my tale, I've told it; and in your hands I leave it.

The Dog's Snout People
(Lettish)

ONG ago there lived in a forest country two peoples: people with dogs' snouts and good people. The former were hunters, and the latter tilled the soil. Once the dog's snout people, while hunting, caught a girl belonging to the good people; she did not come from an adjacent settlement, but from a distant village. The people with dogs' snouts took the girl home and fed her on nuts and sweet milk; then after a while, wishing to judge of her condition, they took a long needle and drove it into her forehead. They licked up the blood, as a bear licks honey from a hive. They fed the girl, till at last she seemed to be suitable for their purpose. 'She will be a delicious morsel!' they said, telling their mother to roast the girl while they were away hunting in the forest. The oven had already been heating for two days. The men's mother now sent the girl to a neighbouring farm for a shovel, upon which the victim could be thrown into the oven, but by chance the girl went for the shovel to a farm belonging to the good people. She arrived and said to their mother, 'Little mother, lend our woman with the dog's snout a shovel.' 'Why does she require a shovel?' 'I do not know.' 'You are a stupid girl,' said the mother of the good people. 'Do you not know that the oven is being heated for you? In carrying the shovel you will be assisting your own death, but I will instruct you, little daughter. Take the shovel with you, and when the woman with the dog's snout says, "Lie upon the shovel!" then lie upon it crossways; and when she says, "Lie more conveniently" beg her to show you how to take your position. As soon as she has lain down lengthways on the shovel throw her as quickly as possible into the oven, and shut the door so tight that she cannot open it. When you have done this strew around you some ashes,

27

and taking off your bast shoes, put them on reversed, so that the front shall become the back and the back shall become the front; then run away with all your might; they will not find you by your traces! Take care that you do not fall into the hands of the dog's snout people, or there will be an end of you!'

The girl took the shovel and returned with it, and the dog's snout woman said to her, 'Lie down upon the shovel!' The girl lay crossways. Then the dog's snout woman said, 'Lie down lengthways; it will be better.' 'I do not understand,' said the girl; 'show me.' They disputed a long while, until the dog's snout woman lay down upon the shovel. The girl immediately seized it, thrust the woman rapidly into the oven and shut the door tight. Then she shod herself, as the mother of the good people had instructed her, and ran away. The dog's snout men came home and looked for their mother unsuccessfully. One said to another, 'Perhaps she has gone on a visit to her neighbours; let us see if the roast meat is ready!'

The Old Woman Against the Stream
(Norwegian)

HERE was once a man who had an old wife, and she was so cross and contrary that she was hard to get along with. The man, in fact, didn't get along with her at all. Whatever *he* wanted, she always wanted the very opposite.

Now one Sunday in late summer it happened that the man and the wife went out to see how the crop was getting along. When they came to a field on the other side of the river, the man said, 'Well, now it's ripe. Tomorrow we'll have to start reaping.'

'Yes, tomorrow we can start to clip it,' said the old woman.

'What's that? Shall we clip? Aren't we going to be allowed to reap either, now?' said the man.

No, clip it they should, the old woman insisted.

'There's nothing worse than knowing too little,' said the man, 'but this time you certainly must have lost what little wits you had. Have you ever seen anyone *clip* the crop?'

'Little do I know, and little do I care to know,' said the old woman, 'but this I know to be sure: the crop is going to be clipped and not reaped!' There was nothing more to be said. Clip it they should, and that was that.

So they walked back, wrangling and quarrelling, until they came to a bridge over the river, just by a deep pool.

'It's an old saying,' said the man, 'that good tools do good work. But I dare say *that'll* be a queer harvest which they clip with sheepshears!' he said. 'Shan't we be allowed to reap the crop at all, now?'

'Nay, nay! – Clip, clip, clip!' shrieked the old woman, hopping up and down, and snipping at the man's nose with her fingers. But in her fury she didn't look where she was going, and she tripped over the end of a post in the bridge and tumbled into the river.

'Old ways are hard to mend,' thought the man, 'but it'd be nice if I were right for once – me too.'

He waded out in the pool and caught hold of the old woman's topknot, just when her head was barely above the water. 'Well, are we going to reap the field?' he said.

'Clip, clip, clip!' shrieked the old woman.

'I'll teach you to clip, I will,' thought the man, and ducked her under. But it didn't help. They were going to clip, she said, when he let her up again.

'I can only believe that the old woman is mad!' said the man to himself. 'Many people are mad and don't know it; many have sense and don't show it. But now I'll have to try once more, all the same,' he said. But hardly had he pushed her under before she thrust her hand up out of the water, and started clipping with her fingers as with a pair of scissors.

Then the man flew into a rage, and ducked her both good and long. But all at once her hand sank down below the surface of the water, and the old woman suddenly became so heavy that he had to let go his hold.

'If you want to drag me down into the pool with you now, you can just lie there, you Troll!' said the man. And so there the old woman stayed.

But after a little while, the man thought it a pity that she should lie there and not have a Christian burial. So he went down along the river, and started looking and searching for her. But for all he looked and for all he searched, he couldn't find her. He took with him folk from the farm, and other folk from the neighbourhood, and they all started digging and dragging down along the whole river. But for all they looked, no old woman did they find.

'No,' said the man. 'That's no use at all. This old woman had a mind of her own,' he said. 'She was so contrary while she was alive that she can't very well be otherwise now. We'll have to start searching upstream, and try above the falls. Maybe she's floated herself upstream.'

Well, they went upstream, and looked and searched above the

falls. There lay the old woman!
She was *the old woman against the stream*, she was!

The Letter Trick
(Surinamese)

HERE was a woman who had a husband. Well, then her husband was in the bush, and she had another man. But when her husband went to the city, then the other man said to her, said 'If you love me, you must let me come sleep in your house.' Then she said to the man, said, 'All right. My husband is in the city, I will let you come. I am going to dress you in one of my skirts and blouses, and I am going to tell my husband that you are my sister from the plantation.' Then when she dressed him in the dress, then that night he came there. And the woman told her husband this was her sister.

Then at night they went to sleep. But in the morning the woman went to the market because she sold things. Then the man lay down upstairs. But when the woman's husband saw she did not come down, then he went to look, and he saw a man. Then the man was angry. He took a stick and came running to the market towards the woman. But when the woman saw him coming, then the woman took a piece of paper, then she read and cried. Then, when the man came he said, 'What are you doing?' Then she made up a speech. 'Hm! I just received a letter that all my sisters on the plantation have changed into men.' Then the man said, 'They do not lie, because the one who came to sleep with you last night, that one, too, changed into a man.' But the man did not know how to read. That is why the woman deceived him with such a trick.

Rolando and Brunilde
(Italy, Tuscan)

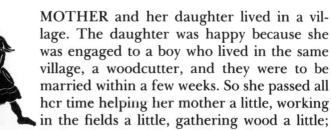 MOTHER and her daughter lived in a village. The daughter was happy because she was engaged to a boy who lived in the same village, a woodcutter, and they were to be married within a few weeks. So she passed all her time helping her mother a little, working in the fields a little, gathering wood a little; and then in her free time she sat at the window and sang . . . as she spun. She spun and she sang, waiting for her fiancé to return from the forest.

One day, a magician passed through town, and he heard singing; she had a pretty voice. He turned around and saw this girl at the window. Seeing her and falling in love with her was one and the same for the magician. And so he sent . . . he sent someone to ask if she would marry him. This prin . . . this girl said, 'No, because I am already engaged to be married. I have a fiancé and I am very fond of him,' she replied, 'and in a few weeks we are getting married,' she said, 'so I don't need a magician or these riches,' because he had told her that he would make her a rich lady because she was poor.

Then the magician, who had become indignant at her refusal, sent an eagle to kidnap the girl, who was called Brunilde, and it carried her to his castle where he showed her all his riches, all his castles, all his gold, all his money, but she didn't care about any of it. She said, 'I will marry Rolando and I want Rolando.' The magician then told her, 'If you don't marry me then you will never leave this castle.' And in fact he locked her up . . . he locked her in a room near his bedroom. Since the magician slept very soundly during the night and snored, for fear that someone would steal her he had an effigy made of himself as big as he was and then he had bells put on it, a thousand tiny bells, so that if

34

anyone bumped into this effigy he would wake up.

Now, her mother and Rolando were worried because the girl didn't come home, and her fiancé wanted to go and kill the magician. But her mother said, 'No, wait, let's wait a little.' She said, 'If not, he could hurt you, too; let's wait a bit.' And they tried one night to get into the garden, but the magician had had a wall built that surrounded the garden and it was so tall that it was impossible to enter. And the girl's mother sat all day and cried.

Finally, one day when she was in the forest she came upon a fairy in the form of an old lady who said to her, 'Tell me, why are you crying so?' And the girl's mother told the old woman about her Brunilde and how she had been carried off. 'Listen,' the fairy said, 'listen, I don't have much power in this case because the magician is much more powerful than I. I can't do anything,' she said. 'However, I can help you,' and she told her that he had closed the girl in a room and that he had had an effigy made of himself. So she said, 'You can't go there because if one of those bells should ring, he'll wake up.' She said: 'Listen to what you should do. This is the season when the cotton falls from the trees. You should go every day and fill a bag with cotton. In the evening when Rolando comes home from the forest, you have him take the cotton to the castle and I'll help you crawl through a hole.' She said: 'I get the bag into the garden and you'll get inside the palace . . . into the castle. In the castle you must stuff a few bells each night with cotton. Until you have stuffed them all, so that they will not ring any more, then we'll see what we can do.' And, in fact, this poor woman said: 'Of course, I'll do it. It will take time but I'll do it gladly.'

So they talked to the young man. During the day the mother gathered the cotton while he went to work, and in the evening they took the bag of cotton to the castle, and the mother stuffed the bells. Until one night the bells had finally all been stuffed. She went back to the old woman in the forest and told her that the last bell had been stuffed that same evening. Then the old woman said, 'Take Rolando with you.' And so the young man was made to enter through the same door that was used to stuff the bells, and the old woman gave him a sword and told him that when they were near enough he should cut off the left ear of the

35

magician. All the power of the magician lies in his left ear, she said . . . In fact they entered the castle and went to get the girl. And the young man went to cut off the magician's ear. After he cut off the ear, the left ear where all his power lay, the entire castle crumbled, everything crumbled. The young couple took all the gold, the silver, and everything that belonged to the magician. They became rich, they got married, and they lived happily ever after.

The Greenish Bird

(Mexican)

HERE were three girls who were orphaned, and Luisa did much sewing. The other two said that they didn't like Luisa's kind of life. They would rather go to bars and such things. Well, that kind of women – gay women. So Luisa stayed home. She kept a jar of water on the window sill, and she sewed and sewed and sewed.

So then he came, the Greenish Bird that was an enchanted prince. And of course he liked Luisa a lot, so he would light there on the window sill and say, 'Luisa, raise your eyes to mine, and your troubles will be over.' But she wouldn't.

On another night he came and said, 'Luisa, give me a drink of water from your little jar.' But she wouldn't look to see if he was a bird or a man or anything. Except she didn't know whether he drank or not, but then she saw he was a man. She gave him some water. So then he came again and proposed to her, and they fell in love. And the bird would come inside; he would lie in her bed. There on the headboard. And he set up a garden for her, with many fruit trees and other things, and a messenger and a maid; so the girl was living in grand style.

What should happen but that her sisters found out. 'Just look at Luisa, how high she has gone overnight. And us,' one of the sisters says, 'just look at us the way we are. Let's spy on her and see who it is that goes in there.' They went and spied on her and saw it was a bird, so they bought plenty of knives. And they put them on the window sill. When the little bird came out, he was wounded all over.

He said, 'Luisa, if you want to follow me, I live in crystal towers on the plains of Merlin. I'm badly wounded,' he said.

So she bought a pair of iron shoes, Luisa did, and she took

37

some clothes with her – what she could carry walking – and a guitar she had. And she went off after him. She came to the house where the Sun's mother lived. She was a blonde, blonde old woman. Very ugly. So she got there and knocked on the door and it opened. The old woman said, 'What are you doing here? If my son the Sun sees you, he'll devour you,' she said.

'I'm searching for the Greenish Bird,' she said.

'He was here. Look, he's badly wounded. He left a pool of blood there, and he just left a moment ago.'

She said, 'All right, then, I'm going.'

'No,' she said, 'hide and let's see if my son can tell you something. He shines on all the world,' she said.

So he came in, very angry:

Whoo! Whoo!
I smell human flesh. Whoo-whoo!
If I can't have it, I'll eat you.

He said this to his mother.

'What do you want me to do, son? There's nobody here.' She calmed him down and gave him food. Then she told him, little by little.

He said, 'Where's the girl,' he said. 'Let her come out so I can see her.' So Luisa came out and asked him about the Greenish Bird. He said, 'Me, I don't know. I haven't heard of him. I don't know where to find him. I haven't seen anything like that, either. It could be that the Moon's mother, or the Moon herself, would know,' he said.

Well then, 'All right, I'm going now.' Without tasting a bite of food. So then the Sun told her to eat first and then go. And so then they gave her something to eat, and she left.

All right, so she got to the house where the Moon's mother lived. And so, 'What are you doing here? If my daughter the Moon sees you, she will devour you.' And I don't know how many other things the old woman said to her.

'Well then, I'll go. I just wanted to ask her if she hadn't seen the Greenish Bird pass by here.'

'He was here. Look, there's the blood; he's very badly wounded,' she said.

All right, so she started to go away, but the Moon said,

'*Hombre*, don't go. Come eat first, and then you can go.' So they also gave her a bite to eat. As soon as they gave her something, she left. 'Why don't you go where the mother of the Wind lives and wait for the Wind to come home? The Wind goes into every nook and cranny; there isn't a place he doesn't visit.'

The mother of the Wind said, 'All right,' so she hid. She said, 'But you'll have to hide, because if my son the Wind sees you, Heaven help us.'

'All right,' she said.

The Wind came home, all vapoury and very angry, and his mother told him to behave, to take a seat, to sit down and have something to eat. So he quieted down. And then the girl told him that she was looking for the Greenish Bird.

But no. 'I can't tell you anything about that. I've never seen anything,' he said.

Well, so the girl went out again, but they gave her breakfast first and all that. The thing is that by the time she did find out, she had worn out the iron shoes she was wearing. It happened that there was an old hermit way out there, who tended to all the birds. He would call them by blowing on a whistle, and they would all come, and all kinds of animals, too. So she went there, too. And he asked her what she was doing out there, in those lonely wilds, and this and that. So she told the hermit, 'I'm in search of the Greenish Bird. Don't you know where he lives?'

'No,' he said. 'What I do know is that he was here. And he's badly wounded. But let me call my birds, and it may be that they know or have heard where he is, or something.'

Well, no. All the birds were called, but the old eagle was missing. The old eagle was right in the middle of it, eating tripe. The prince was to be married, but he had prayed to God that he would get leprosy, something like sores, and he was ill with sores. He was hoping Luisa would get there. But they were getting ready to marry him. The bride was a princess and very rich, but even so he didn't love her. He wanted to wait for his Luisa. Well then, so the old eagle was missing. The old man, the hermit, began blowing and blowing on his whistle until she came.

'What do you want, *hombre*? There I was, peacefully eating tripe, and you have to carry on like that, with all that blowing.'

'Wait, don't be mean,' he said. 'There's a poor girl here

39

looking for the Greenish Bird. She says she's his sweetheart and is going to marry him.'

'She's looking for the Greenish Bird? The Greenish Bird is about to get married. The only reason he hasn't married yet is that he's very sick of some sores. Hmm, yes. But the wedding feast is going on, and the bride's mother is there and everything. But, anyway, if she wants to go, it's all right. I just came from there. I was there eating tripe and guts and all that stuff they throw away. If she wants to go, all she has to do is butcher me a cow, and we'll go.'

The girl heard, and she was very happy, even if he was getting married and all that. The hermit called her, and she came out, and she saw all kinds of birds. And he said, 'The old eagle says that if you butcher a cow, she will take you all the way to the very palace.'

All right, she said she would. For she had plenty of money with her. The bird had made her well off from the beginning. He would have married her then and there, if it hadn't been for those bratty sisters of hers. So all right, so they did go. She slaughtered the cow, and the eagle took her and the cow on her back. She would fly high, high, high; and then she would start coming down.

'Give me a leg,' she would say. And she would eat the meat. That's why we say a person is 'an old eagle' when they ask for meat. She would give her meat. And, 'What do you see?'

'Nothing,' she would say. 'You can't see anything yet. It's a very pretty palace made of nothing but glass. It will shine in the sun,' the eagle would say. 'I don't see anything yet.' And she would keep on going, straight, straight ahead, who knows how far. And then she would fly up, and up, and up.

'What do you see?'

'Well, something like a peak that shines. But it's very far away.'

'Yes, it's very far.'

So the cow was all eaten up, and still they didn't get there. And she said she wanted more meat. Luisa said, 'Here, take the knife.' She told the eagle that. 'Cut off one of my legs, or I'll cut it off myself,' Luisa told the eagle. But she didn't say it whole-heartedly, of course. Not a chance.

Anyway the eagle said, 'No, no. I only said it to test you. I'm

40

going to leave you just outside because there are many cops around – or something like that – guarding the doors. You ask permission to go in from one of them. Tell them to let the ladies know you are coming in to cook. Don't ask for anything else,' she said. 'Get a job as a cook and then, well, we'll see how things go for you.'

All right, so she left Luisa just outside the yard. It was a great big yard made of pure gold or God knows what. As beautiful as could be. She asked the guard to let her in. 'And what is your reason for going in? What are you going to do?'

She said, 'Well, I'm very poor, and I've come from a long way off. And I'm looking for work. Anything I can do to eat, no matter if it is working in the kitchen.' And her carrying a golden comb, and all that the Greenish Bird had given her. And the guitar.

'Let me go ask the mistress,' he said, 'to see if they want to hire some kitchen help.' So he went and told her, 'A woman is looking for work.' And who knows what else.

'What kind of woman is she?'

'Well, she is like this, and this way, and that way.'

'All right, tell her to come in, and have her go around that way, so she won't come in through here in the palace,' she said. She didn't want her to go through the house.

So she went over there. And everybody was very kind to her. Meanwhile the Greenish Bird was a person now, but he was all leprous and very sick. There was a little old woman who had raised him. She was the one who took care of him. They had her there as a servant. First she had raised the boy, when she worked for his parents. Then she had moved over here, to the bride's house. She was no bride when the old woman first came there, but the girl had fallen in love with him. But he loved his Luisa.

And well, the wedding feast was in full swing, you might say, and he began to feel much better, for he heard a guitar being played, and he asked the old woman why they hadn't told him there were strangers in the house.

And when he heard the guitar, he told the woman who was taking care of him, who came to see him when he was sick, 'Who is singing and playing the guitar?'

'Oh, I had forgotten to tell you. A lady came wearing a pair of worn-out iron shoes, and she also has a guitar and a comb.'

'Is there anything on the comb?'

'Well, I don't know.' She couldn't read any more than I can.

'I don't know what's on it. They look like little wreaths or letters or I don't know what.'

'Ask her to lend it to you and bring it here.' And once he heard about the guitar, once he heard the guitar playing and all, he began to get well. He got much better. But neither the mother and father of the girl nor anybody else came to see him there.

He was all alone with the woman who took care of him. Because he looked very ugly. But then the woman went and told the princess who was going to be his mother-in-law, 'You should see how much better the prince is, the Greenish Bird. He is quite well now.'

So they all came to see him. And that made him angrier yet, because they came to see him now that he was well. The girl was very rich and a princess and all that, and Luisa was a poor little thing. But he said, 'Go ask her to lend you her comb and bring it to me.'

The old woman went and asked for the comb as if she wanted to comb her hair, and she went back where he was. He didn't say anything; he just looked at it.

'What do you say?'

'No, nothing,' he said. 'Tomorrow, or this afternoon, when they bring me food, have her bring it to me. She's working here, after all,' he said.

So when it was time to take him his dinner, she said, 'Listen, Luisa, go take the prince his dinner. I'm very tired now. I'm getting old.' Luisa didn't want to go; she was putting on. She hung back and she hung back, but at last she went.

Well, they greeted each other and saw each other and everything. And she said, 'Well, so you are already engaged and are going to get married,' Luisa said. 'And one cannot refuse anything to kings and princes.'

'But I have an idea, ever since I heard the guitar,' said the boy.

'What is it?'

'Everybody is going to make chocolate, and the cup I drink, I'll marry the one who made it.'

And she says, 'But I don't even know how to make chocolate!'

42

The old woman said she would make it for her, the woman who was taking care of him. Because Luisa went and told her about it. 'Just imagine what the prince wants. For all of us to come in, cooks and no cooks and absolutely all the women here, princesses and all. And each one of us must make a cup of chocolate, and the cup he drinks, he'll marry the woman who made it.' And she said, 'I don't know how . . .'

'Now, now,' said the old woman, 'don't worry about that. I'll make it for you. And you can take it to him.'

Well, the first to come in were all the big shots, as is always the case. First the bride, then the mother-in-law, the father-in-law, sisters-in-law, and everybody. And all he said was, 'I don't like it. I don't like it.'

The mother-in-law said, 'Now, I wonder who he wants to marry?' And, 'I wonder who he wants to marry?'

Well . . . nobody. So then the old woman who took care of him came. Neither. Then the other cook went in. And Luisa was the last one. He told them that she was the one he wanted to marry. That she had come searching for him from very far away, and that he would marry her. And he drank all of Luisa's cup of chocolate. Bitter or not, he didn't care. And he married her. And *colorin* so red, the story is finished.

The Crafty Woman
(Lithuanian)

 MAN and his young wife, who had settled down to life in a village, agreed so well that neither of them pronounced a single unpleasant word, they only caressed and kissed each other. For fully six months the Devil did his best to make the pair quarrel, but, at last, irritated by continued failure, he expressed his rage by making a disagreeable noise in his throat and made ready to depart. However, an old woman who was roaming about met him and said, 'Why are you annoyed?' The Devil explained, and the woman, on the understanding that she would receive some new bast shoes and a pair of boots, endeavoured to make the young couple disagree. She went to the wife while the husband was at work in the fields and, having begged for alms, said, 'Ah, my dear! how pretty and good you are! Your husband ought to love you from the depths of his soul. I know you live more amicably than any other couple in the world, but, my daughter! I will teach you to be yet happier. Upon your husband's head, at the very summit, are a few grey hairs, you must cut them off, taking care that he does not notice what you are about.'

'But how shall I do that?'

'When you have given your husband his dinner, tell him to lie down and rest his head upon your lap, then as soon as he goes to sleep, whip a razor out of your pocket and remove the grey hairs.' The young wife thanked her adviser and gave her a present.

The old woman went immediately to the field and warned the husband that a misfortune threatened him, since his amiable wife not only had betrayed him, but intended that afternoon to kill him and later to marry someone richer than himself. When

44

at midday, the wife arrived and, after his meal, placed her husband's head upon her knees, he pretended to be asleep and she took a razor from her pocket in order to remove the grey hairs. Instantly the exasperated man jumped on to his feet and, seizing his wife by the hair, began to abuse and strike her. The Devil saw all and could not believe his eyes; soon he took a long pole, attached loosely to one end of it the promised bast shoes and boots, and without coming close, passed them to the old woman. 'I will not on any account approach nearer to you,' he said, 'lest you should in some way impose upon me, for you really are more crafty and cunning than I am!' Having delivered the boots and bast shoes, the Devil vanished as quickly as if he had been shot from a gun.

Part Two

UP TO SOMETHING –
BLACK ARTS AND DIRTY
TRICKS

Pretty Maid Ibronka

(Hungarian)

HERE was a pretty girl in the village. That is why she was called by the name of Pretty Maid Ibronka. But what of it, if all the other girls – and what a bevy of them used to gather to do their spinning together – had a lover to themselves, and she alone had none? For quite a while she waited patiently, pondering over her chances, but then the thought took hold of her mind: 'I wish God would give me a sweetheart, even if one of the devils he were.'

That evening, when the young were together in the spinning room, in walks a young lad in a sheepskin cape and a hat graced with the feather of a crane. Greeting the others, he takes a seat by the side of Pretty Maid Ibronka.

Well, as is the custom of the young, they start up a conversation, talking about this and that, exchanging news. Then it happened that the spindle slipped from Ibronka's hand. At once she reached down for it and her sweetheart was also bending for it, but as her groping hand touched his foot, she felt it was a cloven hoof. Well, great was her amazement as she picked up her spindle.

Ibronka went to see them out, as on that evening the spinning had been done at her place. Before separating they had a few words together, and then they bid each other goodbye. As is the custom of the young they parted with an embrace. It was then that she felt her hand go into his side, straight through his flesh. That made her recoil with even greater amazement.

There was an old woman in the village. To that woman she went and said, 'Oh mother, put me wise about this. As you may know, for long they have been wagging their tongues in the

49

village, saying that of all the village girls, only Pretty Maid Ibronka is without a sweetheart. And I was waiting and waiting for one, when the wish took hold of my mind that God would give me a sweetheart, even if one of the devils he were. And on that very same evening a young man appeared, in a sheepskin cape and a hat graced with a crane feather. Straight up to me he walked and took a seat by my side. Well, we started up a conversation, as is the custom of the young, talking about this and that. I must have become heedless of my work and let the spindle slip from my hand. At once I reached down to pick it up, and so did he, but as my groping hand chanced to touch his foot, I felt it was a cloven hoof. This was so queer it made me shudder. Now put me wise, mother, what should I be doing now?'

'Well,' she said, 'go and do the spinning at some other place, changing from here to there, so you can see if he will find you.'

She did so and tried every spinning room there was in the village, but wherever she went, he came after her. Again she went to see the old woman. 'Oh mother, didn't he come to every single place I went? I see I shall never get rid of him this way, and I dare not think of what is going to come of all this. I do not know who he is, nor from where he came. And I find it awkward to ask him.'

'Well, here's a piece of advice to you. There are little girls in the village who are just learning to spin, and they find it good practice to wind the thread into balls. Get yourself such a ball, and when they gather again at your place for the spinning, see them out when they leave, and while you are talking to each other before parting, fuss about until you can get the end of the thread tied in a knot round a tuft in his sheepskin cape. When he takes leave and goes his way, let the thread unwind from the ball. When you feel that there is no more to come, make it into a ball again, following the track of the unwound thread.'

Well, they came to her place to do the spinning. The ball of thread she kept in readiness. Her sweetheart was keeping her waiting. The others began teasing her: 'Your sweetheart is going to let you down, Ibronka!'

'To be sure, he won't. He will come; only some business is now keeping him away.'

They hear the door open. They stop in silence and expectation: who is going to open the door? It is Ibronka's sweetheart. He greets them all and takes a seat at her side. And as is the custom of the young, they make conversation, each having something to tell the other. Amid such talk the time passes.

'Let's be going home, it must be close to midnight.'

And they did not tarry long, but quickly rose to their feet and gathered their belongings.

'Good night to you all!'

And they file off and leave the room, one after the other. Outside the house a final goodbye was said, and each went his way and was soon bound homeward.

And the pair drew closer to each other and were talking about this and that. And she was manipulating the thread until she got the end knotted round a tuft of wool in his sheepskin cape. Well, they did not make long with their conversation as they began to feel the chill of the night. 'You better go in now, my dear,' he said to Ibronka, 'or you'll catch cold. When the weather turns mild we may converse at greater leisure.'

And they embraced. 'Good night,' he said.

'Good night,' she said to him.

And he went his way. And she began to unwind the ball as he was walking away. Fast did the thread unwind from the ball. And she began to speculate how much more there would be still to come, but no sooner than this thought came into her head, than it stopped. For a while she kept waiting. But no more thread came off the ball. Then she started to rewind it. And bravely she followed the track of the thread as she went winding it into a ball again. Rapidly the ball was growing in her hand. And she was thinking to herself that she would not have to go very much farther. But where would the thread be leading her? It led her straight to the church.

'Well,' she thought, 'he must have passed this way.'

But the thread led her further on, straight to the churchyard. And she walked over to the door. And through the keyhole the light shone from the inside. And she bent down and peeped

51

through the keyhole. And whom does she behold there? Her own sweetheart. She keeps her eye on him to find out what he was doing. Well, he was busy sawing the head of a dead man in two. She saw him separate the two parts, just the same way we cut a melon in two. And then she saw him feasting on the brains from the halved head. Seeing that, she grew even more horrified. She broke the thread, and in great haste made her way back to the house.

But her sweetheart must have caught sight of her and briskly set out after her. No sooner had she reached home in great weariness and bolted the door safely on the inside, than her sweetheart was calling to her through the window, 'Pretty Maid Ibronka, what did you see looking through the keyhole?'

She answered, 'Nothing did I see.'

'You must tell me what you saw, or your sister shall die.'

'Nothing did I see. If she dies, we'll bury her.'

Then her sweetheart went away.

First thing in the morning she went to the old woman. In great agitation did she appeal to her, as her sister had died. 'Oh mother, I need your advice.'

'What about?'

'Well, I did what you advised me to do.'

'What happened then?'

Oh, just imagine where I was led in following the thread. Straight to the churchyard.'

'Well, what was his business there?'

'Oh, just imagine, he was sawing a dead man's head in two, just the same way we'd go about cutting up a melon. And there I stayed and kept my eye on him, to see what he'd be doing next. And he set to feasting on the brains from the severed head. I was so horrified that I broke the thread and in great haste made my way back home. But he must have caught sight of me, because as soon as I had the door safely bolted on the inside, he was calling to me through the window, "Pretty Maid Ibronka, what did you see looking through the keyhole?" "Nothing did I see." "You must tell me what you saw, or your sister shall die." I said then, "If she dies, we will bury her, but nothing did I see through the

52

keyhole."'

'Now listen,' the old woman said, 'take my advice and put your dead sister in the outhouse.'

Next evening she did not dare to go spinning with her friends, but her sweetheart was calling again through her window, 'Pretty Maid Ibronka, what did you see through the keyhole?'

'Nothing did I see.'

'You must tell me what you saw,' he said, 'or your mother shall die.'

'If she dies, we will bury her, but nothing did I see looking through the keyhole.'

He turned away from the window and was off. Ibronka was preparing for a night's rest. When she rose in the morning, she found her mother dead. She went to the old woman. 'Oh, mother, what will all this lead to? My mother too – she's dead.'

'Do not worry about it, but put her corpse in the outhouse.'

In the evening her sweetheart came again. He was calling her through the window, 'Pretty Maid Ibronka, tell me, what did you see looking through the keyhole?'

'Nothing did I see.'

'You must tell me what you saw,' he said, 'or your father shall die.'

'If he dies, we will bury him, but nothing did I see looking through the keyhole.'

Her sweetheart turned away from the window and was off, and she retired for the night. But she could not help musing over her lot; what would come of all this? And she went on speculating until she felt sleepy and more at ease. But she could not rest for long. Soon she lay wide awake and was pondering over her fate. 'I wonder what the future keeps in store for me?' And when the day broke she found her father dead. 'Now I am left alone.'

She took the corpse of her father into the outhouse, and then she went as fast as she could to the old woman again. 'Oh, mother, mother! I need your comfort in my distress. What is going to happen to me?'

'You know what's going to happen to you? I may tell you. You are going to die. Now go and ask your friends to be there when you die. And when you die, because die you will for certain, they must not take out the coffin either through the door or the window when they carry it to the churchyard.'

'How then?'

'They must cut a hole through the wall and must push the coffin through that hole. But they should not carry it along the road but cut across through the gardens and the bypaths. And they should not bury it in the burial ground but in the ditch of the churchyard.'

Well, she went home. Then she sent word to her friends, the girls in the village, and they appeared at her call.

In the evening her sweetheart came to the window. 'Pretty Maid Ibronka, what did you see looking through the keyhole?'

'Nothing did I see.'

'You must tell me at once,' he said, 'or you shall die.'

'If I die, they will bury me, but nothing did I see through the keyhole.'

He turned away from the window and took off.

Well, for a while she and her friends kept up their conversation. They were only half inclined to believe that she would die. When they grew tired they went to sleep. But when they awoke, they found Ibronka dead. They were not long in bringing a coffin and cutting a hole through the wall. They dug a grave for her in the ditch of the churchyard. They pushed the coffin through the hole in the wall and went off with it. They did not follow the road, but went cross-country, cutting through the gardens and the bypaths. When they came to the churchyard they buried her. Then they returned to the house and filled in the hole they had cut through the wall. It so happened that before she died, Ibronka enjoined them to take care of the house until further events took place.

Before long, a beautiful rose grew out of Ibronka's grave. The grave was not far from the road, and a prince, driving past in his coach, saw it. So much was he taken by its beauty that he stopped the coachman at once. 'Hey! Rein in the horses and get me that rose from the grave. Be quick about it!'

At once the coachman came to a halt. He jumps from the coach and goes to fetch the rose. But when he wants to break it off, the rose will not yield. He is pulling harder now, but still it does not yield. He is pulling the rose with all his might, but all in vain.

'Oh, what a dummy you are! Haven't you got the brains to pick a rose? Come on here, get back on the coach and let me go and get the flower.'

The coachman got back on to his seat, and the prince gave him the reins, which he had been holding while the other went for the rose. The prince then jumped down from the coach and went to the grave. No sooner had he grasped the rose, than it came off at once and he was holding it in his hand.

'Look here, you idiot, with all your tearing and pulling you could not get me this rose, and hardly did I touch it and off it came into my hand.'

Well, they took off, driving back home at great speed. The prince pinned the rose on his breast. At home, he found a place for it in front of the dining-room mirror so that he should be able to look at it even while he was having his meals.

There the rose stayed. One evening some leftovers remained on the table after supper. The prince left them there. 'I may eat them some other time.'

This happened every now and again. Once the servant asked the prince, 'Did your majesty eat the leftovers?'

'Not I,' said the prince. 'I guessed it was you who finished off what was left.'

'No, I did not,' he says.

'Well, there's something fishy about it.'

Says the servant, 'I am going to find out who's in this – the cat, or whoever.'

Neither the prince nor the servant would have guessed that the rose was eating the remains.

'Well,' said the prince, 'we must leave some more food on the table. And you will lie in wait and see who's going to eat it up.'

They left plenty of food on the table. And the servant was lying in wait, but never for a moment did he suspect the rose.

And the rose alighted from her place by the mirror, and shook itself, and at once it turned into such a beautiful maiden that you could not find a second to her, not in all Hungary, not in all the wide world. Well, she sat down on a chair at the table and supped well off the dishes. She even found a glass of water to finish off her supper. Then she shook herself a little and back again she was in her place in front of the mirror, in the shape of a rose.

Well, the servant was impatiently waiting for day to break. Then he went to the prince and reported, 'I've found it out, your royal majesty, it was the rose.'

'This evening you must lay the table properly and leave plenty of food on it. I am going to see for myself whether you are telling me the truth.'

And as they were lying in wait, the prince and the servant, they saw the rose alight from her place. She made a slight movement, then shook herself and at once turned into a fine and beautiful maiden. She takes a chair, sits down at the table, and sups well on the dishes. The prince was watching her as he sat under the mirror. And when she finished her supper and poured herself a glass of water and was about to shake herself into a rose again, the prince clasped his arms round her and took her into his lap.

'My beautiful and beloved sweetheart. You are mine, and I am yours for ever, and nothing but death can us part.'

'Oh, it cannot be so,' said Ibronka.

'To be sure, it can be,' he says. 'And why not?'

'There is more to it than you think.'

Well, I just remember a slip I have made in the story. Here goes then. On the day she was buried, her sweetheart appeared at her window as usual. He called in to her. But no answer came. He goes to the door and kicks it open. 'Tell me, you door, was it through you they took out Ibronka's coffin?'

'No, it was not.'

He goes then to the window. 'Tell me, you window, was it through you they took the coffin out?'

'No, it was not.'

He takes himself off to the road. 'Tell me, you road, was it this way they took the coffin?'

'No, it was not.'

He goes to the churchyard. 'Tell me, you churchyard, was it in your ground they buried Pretty Maid Ibronka?'

'No, it was not.'

Well, that is the missing part.

Fervently the prince is now wooing her and tries to win her consent to their marriage. But she resorts to evasion. And finally she made her condition, 'I will marry you only if you never compel me to go to church.'

Said the prince, 'Well then, we could get along without you going to church. Even if I sometimes go myself. I shall never compel you to come with me.'

Here is another part of the story I missed telling in its proper order. As he did not get any the wiser from the answer of the road, and the churchyard either, her sweetheart said to himself, 'Well, I see I must get myself a pair of iron moccasins and an iron staff and then I shall not stop until I find you, Pretty Maid Ibronka, even if I have to wear them away to naught.'

The time comes when Ibronka is expecting a child. The couple are living happily, only she never goes along with him to church. Day follows day, the years slip by. Again she is with child. They have already two children, and they are no longer babes, but a boy of five and six years of age. And it is their father who takes them to church. True enough, he himself had found it strange enough that only his children went with him while all other folks appeared together with their wives. And he knew that they rebuked him for it and said, 'Why does not your majesty bring along the queen?'

He says, 'Well, that is the custom with us.'

But all the same he felt embarrassed after this rebuke, and next Sunday, when he was getting ready with the boys to go to church, he said to his wife, 'Look here, missus, why won't you come with us too?'

She answered, 'Look here, husband, don't you remember your promise?'

'How then? Must we stick to it for ever and aye? I've been hearing their scorn long enough. And how could I give up going to church when the kids want me to go with them? Whatever we were saying then, let us forget about it.'

'All right, let it be as you wish, but it will give rise to trouble between us two. However, as I see you've set your mind on it, I am willing to go with you. Now let me go and dress for church.'

So they went, and it made the people rejoice to see them together. 'That is the right thing, your majesty,' they said, 'coming to church with your wife.'

The mass is drawing to a close, and when it ends, a man is walking up to the couple wearing a pair of iron moccasins worn to holes, and with an iron staff in his hand. He calls out loudly, 'I pledged myself, Ibronka, that I would put on a pair of iron moccasins and take an iron staff, and go out looking for you, even if I should wear them to naught. But before I had worn them quite away, I found you. Tonight I shall come to you.'

And he disappeared. On their way home the king asked his wife, 'What did that man mean by threatening you?'

'Just wait and see, and you will learn what will come of it.'

So both were anxiously waiting for the evening to come. The day was drawing to a close. Suddenly there was someone calling through the window, 'Pretty Maid Ibronka, what did you see through the keyhole?'

Pretty Maid Ibronka then began her speech: 'I was the prettiest girl in the village, but to a dead and not a living soul am I speaking – and all the other girls had a sweetheart – but to a dead and not to a living soul am I speaking. Once I let it out, I wish God would give me one, even if one of the devils he were. There must have been something in the way I said it, because that evening, when we gathered to do our spinning, there appeared a young lad in a sheepskin cape, and a hat graced with a feather of a crane. He greets us and takes a seat at my side and we are conversing, as is the custom of the young. And then it so happened – but to a dead and not to a living soul am I speaking – that my spindle slipped from my hand. I bent to pick it up and so did my sweetheart, but as my groping hand touched his foot, I felt at once – but to a dead and not to a living soul am I speaking – that it was a cloven hoof. And I recoiled in horror that God had given me a devil for a sweetheart – but to a dead and not to a living soul am I speaking.'

And he is shouting at the top of his voice through the window. 'Pretty Maid Ibronka, what did you see looking through the keyhole?'

'But when at the parting, as is the custom with the young, we embraced, my hand went straight through his flesh. At that I grew even more horrified. There was a woman in the village, and I went to ask for her advice. And she put me wise – but to a dead and not to a living soul am I speaking.'

And he kept shouting through the window, 'Pretty Maid Ibronka, what did you see looking through the keyhole?'

'And then my sweetheart took leave and went away. And I wished he would never come again – but to a dead and not to a living soul am I speaking. The woman said, I was to try to do the spinning at some other place, once here, once there, so that he might not find me. But wherever I went, there he came. And again I went for advice to the woman – but to a dead and not to a living soul am I speaking.'

And he was shouting through the window, 'Pretty Maid Ibronka, what did you see looking through the keyhole?'

'Then the woman advised me to get myself a ball of thread, which I was to fasten on to his sheepskin cape. And when he asked me and I said "Nothing did I see", he said, "Tell me at once, or your sister shall die," "If she dies, we will bury her, but nothing did I see looking through the keyhole." And he came again next evening and asked me what I had seen through the keyhole – but to a dead and not to a living soul am I speaking.'

And all the while he never stops shouting through the window.

'And my sister died. And the next evening he came again and was calling to me through the window – but to a dead and not to a living soul am I speaking. "Tell me what you saw, or your mother shall die." "If she dies, we will bury her." Next evening he is calling to me again, "Pretty Maid Ibronka, what did you see looking through the keyhole?" – but to a dead and not to a living soul am I speaking. "Tell me what you saw, or your father shall die." "If he dies, we will bury him, but nothing did I see looking through the keyhole." On that day I sent word to my friends, and they came and it was arranged that when I died they would not take my coffin either through the door or the window. Nor were they to take me along the road or bury me in the churchyard.'

And he went on shouting through the window, 'Pretty Maid Ibronka, what did you see looking through the keyhole?'

'And my friends cut a hole through the wall and went along the road when they took me to the churchyard where they buried me in the ditch – but to a dead and not to a living soul am I speaking.'

And then he collapsed under the window. He uttered a shout which shook the castle to its bottom, and it was he who died then. Her mother and her father and her sister rose from their long sleep. And that is the end of it.

Enchanter and Enchantress
(Mordvin)

MAN who was a magician took a girl-magician as his wife. The man went to the bazaar, whereupon his wife, who had a lover, called him, and they drank and ate together. In the evening the husband returned late from the bazaar and, looking through the window, saw his wife and her lover drinking and eating. The lover caught a glimpse of the husband and said to the woman, 'Who peered through the window just now?'

'I know,' said the woman; she took a small whip, and going out, struck her husband with the whip and said, 'Be no more a man; become a yellow dog!' The peasant became a yellow dog. It grew day, and the other dogs seeing the yellow dog, began to tear him. The yellow dog galloped along the road; bounded and leapt; he saw some shepherds feeding their flock, and he went to them. Pleased that the yellow dog had joined them, the shepherds fed him and gave him water. The dog looked after the flock so well that there was nothing left for the shepherds to do. As they saw that the dog acted efficiently they began to stay away from the field.

Once, when the dog was guarding the flock, the shepherds were in the tavern. A merchant entered this tavern and said, 'A thief is pestering me; he comes every night.' 'You should have our dog!' said the shepherds, and they related the dog's services. The merchant made an offer for the dog, and though the shepherds did not wish to sell him, they were overcome by the thought of the money. The merchant bought the dog and led him home. Night came, and with it the magician-wife of the yellow dog arrived to commit a theft. The woman entered the merchant's house and began to remove his money chest. The yellow dog threw himself upon his wife, took away the money chest and lay down upon it. In the morning the merchant rose and saw that the chest was gone; pushing the yellow dog, he said, 'I bought a dog to no purpose, for thieves have got hold of my money.' No sooner had the merchant pushed the dog, than he saw his coffer. The yellow dog slept three nights at the merchant's, and each night deprived his wife of the merchant's money. The wife ceased to visit the merchant for the purpose of theft.

The queen bore two sons, but both disappeared in the night; the wife of the yellow dog had stolen them. When the queen was again about to give birth to a child the king, who had heard of the yellow dog, went to the merchant and asked for him. The queen bore a son, but the wife of the yellow dog came by night and tried to steal him. However, no sooner had the wife of the yellow dog entered the royal dwelling and seized the third little prince, than the yellow dog rushed up and snatched the infant from her. In the morning the child was found safe and protected by the dog in the middle of a field. The king took his son and said to the yellow dog, 'If you were a man I would give you half my kingdom.'

The yellow dog lived well now at the king's house; nevertheless, he longed for his wife. He left the king and galloped to his own home, where he looked in at the window and found his wife again drinking with her lover. The lover saw the yellow dog and said, 'Someone looked through the window.' 'I know him,' answered the woman. She went out and struck the yellow dog with a whip, and he became a sparrow. For a long time he flew about as a sparrow.

Then the wife began to long for her husband. She went into the forest and, having made a cage, threw into it some millet seeds and hoped to effect a capture. The husband was roaming about in the form of a sparrow and was very hungry. He flew into the forest, found the cage, and, stepping in to peck at the grains, was caught. The wife came and took the cage, dragged her husband out of it, made him once more a man, and said, 'Return home, take the king's two first children from the cellar, and restore them to him.' The peasant accompanied his wife home, and, having taken the king's children from the cellar, carried them to the king. When the king saw his eldest sons his delight knew no bounds, and he loaded the peasant with gifts.

The peasant took the money and went home and said, 'Well, woman, we have enough money now!' 'Come old man,' his wife replied, 'let us build a stone house and sell the square logs.' But the peasant had not forgotten the tortures inflicted on him by his wife, and he said, 'Woman, become a chestnut mare; I will use you to transport both stones and logs.' The peasant-magician had scarcely spoken when his wife became a chestnut mare, and by harnessing her and setting her to transport stones he was enabled to erect a stone house. When it was completed he harnessed the chestnut, and transported the logs, a great number of them. The yard was now filled with the timber, and the old man said, 'Wife, change again to a woman.' Immediately the mare became a woman. The woman had taught the peasant and the peasant had taught the woman. Now she is always baking pancakes and feeding her husband, and he sells logs and they live very well.

The Telltale Lilac Bush
(USA, Hillbilly)

N OLD MAN and woman once lived by themselves along the Tygart Valley River. There had been trouble between them for many years. Few people visited them, and it was not immediately noticed that the wife had unaccountably disappeared. People suspected that the old man had killed her, but her body could not be found, and the question was dropped.

The old man lived a gay life after his wife's disappearance, until one night when a group of young men were sitting on his porch, talking of all the parties which the old man was giving. While they were talking, a large lilac bush growing nearby began beating on the window pane and beckoning towards them as though it were trying to tell them something. No one would have thought anything of this if the wind had been blowing. But there was no wind – not even a small breeze.

Paying no attention to the old man's protests, the young men dug up the lilac bush. They were stunned when the roots were found to be growing from the palm of a woman's hand.

The old man screamed and ran down the hill towards the river, never to be seen again.

Tatterhood

(Norwegian)

NCE on a time there was a king and a queen who had no children, and that gave the queen much grief; she scarce had one happy hour. She was always bewailing and bemoaning herself, and saying how dull and lonesome it was in the palace.

'If we had children there'd be life enough,' she said.

Wherever she went in all her realm she found God's blessing in children, even in the vilest hut; and wherever she came she heard the Goodies scolding the bairns, and saying how they had done that and that wrong. All this the queen heard, and thought it would be so nice to do as other women did. At last the king and queen took into their palace a stranger lassie to rear up, that they might have her always with them, to love her if she did well, and scold her if she did wrong, like their own child.

So one day the little lassie whom they had taken as their own, ran down into the palace-yard, and was playing with a gold apple. Just then an old beggar wife came by, who had a little girl with her, and it wasn't long before the little lassie and the beggar's bairn were great friends, and began to play together, and to toss the gold apple about between them. When the queen saw this, as she sat at a window in the palace, she tapped on the pane for her foster-daughter to come up. She went at once, but the beggar girl went up too; and as they went into the queen's bower, each held the other by the hand. Then the queen began to scold the little lady, and to say, 'You ought to be above running about and playing with a tattered beggar's brat.' And so she wanted to drive the lassie downstairs.

'If the queen only knew my mother's power, she'd not drive

me out,' said the little lassie; and when the queen asked what she meant more plainly, she told her how her mother could get her children if she chose. The queen wouldn't believe it, but the lassie held her own, and said every word of it was true, and bade the queen only to try and make her mother do it. So the queen sent the lassie down to fetch up her mother.

'Do you know what your daughter says?' asked the queen of the old woman, as soon as ever she came into the room.

No; the beggar wife knew nothing about it.

'Well, she says you can get me children if you will,' answered the queen.

'Queens shouldn't listen to beggar lassies' silly stories,' said the old wife, and strode out of the room.

Then the queen got angry, and wanted again to drive out the little lassie; but she declared it was true every word that she had said.

'Let the queen only give my mother a drop to drink,' said the lassie. 'When she gets merry she'll soon find out a way to help you.'

The queen was ready to try this; so the beggar wife was fetched up again once more, and treated both with wine and mead as much as she chose; and so it was not long before her tongue began to wag. Then the queen came out again with the same question she had asked before.

'One way to help you perhaps I know,' said the beggar wife. 'Your Majesty must make them bring in two pails of water some evening before you go to bed. In each of them you must wash yourself, and afterwards throw away the water under the bed. When you look under the bed next morning, two flowers will have sprung up, one fair and one ugly. The fair one you must eat, the ugly one you must let stand; but mind you don't forget the last.'

That was what the beggar wife said.

Yes; the queen did what the beggar wife advised her to do. She had the water brought up in two pails, washed herself in them, and emptied them under the bed; and lo! when she looked under the bed next morning, there stood two flowers. One was ugly and foul, and had black leaves; but the other was so bright and fair, and lovely, she had never seen its like; so she ate it up at once. But the pretty flower tasted so sweet, that she couldn't help herself. She ate the other up too, for, she thought, 'It can't hurt or help one much either way, I'll be bound.'

Well, sure enough, after a while the queen was brought to bed. First of all, she had a girl who had a wooden spoon in her hand, and rode upon a goat; loathly and ugly she was, and the very moment she came into the world she bawled out 'Mamma.'

'If I'm your mamma,' said the queen, 'God give me grace to mend my ways.'

'Oh, don't be sorry,' said the girl, who rode on the goat, 'for one will soon come after me who is better looking.'

So, after a while, the queen had another girl, who was so fair and sweet, no one had ever set eyes on such a lovely child, and with her you may fancy the queen was very well pleased. The elder twin they called 'Tatterhood', because she was always so ugly and ragged, and because she had a hood which hung about her ears in tatters. The queen could scarce bear to look at her, and the nurses tried to shut her up in a room by herself, but it was all no good; where the younger twin was, there she must also be, and no one could ever keep them apart.

Well, one Christmas eve, when they were half grown up, there rose such a frightful noise and clatter in the gallery outside the queen's bower. So Tatterhood asked what it was that dashed and crashed so out in the passage.

'Oh!' said the queen, 'it isn't worth asking about.'

But Tatterhood wouldn't give over till she found out all about it; and so the queen told her it was a pack of Trolls and witches who had come there to keep Christmas. So Tatterhood said she'd just go out and drive them away, and in spite of all they could say, and however much they begged and prayed her to let the Trolls alone, she must and would go out to drive the witches off; but she begged the queen to mind and keep all the doors close shut, so that not one of them came so much as the least bit ajar. Having said this, off she went with her wooden spoon, and began to hunt and sweep away the hags; and all this while there

67

was such a pother out in the gallery, the like of it was never heard. The whole palace creaked and groaned as if every joint and beam were going to be torn out of its place.

Now, how it was, I'm sure I can't tell; but somehow or other one door did get the least bit ajar. Then her twin sister just peeped out to see how things were going with Tatterhood, and put her head a tiny bit through the opening. But, POP! up came an old witch, and whipped off her head, and stuck a calf's head on her shoulders instead; and so the princess ran back into the room on all fours, and began to 'moo' like a calf. When Tatterhood came back and saw her sister, she scolded them all round, and was very angry because they hadn't kept better watch, and asked them what they thought of their heedlessness now, when her sister was turned into a calf.

'But still I'll see if I can't set her free,' she said.

Then she asked the king for a ship in full trim, and well fitted with stores; but captain and sailors she wouldn't have. No, she would sail away with her sister all alone; and as there was no holding her back, at last they let her have her own way.

Then Tatterhood sailed off, and steered her ship right under the land where the witches dwelt, and when she came to the landing place, she told her sister to stay quite still on board the ship; but she herself rode on her goat up to the witches' castle. When she got there, one of the windows in the gallery was open, and there she saw her sister's head hung up on the window frame; so she leapt her goat through the window into the gallery, snapped up the head, and set off with it. After her came the witches to try to get the head again, and they flocked about her as thick as a swarm of bees or a nest of ants; but the goat snorted and puffed, and butted with his horns, and Tatterhood beat and banged them about with her wooden spoon; and so the pack of witches had to give it up. So Tatterhood got back to her ship, took the calf's head off her sister, and put her own on again, and then she became a girl as she had been before. After that she sailed a long, long way, to a strange king's realm.

Now the king of that land was a widower, and had an only son. So when he saw the strange sail, he sent messengers down to the strand to find out whence it came, and who owned it; but when the king's men came down there, they saw never a living soul on board but Tatterhood, and there she was, riding round and round the deck on her goat at full speed, till her elf locks streamed again in the wind. The folk from the palace were all amazed at this sight, and asked were there not more on board. Yes, there were; she had a sister with her, said Tatterhood. Her, too, they wanted to see, but Tatterhood said 'No.'

'No one shall see her, unless the king comes himself,' she said, and so she began to gallop about on her goat till the deck thundered again.

So when the servants got back to the palace, and told what they had seen and heard down at the ship, the king was for setting out at once, that he might see the lassie that rode on the goat. When he got down, Tatterhood led out her sister, and she was so fair and gentle, the king fell over head and ears in love with her as he stood. He brought them both back with him to the palace, and wanted to have the sister for his queen; but Tatterhood said 'No': the king couldn't have her in any way, unless the king's son chose to have Tatterhood. That you may fancy the prince was very loath to do, such an ugly hussy as Tatterhood was; but at last the king and all the others in the palace talked him over, and he yielded, giving his word to take her for his queen; but it went sore against the grain, and he was a doleful man.

Now they set about the wedding, both with brewing and baking, and when all was ready they were to go to church; but the prince thought it the weariest churching he had ever had in all his life. First, the king drove off with his bride, and she was so lovely and so grand, all the people stopped to look after her all along the road, and they stared at her till she was out of sight. After them came the prince on horseback by the side of Tatterhood, who trotted along on her goat with her wooden spoon in her fist, and to look at him, it was more like going to a burial than a wedding, and that his own; so sorrowful he seemed, and with never a word to say.

'Why don't you talk?' asked Tatterhood, when they had ridden a bit.

'Why, what should I talk about?' answered the prince.

'Well, you might at least ask me why I ride upon this ugly goat,' said Tatterhood.

'Why do you ride on that ugly goat?' asked the prince.

'Is it an ugly goat? why, it's the grandest horse a bride ever rode on,' answered Tatterhood; and in a trice the goat became a horse, and that the finest the prince had ever set eyes on.

Then they rode on again a bit, but the prince was just as woeful as before, and couldn't get a word out. So Tatterhood asked him again why he didn't talk, and when the prince answered, he didn't know what to talk about, she said, 'You can at least ask me why I ride with this ugly spoon in my fist.'

'Why do you ride with that ugly spoon?' asked the prince.

'Is it an ugly spoon? why, it's the loveliest silver wand a bride ever bore,' said Tatterhood; and in a trice it became a silver wand, so dazzling bright, the sunbeams glistened from it.

So they rode on another bit, but the prince was just as sorrowful, and said never a word. In a little while Tatterhood asked him again why he didn't talk, and bade him ask why she wore that ugly grey hood on her head.

'Why do you wear that ugly grey hood on your head?' asked the prince.

'Is it an ugly hood? why, it's the brightest golden crown a bride ever wore,' answered Tatterhood, and it became a crown on the spot.

Now they rode on a long while again, and the prince was so woeful that he sat without sound or speech, just as before. So his bride asked him again why he didn't talk and bade him ask now why her face was so ugly and ashen-grey?

'Ah!' asked the prince, 'why is your face so ugly and ashen-grey?'

'I ugly?' said the bride. 'You think my sister pretty, but I am ten times prettier'; and lo! when the prince looked at her, she was so lovely he thought there never was so lovely a woman in all the world. After that, I shouldn't wonder if the prince found his tongue, and no longer rode along hanging down his head.

So they drank the bridal cup both deep and long, and, after

that, both prince and king set out with their brides to the princess's father's palace, and there they had another bridal feast, and drank anew, both deep and long. There was no end to the fun; and, if you make haste and run to the king's palace, I dare say you'll find there's still a drop of the bridal ale left for you.

The Witchball
(USA Hillbilly)

NCE there was a poor boy who wanted to marry a girl, but her folks didn't want him. His grandma was a witch, an' she said she'd fix it up. She made a horsehair witchball, an' put it under the girl's doorstep. The girl come outside, passin' over the witchball, an' went back in the house. She started to say somethin' to her mother, an' ripped out, an' every time she spoke a word, she'd rip out. Her mother told her to stop that or she'd lick her. Then the mother went out for somethin', an' when she came back in, she broke wind, too, every time she spoke. The father come in an' he did the same thing.

He thought somethin' was the matter, so he called the doctor, an' when the doctor come in over the doorstep, he started to poop with every word he said, and they were all atalkin' an' apoopin' when the ole witch come in, an' told 'em God had probably sent that on them as a curse because they wouldn' allow their daughter to marry the poor boy. They told her to run an' git the boy, 'cause he could marry their girl right away, if God would only take that curse offa them. The ole witch went an' got the boy, an' on her way out, she slipped the witchball out from under the doorstep. The boy an' girl got married an' lived happy ever after.

The Werefox
(Chinese)

ANY years ago, a Buddhist monk, named Chi Hsüan, led a very holy and mortified life. He never wore silk, tramped from town to town on foot, and slept in the open. One moonlight night, he was preparing to sleep in a copse adjoining a grave, ten miles from a city in Shan Si. By the light of the moon he saw a wild fox place on its head a skull and some withered bones, go through several mysterious movements, and then deck itself out with grass and leaves. Presently the fox assumed the form of a beautiful woman, very quietly and plainly dressed, and in this guise it wandered out of the copse on to the adjoining high road. As the trampling of a horseman's mount became audible, coming from the north-west, the woman began to weep and wail, her attitude and gestures showing extreme grief. A man on horseback approached, pulled his horse up, and alighted.

'Lady,' he cried, 'what brings you here, alone, in the night? Can I help you?'

The woman stopped crying and told her tale. 'I am the window of So-and-so. My husband died suddenly last year, leaving me penniless; my parents live a long way off. I do not know the way, and there is no one I can turn to, to help me to get back to my home.'

When he heard where her parents lived, the horseman said, 'I come from that place, and I am now on my way home again. If you do not mind rough travelling, you may ride my horse, and I will walk beside it.'

The woman accepted gratefully, and vowed she would never forget the horseman's kindness. She was just on the point of mounting, when the monk, Chi Hsüan, came out of the copse, crying to the horseman, 'Beware! She is not human; she is a werefox. If you do not believe me, wait a few moments and I will make her resume her true shape.'

So he made a sign, or mudra, with his fingers, uttered a *dhârani* (or spell) and cried in a loud voice, 'Why do you not return at once to your original form?'

The woman immediately fell down, turned into an old fox, and expired. Her flesh and blood flowed away like a stream, and nothing remained but the dead fox, a skull, a few dry bones and some leaves and blades of grass.

The cavalier, quite convinced, prostrated himself several times before the priest, and went away full of astonishment.

The Witches' Piper
(Hungarian)

 Y elder brother was piping for some people at a certain place, while another fellow, a man from Etes, was playing for the children at the same house. It must have been on a day before Ash Wednesday. At eleven o'clock or so, the children were taken home. The man who had been playing for them, Uncle Matyi, was paid for his piping. He took leave of my brother and left for home.

On his way home, three women stepped up to him and said, 'Come along, Uncle Matyi! We want you to play for us. Let's go to that house over there, at the end of the street. And have no fear, we're going to pay for your piping.'

When he went in, they took him by the arms (by the way, the man is still living in the village) and made him stand on the bench near the wall. And there he was piping for them. Money came in showers at his feet. 'Gee, I'm not doing badly at all!' he said to himself.

At about midnight, there came a terrible crash, and in a wink he found himself standing right in the top of the white poplar, at the end of the village.

'Damn it! How the dickens can I get down from this tree?'

Suddenly a cart came up the road. When it reached the tree, he called down, 'Oh, brother, do help me!' But the man drove on, taking no heed of Uncle Matyi. Before long another cart drove up towards the tree. On the cart was Péter Barta, a fellow from Karancsság. 'I say, brother, stop your horses and help me get down.' The man brought his horses to a halt and said, 'Is that you, Uncle Matyi?'

'Damn it, to be sure it's me.'

'What on earth are you doing up there?'

'Well, brother, three women stopped me on my way home. They asked me to follow them to a house at the end of the street. When I went in, they made me stand on a bench and there I was to pipe for them. And they've given me a lot of money for it.'

When the man got him down from the tree, Uncle Matyi began looking for the money he had tucked into the hem of his cloak. But there was no money. There was only a lot of broken crockery and little chips of glass.

Such strange things sometimes still happen.

Vasilissa the Fair
(Russian)

MERCHANT and his wife living in a certain country had an only daughter, the beautiful Vasilissa. When the child was eight years old the mother was seized with a fatal illness, but before she died she called Vasilissa to her side and, giving her a little doll, said, 'Listen, dear daughter! remember my last words. I am dying, and bequeath to you now, together with a parent's blessing, this doll. Keep it always beside you, but show it to nobody; if at any time you are in trouble, give the doll some food and ask its advice.' Then the mother kissed her daughter, sighed deeply and died.

After his wife's death the merchant grieved for a long time, and next began to think whether he should not wed again. He was handsome and would have no difficulty in finding a bride; moreover, he was especially pleased with a certain little widow, no longer young, who possessed two daughters of about the same age as Vasilissa.

The widow was famous as both a good housekeeper and a good mother to her daughters, but when the merchant married her he quickly found she was unkind to his daughter. Vasilissa, being the chief beauty in the village, was on that account envied by her stepmother and stepsisters. They found fault with her on every occasion, and tormented her with impossible tasks; thus, the poor girl suffered from the severity of her work and grew dark from exposure to wind and sun. Vasilissa endured all and became every day more beautiful; but the stepmother and her daughters who sat idle with folded hands, grew thin and almost lost their minds from spite. What supported Vasilissa? This. She received assistance from her doll; otherwise she could not have surmounted her daily difficulties.

Vasilissa, as a rule, kept a dainty morsel for her doll, and in the evening when everyone had gone to bed she would steal to her closet and regale her doll and say, 'Now, dear, eat and listen to my grief! Though I am living in my father's house, my life is joyless; a wicked stepmother makes me wretched; please direct my life and tell me what to do.'

The doll tasted the food, and gave advice to the sorrowing child, and in the morning performed her work, so that Vasilissa could rest in the shade or pluck flowers; already the beds had been weeded, and the cabbages watered, and the water carried, and the stove heated. It was nice for Vasilissa to live with her doll.

Several years passed. Vasilissa grew up, and the young men in the town sought her hand in marriage; but they never looked at the stepsisters. Growing more angry than ever, the stepmother answered Vasilissa's suitors thus: 'I will not let you have my youngest daughter before her sisters.' She dismissed the suitors and vented her spite on Vasilissa with harsh words and blows.

But it happened that the merchant was obliged to visit a neighbouring country, where he had business; and in the meanwhile the stepmother went to live in a house situated close to a thick forest. In the forest was a glade, in which stood a cottage, and in the cottage lived Baba-Yaga, who admitted nobody to her cottage, and devoured people as if they were chickens. Having moved to the new house, the merchant's wife continually, on some pretext or other, sent the hated Vasilissa into the forest, but the girl always returned home safe and unharmed, because the doll directed her and took care she did not enter Baba-Yaga's cottage.

Spring arrived, and the stepmother assigned to each of the three girls an evening task; thus, she set one to make lace, a second to knit stockings, and Vasilissa to spin. One evening, having extinguished all the lights in the house except one candle in the room where the girls sat at work, the stepmother went to bed. In a little while the candle needed attention, and one of the stepmother's daughters took the snuffers and, beginning to cut the wick, as if by accident, put out the light.

'What are we to do now?' said the girls. 'There is no light in the whole house, and our tasks are unfinished; someone must run for a light to Baba-Yaga.'

'I can see my pins,' said the daughter who was making lace. 'I shall not go.'

'Neither shall I,' said the daughter who was knitting stockings; 'my needles are bright.'

'You must run for a light. Go to Baba-Yaga's,' they both cried, pushing Vasilissa from the room.

Vasilissa went to her closet, placed some supper ready for the doll, and said, 'Now, little doll, have something to eat and hear my trouble. They have sent me to Baba-Yaga's for a light, and she will eat me.'

'Do not be afraid!' answered the doll. 'Go on your errand, but take me with you. No harm will befall you while I am present.' Vasilissa placed the doll in her pocket, crossed herself and entered the thick forest, but she trembled.

Suddenly a horseman galloped past; he was white and dressed in white, his steed was white and had a white saddle and bridle. The morning light was appearing.

The girl went further and another horseman rode past; he was red and dressed in red and his steed was red. The sun rose.

Vasilissa walked all night and all day, but on the following evening she came out in a glade, where stood Baba-Yaga's cottage. The fence around the cottage was made of human bones, and on the fence there were fixed human skulls with eyes. Instead of doorposts at the gates there were human legs; instead of bolts there were hands, instead of a lock there was a mouth with sharp teeth. Vasilissa grew pale from terror and stood as if transfixed. Suddenly another horseman rode up; he was black and dressed in black and upon a black horse; he sprang through Baba-Yaga's gates and vanished, as if he had been hurled into the earth. Night came on. But the darkness did not last long; the eyes in all the skulls on the fence lighted up, and at once it became as light throughout the glade as if it were midday. Vasilissa trembled from fear, and not knowing whither to run, she remained motionless.

Suddenly she heard a terrible noise. The trees cracked, the dry leaves rustled, and out of the forest Baba-Yaga appeared, riding in a mortar which she drove with a pestle, while she swept away traces of her progress with a broom. She came up to the gates and stopped; then sniffing about her, cried, 'Phoo, phoo, I smell a Russian! Who is here?'

Vasilissa approached the old woman timidly and gave her a low bow; then she said, 'It is I, granny! My stepsisters have sent me to you for a light.'

'Very well,' said Baba-Yaga, 'I know them. If you first of all live with me and do some work, then I will give you a light. If you refuse, I will eat you.' Then she turned to the gates and exclaimed, 'Strong bolts, unlock; wide gates, open!' The gates opened, and Baba-Yaga went out whistling. Vasilissa followed, and all again closed.

Having entered the room, the witch stretched herself and said to Vasilissa, 'Hand me everything in the oven; I am hungry.' Vasilissa lit a torch from the skulls upon the fence and, drawing the food from the oven, handed it to the witch. The meal would have been sufficient for ten men. Moreover, Vasilissa brought up from the cellar kvass, and honey, and beer and wine. The old woman ate and drank almost everything. She left nothing for Vasilissa but some fragments, end-crusts of bread and tiny morsels of sucking pig. Baba-Yaga lay down to sleep and said, 'When I go away tomorrow, take care that you clean the yard, sweep out the cottage, cook the dinner and get ready the linen. Then go to the cornbin, take a quarter of the wheat and cleanse it from impurities. See that all is done! otherwise I shall eat you.'

After giving these injunctions Baba-Yaga began to snore. But Vasilissa placed the remains of the old woman's meal before her doll and, bursting into tears, said, 'Now, little doll, take some food and hear my grief. Baba-Yaga has set me a terrible task, and has threatened to eat me if I fail in any way; help me!'

The doll answered, 'Have no fear, beautiful Vasilissa! Eat your supper, say your prayers and lie down to sleep; morning is wiser than evening.'

It was early when Vasilissa woke, but Baba-Yaga, who had

already risen, was looking out of the window. Suddenly the light from the eyes in the skulls was extinguished; then a pale horseman flashed by, and it was altogether daylight. Baba-Yaga went out and whistled; a mortar appeared before her with a pestle and a hearth broom. A red horseman flashed by, and the sun rose. Then Baba-Yaga took her place in the mortar and went forth, driving herself with the pestle and sweeping away traces of her progress with the broom.

Vasilissa remained alone and, eyeing Baba-Yaga's house, wondered at her wealth. The girl did not know which task to begin with. But when she looked she found that the work was already done: the doll had separated from the wheat the last grains of impurity.

'Oh, my dear liberator,' said Vasilissa to the doll, 'you have rescued me from misfortune!'

'You have only to cook the dinner,' said the doll, climbing into Vasilissa's pocket. 'God help you to prepare it; then rest in peace!'

Towards evening Vasilissa laid the table and awaited Baba-Yaga's return. It became dusk, and a black horseman flashed by the gates; it had grown altogether dark. But the eyes in the skulls shone and the trees cracked and the leaves rustled. Baba-Yaga came. Vasilissa met her. 'Is all done?' asked the witch. 'Look for yourself, granny!'

Baba-Yaga examined everything and, vexed that she had no cause for anger, said, 'My true servants, my bosom friends, grind my wheat!' Three pairs of hands appeared, seized the wheat and bore it from sight.

Baba-Yaga ate to repletion, prepared for sleep, and again gave an order to Vasilissa. 'Tomorrow repeat your task of today; in addition remove the poppies from the cornbin and cleanse them from earth, seed by seed; you see, someone has maliciously mixed earth with them!' Having spoken, the old woman turned to the wall and snored.

Vasilissa began to feed her doll, who said, as on the previous day, 'Pray to God and go to sleep; morning is wiser than evening; all will be done, dear Vasilissa!'

In the morning Baba-Yaga departed again in her mortar, and immediately Vasilissa and the doll set to work at their tasks. The old woman returned, observed everything and cried out, 'My faithful servants, my close friends, squeeze the oil from the poppies!' Three pairs of hands seized the poppies and bore them from sight. Baba-Yaga sat down to dine, and Vasilissa stood silent.

'Why do you say nothing?' remarked the witch. 'You stand as if you were dumb.'

Timidly Vasilissa replied, 'If you would permit me, I should like to ask you a question.'

'Ask, but remember, not every question leads to good. You will learn much; you will soon grow old.'

'I only wish to ask you,' said the girl, 'about what I have seen. When I came to you a pale horseman dressed in white on a white horse overtook me. Who was he?'

'He is my clear day,' answered Baba-Yaga.

'Then another horseman, who was red and dressed in red, and who rode a red horse, overtook me. Who was he?'

'He was my little red sun!' was the answer.

'But who was the black horseman who passed me at the gate granny?'

'He was my dark night; all three are my faithful servants.'

Vasilissa recalled the three pairs of hands, but was silent. 'Have you nothing more to ask?' said Baba-Yaga.

'I have, but you said, granny, that I shall learn much as I grow older.'

'It is well,' answered the witch, 'that you have enquired only about things outside and not about anything here! I do not like my rubbish to be carried away, and I eat over-inquisitve people! Now I will ask you something. How did you succeed in performing the tasks which I set you?'

'My mother's blessing assisted me,' answered Vasilissa.

'Depart, favoured daughter! I do not require people who have been blessed.' Baba-Yaga dragged Vasilissa out of the room and pushed her beyond the gate, took down from the fence a skull with burning eyes and, putting it on a stick, gave it to the girl and said, 'Take this light to your stepsisters; they sent you here for it.'

Vasilissa ran off, the skull giving her light, which only went out in the morning; and at last, on the evening of the second day, she reached home. As she approached the gates, she was on the point of throwing away the skull, for she thought that there would no longer be any need for a light at home. Then suddenly a hollow voice from the skull was heard to say, 'Do not cast me aside, but carry me to your stepmother.' Glancing at the house, and not seeing a light in any of the windows, she decided to enter with the skull.

At first her stepmother and stepsisters met her with caresses, telling her that they had been without a light from the moment of her departure; they could not strike a light in any way, and if anybody brought one from the neighbours, it went out directly it was carried into the room. 'Perhaps your light will last,' said the stepmother. When they carried the skull into the room its eyes shone brightly and looked continually at the stepmother and her daughters. All their efforts to hide themselves were vain; wherever they rushed they were ceaselessly pursued by the eyes, and before dawn had been burnt to ashes, though Vasilissa was unharmed.

In the morning the girl buried the skull in the ground, locked up the house and visited the town, where she asked admission into the home of a certain old woman who was without kindred. Here she lived quietly and awaited her father. But one day she said to the old woman, 'It tires me to sit idle, granny! Go off and buy me some of the best flax; I will busy myself with spinning.'

The old woman purchased the flax and Vasilissa sat down to spin. The work proceeded rapidly, and the thread when spun was as smooth and fine as a small hair. The thread lay in heaps, and it was time to begin weaving, but a weaver's comb could not be found to suit Vasilissa's thread, and nobody would undertake to make one. Then the girl had recourse to her doll, who said, 'Bring me an old comb that has belonged to a weaver, and an old shuttle, and a horse's mane, and I will do everything for you.' Vasilissa obtained everything necessary, and lay down to sleep. The doll, in a single night, made a first-rate loom. Towards the end of winter linen had been woven of so fine a texture that it could be drawn through the needle where the thread should pass.

In spring the linen was bleached, and Vasilissa said to the old woman, 'Sell this linen, granny, and keep the money for yourself.'

The old woman glanced at the work and said with a sigh, 'Ah! my child, nobody but a tsar would wear such linen. I will take it to the palace.'

She went to the royal dwelling, and walked up and down in front of the windows. When the tsar saw her he said, 'What do you desire, old woman?'

'Your Majesty,' she answered, 'I have brought some wonderful material, and will show it to nobody but yourself.'

The tsar ordered that she should be admitted, and marvelled when he saw the linen. 'How much do you ask for it?' he enquired.

'It is not for sale, Tsar and Father! I have brought it as a gift.' The tsar thanked her, and sent her away with some presents.

Some shirts for the tsar were cut out from this linen, but a seamstress could nowhere be found to complete them. At last the tsar summoned the old woman and said to her, 'You were able to spin and weave this linen, so you will be able to sew together some shirts from it.'

'Tsar, it was not I who spun and wove the linen; it is the work of a beautiful maiden.'

'Well, let her sew them!'

The old woman returned home and related everything to Vasilissa. The girl said in reply, 'I knew that this work would not pass out of my hands.' She shut herself in her room and began the undertaking; soon without resting her hands, she had completed a dozen shirts.

The old woman bore them to the tsar, while Vasilissa washed herself and combed her hair, dressed and then took a seat at the window, and there awaited events. She saw a royal servant come to the old woman's house. He entered the room and said, 'The Tsar-Emperor desires to see the skilful worker who made his shirts, and to reward her out of his royal hands.'

Vasilissa presented herself before the tsar. So much did she please him that he said, 'I cannot bear to separate from you; become my wife!' The tsar took her by her white hands, placed her beside himself, and the wedding was celebrated.

Vasilissa's father quickly returned to rejoice at his daughter's good fortune and to live with her. Vasilissa took the old woman into the palace, and never separated from the little doll, which she kept in her pocket.

The Midwife and the Frog
(Hungarian)

MY grandmother's mother was a midwife – the queen's midwife, as we used to say, because she drew her pay from the parish, which in our eyes meant the whole country.

One night she was called away to assist at a childbirth. It was about midnight. It was pitch dark on the road and it was raining. When the woman was delivered of her babe – God let her have a good one – my great-grandmother started off homeward. On the road she came across a big frog. It was hopping along right in front of her. My great-grandmother had always had a holy fear of frogs, and she cried out in terror, 'Get out of my way, you hideous creature! Why on earth are you hopping around me? Is it a midwife you may be wanting?'

And thus she was conversing with the frog as she proceeded on her way, and the frog jumped closer and closer to her. Once it got right under her feet, and she stepped on it. It gave such a shriek that my great-grandmother almost jumped out of her shoes. Well, she went home leaving the frog on the road, and the frog hopped off to some place, wherever it had its abode.

Back at home, my great-grandmother went to bed. Suddenly she heard a cart driving into the yard. She thought there was another childbirth where her assistance would be needed. Soon she saw the door open. Two men came in; both were very dark-skinned. They were both spindleshanks; their legs looked like a pair of pipestems, and their heads were as big as a bushel. They greeted her with, 'Good evening,' and then said, 'We want to take you along, mother; you must come and help with a birth.'

She said, 'Who is it?' as it is the custom of a midwife to enquire where her assistance is wanted.

One of the men said, 'On the road you promised my wife to

help her with the child when her time came.'

And this gave my great-grandmother something to think of, because she had not met a single soul on her way back, except the frog. 'It's true' she thought to herself, 'I asked her by way of a joke "Is it a midwife you're looking for? I might come and help you too."'

The two men said to her, 'Do not tarry, mother.'

But she said to them, 'I'm not going with you because I've met no human creature and I've promised nothing.'

But they were so insistent that she should keep her promise that finally she said, 'Well, as you are so keen on taking me along, I'll go with you.'

She thought to herself that in any case she'd take her rosary with her, and that if she would pray, God would not forsake her, wherever she'd be taken by the two men. And then the men left her alone, and she began to dress. She dressed herself quite neatly, and when she was ready she asked the men, 'Is it a long journey? Shall I put on more warm clothes?'

'We aren't going far. It will take us an hour and a half or so to get back. But hurry up, mother, because my wife was in a bad state when I left her.'

Then she finished dressing and went out with the two men. They put her in their black coach and soon were driving up a big mountain. It was Magyarós Mountain, not far from the banks of the Szucsáva. As they were driving along, suddenly the mountain opened up before them, and they drove straight through the split, right into the centre of the mountain. They pulled up before a house and one of the men opened the door for her.

'Well, you go in to her,' he said. 'You'll find my wife there. She's lying on the floor.'

And as she stepped through the door, she beheld a small woman lying on the floor. She, too, had a head as big as a bushel. She looked ill and was groaning terribly.

My great-grandmother said to her, 'You're in a bad state, daughter, aren't you? But have no fear, God will deliver you of your burden, and then you'll feel well again.'

The woman then said to my great-grandmother, 'Don't say that God will help me. My husband must not hear you saying it.'

The midwife asked, 'What else could I say?'

'Say the *gyivák* [a type of devil] will help you.'

Then my great-grandmother – we had it from her own mouth – felt as if the words had frozen on her lips, so alarmed did she grow at the thought of what place she had been brought to. No sooner had she thought about it than the child was born, a spindleshanks, with legs as thin as pipestems and a head as big as a stewpot. My great-grandmother thought to herself, 'Well, I was brought here, but how am I to get back? So she turned to the woman. 'Well, your men have brought me to your place, but how can I get back? It's pitch dark outside. I couldn't find my way back home alone.'

The sick woman then said, 'Do not worry about that. My husband will take you back to the same place he brought you from.' And then she asked my great-grandmother, 'Well, mother, do you know who I am?'

'I couldn't say I do. I've asked your husband a few questions about you, but he didn't tell me a thing. He said I should go with them and I'd learn in time who you were.'

'Well, you know who I am? I am the frog you kicked about on the road and trod under your feet. Now, this should serve as a lesson that if you happen to come across some creature like me at about midnight or an hour past it, do not speak to it, nor take heed of what you see. Just pass along on your way. You see, you stopped to talk to me and made a promise to me. So you had to be brought here, because I was that frog you met on the road.'

Then my great-grandmother said, 'I've done my job here; now get me back to my home.'

Then the man came in and asked her, 'Well, what would you want me to pay for your troubles?'

Then the old midwife said, 'I don't want you to pay me anything. Get me right back to the place you brought me from.'

The man said, 'Do not worry. We still have half an hour or so to get you back. But now let me take you to our larder so that you may see for yourself that we are doing well. You needn't fear that we haven't the wherewithal to pay for your services.'

And my great-grandmother followed him to the larder. In the larder she beheld all sorts of food heaped on the shelves: flour and bacon and firkins of lard here, and loaves of bread and cream there and a lot of other things, all arranged in neat order, to say nothing of veritable mounds of gold and silver.

'Now you can see for yourself what plenty there is. Whatever the rich men and the wealthy farmers deny to the poor in their greed becomes ours and goes into our storeroom.' And he turned to my great-grandmother and said, 'Well, mother, let's get along. There isn't much time left for us to get you back to your home. Take of this gold an apronful, as I see you have on your Sunday apron.'

And he insisted on her taking an apronful of gold. He wouldn't let her leave the larder until she had filled her apron with it.

When she had put the gold in her apron, she was taken to the top of Magyarós Mountain by the same coach in which she had first come. But dawn was already coming on, and soon the cock uttered its first crow. Then the men pushed her from the black coach – though they were still near the top – and said to her, 'Trot along, mother, you can find your way home from here.'

And when she took a look at her apron to make sure that she had the gold, there was nothing whatever in her apron; that heap of gold had vanished into thin air.

And that is all there is to the story; you can take it from me.

Part Three

BEAUTIFUL PEOPLE

Fair, Brown and Trembling
(Irish)

ING Aedh Cúrucha lived in Tir Conal, and he had three daughters, whose names were Fair, Brown, and Trembling.

Fair and Brown had new dresses, and went to church every Sunday. Trembling was kept at home to do the cooking and work. They would not let her go out of the house at all; for she was more beautiful than the other two, and they were in dread she might marry before themselves.

They carried on in this way for seven years. At the end of seven years the son of the king of Omanya fell in love with the eldest sister.

One Sunday morning, after the other two had gone to church, the old henwife came into the kitchen to Trembling, and said, 'It's at church you ought to be this day, instead of working here at home.'

'How could I go?' said Trembling. 'I have no clothes good enough to wear at church. And if my sisters were to see me there, they'd kill me for going out of the house.'

'I'll give you,' said the henwife, 'a finer dress than either of them has ever seen. And now tell me what dress will you have?'

'I'll have,' said Trembling, 'a dress as white as snow, and green shoes for my feet.'

Then the henwife put on the cloak of darkness, clipped a piece from the old clothes the young woman had on, and asked for the whitest robes in the world and the most beautiful that could be found, and a pair of green shoes.

That moment she had the robe and the shoes, and she brought them to Trembling, who put them on. When Trembling was dressed and ready, the henwife said, 'I have a honey-bird here to sit on your right shoulder, and a honey-finger to put on

95

your left. At the door stands a milk-white mare, with a golden saddle for you to sit on, and a golden bridle to hold in your hand.'

Trembling sat on the golden saddle. And when she was ready to start, the henwife said, 'You must not go inside the door of the church, and the minute the people rise up at the end of mass, do you make off, and ride home as fast as the mare will carry you.'

When Trembling came to the door of the church there was no one inside who could get a glimpse of her but was striving to know who she was; and when they saw her hurrying away at the end of mass, they ran out to overtake her. But no use in their running; she was away before any man could come near her. From the minute she left the church till she got home, she overtook the wind before her, and outstripped the wind behind.

She came down at the door, went in, and found the henwife had dinner ready. She put off the white robes, and had on her old dress in a twinkling.

When the two sisters came home the henwife asked, 'Have you any news today from the church?'

'We have great news,' said they. 'We saw a wonderful, grand lady at the church door. The like of the robes she had we have never seen on woman before. It's little that was thought of our dresses beside what she had on. And there wasn't a man at the church, from the king to the beggar, but was trying to look at her and know who she was.'

The sisters would give no peace till they had two dresses like the robes of the strange lady; but honey-birds and honey-fingers were not to be found.

Next Sunday the two sisters went to church again, and left the youngest at home to cook the dinner.

After they had gone, the henwife came in and asked, 'Will you go to church today?'

'I would go,' said Trembling, 'if I could get the going.'

'What robe will you wear?' asked the henwife.

'The finest black satin that can be found, and red shoes for my feet.'

'What colour do you want the mare to be?'

'I want her to be so black and so glossy that I can see myself in her body.'

The henwife put on the cloak of darkness, and asked for the robes and the mare. That moment she had them. When Trembling was dressed, the henwife put the honey-bird on her right shoulder and the honey-finger on her left. The saddle on the mare was silver, and so was the bridle.

When Trembling sat in the saddle and was going away, the henwife ordered her strictly not to go inside the door of the church, but to rush away as soon as the people rose at the end of mass, and hurry home on the mare before any man could stop her.

That Sunday the people were more astonished than ever, and gazed at her more than the first time, and all they were thinking of was to know who she was. But they had no chance, for the moment the people rose at the end of mass she slipped from the church, was in the silver saddle, and home before a man could stop her or talk to her.

The henwife had the dinner ready. Trembling took off her satin robe, and had on her old clothes before her sisters got home.

'What news have you today?' asked the henwife of the sisters when they came from the church.

'Oh, we saw the grand strange lady again! And it's little that any man could think of our dresses after looking at the robes of satin that she had on! And all at church, from high to low, had their mouths open, gazing at her, and no man was looking at us.'

The two sisters gave neither rest nor peace till they got dresses as nearly like the strange lady's robes as they could find. Of course they were not so good, for the like of those robes could not be found in Erin.

When the third Sunday came, Fair and Brown went to church dressed in black satin. They left Trembling at home to work in the kitchen, and told her to be sure and have dinner ready when they came back.

After they had gone and were out of sight, the henwife came to the kitchen and said, 'Well, my dear, are you for church today?'

'I would go if I had a new dress to wear.'

'I'll get you any dress you ask for. What dress would you like?' asked the henwife.

97

'A dress red as a rose from the waist down, and white as snow from the waist up; a cape of green on my shoulders; and a hat on my head with a red, a white, and a green feather in it; and shoes for my feet with the toes red, the middle white, and the backs and heels green.'

The henwife put on the cloak of darkness, wished for all these things, and had them. When Trembling was dressed, the henwife put the honey-bird on her right shoulder and the honey-finger on her left, and placing the hat on her head, clipped a few hairs from one lock and a few from another with her scissors, and that moment the most beautiful golden hair was flowing down over the girl's shoulders. Then the henwife asked what kind of a mare she would ride. She said white, with blue and gold-coloured diamond-shaped spots all over her body, on her back a saddle of gold, and on her head a golden bridle.

The mare stood there before the door, and a bird sitting between her ears, which began to sing as soon as Trembling was in the saddle, and never stopped till she came home from the church.

The fame of the beautiful strange lady had gone out through the world, and all the princes and great men that were in it came to church that Sunday, each one hoping that it was himself would have her home with him after mass.

The son of the king of Omanya forgot all about the eldest sister, and remained outside the church, so as to catch the strange lady before she could hurry away.

The church was more crowded than ever before, and there were three times as many outside. There was such a throng before the church that Trembling could only come inside the gate.

As soon as the people were rising at the end of mass, the lady slipped out through the gate, was in the golden saddle in an instant, and sweeping away ahead of the wind. But if she was, the prince of Omanya was at her side, and seizing her by the foot, he ran with the mare for thirty perches, and never let go of the beautiful lady till the shoe was pulled from her foot, and he was left behind with it in his hand. She came home as fast as the mare could carry her, and was thinking all the time that the henwife would kill her for losing the shoe.

Seeing her so vexed and so changed in the face, the old woman asked, 'What's the trouble that's on you now?'

'Oh! I've lost one of the shoes off my feet,' said Trembling.

'Don't mind that; don't be vexed,' said the henwife. 'Maybe it's the best thing that ever happened to you.'

Then Trembling gave up all the things she had to the henwife, put on her old clothes, and went to work in the kitchen. When the sisters came home, the henwife asked, 'Have you any news from the church?'

'We have indeed,' said they; 'for we saw the grandest sight today. The strange lady came again, in grander array than before. On herself and the horse she rode were the finest colours of the world, and between the ears of the horse was a bird which never stopped singing from the time she came till she went away. The lady herself is the most beautiful woman ever seen by man in Erin.'

After Trembling had disappeared from the church, the son of the king of Omanya said to the other kings' sons, 'I will have that lady for my own.'

They all said, 'You didn't win her just by taking the shoe off her foot, you'll have to win her by the point of the sword. You'll have to fight for her with us before you can call her your own.'

'Well,' said the son of the king of Omanya, 'when I find the lady that shoe will fit, I'll fight for her, never fear, before I leave her to any of you.'

Then all the kings' sons were uneasy, and anxious to know who was she that lost the shoe; and they began to travel all over Erin to know could they find her. The prince of Omanya and all the others went in a great company together, and made the round of Erin. They went everywhere – north, south, east and west. They visited every place where a woman was to be found, and left not a house in the kingdom they did not search, to know could they find the woman the shoe would fit, not caring whether she was rich or poor, of high or low degree.

The prince of Omanya always kept the shoe. And when the young women saw it they had great hopes, for it was of proper size, neither large nor small, and it would beat any man to know of what material it was made. One thought it would fit her if she cut a little from her great toe; and another, with too short a foot, put something in the tip of her stocking. But no use, they only spoiled their feet, and were curing them for months afterwards.

The two sisters, Fair and Brown, heard that the princes of the world were looking all over Erin for the woman that could wear the shoe, and every day they were talking of trying it on. And one day Trembling spoke up and said, 'Maybe it's my foot that the shoe will fit.'

'Oh, the breaking of the dog's foot on you! Why say so when you were at home every Sunday?'

They were that way waiting, and scolding the younger sister, till the princes were near the place. The day they were to come, the sisters put Trembling in a closet, and locked the door on her. When the company came to the house, the prince of Omanya gave the shoe to the sisters. But though they tried and tried, it would fit neither of them.

'Is there any other young woman in the house?' asked the prince.

'There is,' said Trembling, speaking up in the closet. 'I'm here.'

'Oh! we have her for nothing but to put out the ashes,' said the sisters.

But the prince and the others wouldn't leave the house till they had seen her. So the two sisters had to open the door. When Trembling came out, the shoe was given to her, and it fitted exactly.

The prince of Omanya looked at her and said, 'You are the woman the shoe fits, and you are the woman I took the shoe from.'

Then Trembling spoke up, and said, 'Do you stay here till I return.'

Then she went to the henwife's house. The old woman put on the cloak of darkness, got everything for her she had the first Sunday at church, and put her on the white mare in the same fashion. Then Trembling rode along the highway to the front of the house. All who saw her the first time said, 'This is the lady we saw at church.'

Then she went away a second time, and a second time came back on the black mare in the second dress which the henwife gave her. All who saw her the second Sunday said, 'That is the lady we saw at church.'

A third time she asked for a short absence, and soon came back on the third mare and in the third dress. All who saw her the third time said, 'That is the lady we saw at church.' Every man was satisfied, and knew that she was the woman.

Then all the princes and great men spoke up, and said to the son of the king of Omanya, 'You'll have to fight now for her before we let her go with you.'

'I'm here before you, ready for combat,' answered the prince.

Then the son of the king of Lochlin stepped forth. The struggle began, and a terrible struggle it was. They fought for nine hours. And then the son of the king of Lochlin stopped, gave up his claim, and left the field. Next day the son of the king of Spain fought six hours, and yielded his claim. On the third day the son of the king of Nyerfói fought eight hours, and stopped. The fourth day the son of the king of Greece fought six hours, and stopped. On the fifth day no more strange princes wanted to fight. And all the sons of kings in Erin said they would not fight with a man of their own land, that the strangers had had their chance, and as no others came to claim the woman, she belonged of right to the son of the king of Omanya.

The marriage day was fixed, and the invitations were sent out. The wedding lasted for a year and a day. When the wedding was over, the king's son brought home the bride, and when the time came a son was born. The young woman sent for her eldest sister, Fair, to be with her and care for her. One day, when Trembling was well, and when her husband was away hunting, the two sisters went out to walk. And when they came to the seaside, the eldest pushed the youngest sister in. A great whale came and swallowed her.

The eldest sister came home alone, and the husband asked, 'Where is your sister?'

'She has gone home to her father in Ballyshannon. Now that I am well, I don't need her.'

'Well,' said the husband, looking at her, 'I'm in dread it's my wife that has gone.'

'Oh! no,' said she. 'It's my sister Fair that's gone.'

Since the sisters were very much alike, the prince was in doubt. That night he put his sword between them, and said, 'If you are my wife, this sword will get warm; if not, it will stay cold.'

In the morning when he rose up, the sword was as cold as when he put it there.

It happened when the two sisters were walking by the seashore that a little cowboy was down by the water minding cattle, and saw Fair push Trembling into the sea; and next day, when the tide came in, he saw the whale swim up and throw her out on the sand. When she was on the sand she said to the cowboy, 'When you go home in the evening with the cows, tell the master that my sister Fair pushed me into the sea yesterday; that a whale swallowed me, and then threw me out, but will come again and swallow me with the coming of the next tide; then he'll go out with the tide, and come again with tomorrow's tide, and throw me again on the strand. The whale will cast me out three times. I'm under the enchantment of this whale, and cannot leave the beach or escape myself. Unless my husband saves me before I'm swallowed a fourth time, I shall be lost. He must come and shoot the whale with a silver bullet when he turns on the broad of his back. Under the breast-fin of the whale is a reddish-brown spot. My husband must hit him in that spot, for it is the only place in which he can be killed.'

When the cowboy got home, the eldest sister gave him a draught of oblivion, and he did not tell.

Next day he went again to the sea. The whale came and cast Trembling on shore again. She asked the boy, 'Did you tell the master what I told you to tell him?'

'I did not,' said he. 'I forgot.'

'How did you forget?' asked she.

'The woman of the house gave me a drink that made me forget.'

'Well, don't forget telling him this night. And if she gives you a drink, don't take it from her.'

As soon as the cowboy came home, the eldest sister offered him a drink. He refused to take it till he had delivered his message and told all to the master. The third day the prince went down with his gun and a silver bullet in it. He was not long down when the whale came and threw Trembling upon the beach as the two days before. She had no power to speak to her husband till he had killed the whale. Then the whale went out, turned over once on the broad of his back, and showed the spot for a moment only. That moment the prince fired. He had but the one chance, and a short one at that. But he took it, and hit the spot, and the whale, mad with pain, made the sea all around red with blood, and died.

That minute Trembling was able to speak, and went home with her husband, who sent word to her father what the eldest sister had done. The father came, and told him any death he chose to give her to give it. The prince told the father he would leave her life and death with himself. The father had her put out then on the sea in a barrel, with provisions in it for seven years.

In time Trembling had a second child, a daughter. The prince and she sent the cowboy to school, and trained him up as one of their own children, and said, 'If the little girl that is born to us now lives, no other man in the world will get her but him.'

The cowboy and the prince's daughter lived on till they were married. The mother said to her husband, 'You could not have saved me from the whale but for the little cowboy. On that account I don't grudge him my daughter.'

The son of the king of Omanya and Trembling had fourteen children, and they lived happily till the two died of old age.

Diirawic and Her Incestuous Brother
(Sudan, Dinka)

GIRL called Diirawic was extremely beautiful. All the girls of the tribe listened to her words. Old women all listened to her words. Small children all listened to her words. Even old men all listened to her words. A man called Teeng wanted to marry her, but her brother, who was also called Teeng, refused. Many people each offered a hundred cows for her bridewealth, but her brother refused. One day Teeng spoke to his mother and said, 'I would like to marry my sister Diirawic.'

His mother said, 'I have never heard of such a thing. You should go and ask your father.'

He went to his father and said, 'Father, I would like to marry my sister.'

His father said, 'My son, I have never heard of such a thing. A man marrying his sister is something I cannot even speak about. You had better go and ask your mother's brother.'

He went to his mother's brother and said, 'Uncle, I would like to marry my sister.'

His maternal uncle exclaimed, 'My goodness! Has anybody ever married his sister? Is that why you have always opposed her marriage? Was it because you had it in your heart to marry her yourself? I have never heard of such a thing! But what did your mother say about this?'

'My mother told me to ask my father. I agreed and went to my father. My father said he had never heard such a thing and told me to come to you.'

'If you want my opinion,' said his uncle, 'I think you should ask your father's sister.'

He went around to all his relatives that way. Each one

expressed surprise and suggested that he should ask another. Then he came to his mother's sister and said, 'Aunt, I would like to marry my sister.'

She said, 'My child, if you prevented your sister from being married because you wanted her, what can I say! Marry her if that is your wish. She is your sister.'

Diirawic did not know about this. One day she called all the girls and said, 'Girls, let us go fishing.' Her words were always listened to by everyone, and when she asked for anything, everyone obeyed. So all the girls went, including little children. They went and fished.

In the mean time, her brother Teeng took out his favourite ox, Mijok, and slaughtered it for a feast. He was very happy that he was allowed to marry his sister. All the people came to the feast.

Although Diirawic did not know her brother's plans, her little sister had overheard the conversation and knew what was happening. But she kept silent; she did not say anything.

A kite flew down and grabbed up the tail of Teeng's ox, Mijok. Then it flew to the river where Diirawic was fishing and dropped it in her lap. She looked at the tail and recognised it. 'This looks like the tail of my brother's ox, Mijok,' she said. 'What has killed him? I left him tethered and alive!'

The girls tried to console her, saying, 'Diirawic, tails are all the same. But if it is the tail of Mijok, then perhaps some important guests have arrived. It may be that they are people wanting to marry you. Teeng may have decided to honour them with his favourite ox. Nothing bad has happened.'

Diirawic was still troubled. She stopped the fishing and suggested that they return to find out what had happened to her brother's ox.

They went back. As they arrived, the little sister of Diirawic came running to her and embraced her, saying, 'My dear sister Diirawic, do you know what has happened?'

'I don't know,' said Diirawic.

'Then I will tell you a secret,' continued her sister, 'but please don't mention it to anyone, not even to our mother.'

'Come on, sister, tell me,' said Diirawic.

'Teeng has been preventing you from being married because *he* wants to marry you,' her sister said. 'He has slaughtered his ox, Mijok, to celebrate his engagement to you. Mijok is dead.'

Diirawic cried and said, 'So that is why God made the kite fly with Mijok's tail and drop it in my lap. So be it. There is nothing I can do.'

'Sister,' said her little sister, 'let me continue with what I have to tell you. When your brother bedevils you and forgets that you are his sister, what do you do? I found a knife for you. He will want you to sleep with him in the hut. Hide the knife near the bed. And at night when he is fast asleep, cut off his testicles. He will die. And he will not be able to do anything to you.'

'Sister,' said Diirawic, 'you have given me good advice.'

Diirawic kept the secret and did not tell the girls what had occurred. But she cried whenever she was alone.

She went and milked the cows. People drank the milk. But when Teeng was given milk, he refused. And when he was given food, he refused. His heart was on his sister. That is where his heart was.

At bedtime, he said, 'I would like to sleep in that hut, Diirawic, sister, let us share the hut.'

Diirawic said, 'Nothing is bad, my brother. We can share the hut.'

They did. Their little sister also insisted on sleeping with them in the hut. So she slept on the other side of the hut. In the middle of the night, Teeng got up and moved the way men do! At that moment, a lizard spoke and said, 'Come, Teeng, have you really become an imbecile? How can you behave like that towards your sister?

He felt ashamed and lay down. He waited for a while and then got up again. And when he tried to do what men do, the grass on the thatching spoke and said, 'What an imbecile! How can you forget that she is your sister?'

He felt ashamed and cooled down. This time, he waited much longer. Then his desire rose and he got up. The rafters spoke and said, 'O, the man has really become an idiot! How can your heart be on your mother's daughter's body? Have you become a hopeless imbecile?'

He cooled down. This time he remained quiet for a very long time, but then his mind returned to it again.

This went on until very close to dawn. Then he reached that point when a man's heart fails him. The walls spoke and said, 'You monkey of a human being, what are you doing?' The utensils rebuked him. The rats in the hut laughed at him. Everything started shouting at him, 'Teeng, imbecile, what are you doing to your sister?'

At that moment, he fell back ashamed and exhausted and fell into a deep sleep.

The little girl got up and woke her older sister, saying, 'You fool, don't you see he is now sleeping? This is the time to cut off his testicles.'

Diirawic got up and cut them off. Teeng died.

Then the two girls got up and beat the drums in a way that told everybody that there was an exclusive dance for girls. No men could attend that dance. Nor could married women and children. So all the girls came out running from their huts and went to the dance.

Diirawic then spoke to them and said, 'Sisters, I called you to say that I am going into the wilderness.' She then went on to explain to them the whole story and ended, 'I did not want to leave you in secret. So I wanted a chance to bid you farewell before leaving.'

All the girls decided they would not remain behind.

'If your brother did it to you,' they argued, 'what is the guarantee that our brothers will not do it to us? We must all leave together!'

So all the girls of the tribe decided to go. Only very small girls remained. As they left, the little sister of Diirawic said, 'I want to go with you.'

But they would not let her. 'You are too young,' they said. 'You must stay.'

'In that case,' she said, 'I will cry out loud and tell everyone your plan!' And she started to cry out.

'Hush, hush,' said the girls. Then turning to Diirawic they said, 'Let her come with us. She is a girl with a heart. She has already taken our side. If we die, we die together with her!'

Diirawic accepted and they went. They walked; they walked and walked and walked, until they came to the borders between the human territory and the lion world. They carried their axes and their spears; they had everything they might need.

They divided the work among themselves. Some cut the timber for rafters and poles. Others cut the grass for thatching. And they built for themselves an enormouse house – a house far larger even than a cattle-byre. The number of girls was tremendous. They built many beds for themselves inside the hut and made a very strong door to make sure of their safety.

Their only problem was that they had no food. But they found a large anthill, full of dried meat, grain, and all the other foodstuffs that they needed. They wondered where all this could have come from. But Diirawic explained to them. 'Sisters, we are women and it is the woman who bears the human race. Perhaps God has seen our plight, and not wanting us to perish, has provided us with all this. Let us take it in good grace!'

They did. Some went for firewood. Others fetched water. They cooked and ate. Every day they would dance the women's dance in great happiness and then sleep.

One evening a lion came in search of insects and found them dancing. But seeing such a large number of girls, he became frightened and left. Their number was such as would frighten anyone.

It then occurred to the lion to turn into a dog and go into their compound. He did. He went there looking for droppings of food. Some girls hit him and chased him away. Others said, 'Don't kill him. He is a dog and dogs are friends!'

But the sceptical ones said, 'What kind of dog would be in this isolated world? Where do you think he came from?'

Other girls said, 'Perhaps he came all the way from the cattle camp, following us! Perhaps he thought the whole camp was moving and so he ran after us!'

Diirawic's sister was afraid of the dog. She had not seen a dog following them. And the distance was so great that the dog could not have travelled all the way alone. She worried but said nothing. Yet she could not sleep; she stayed awake while all the others slept.

One night the lion came and knocked at the door. He had overheard the names of the older girls, one of them, Diirawic. After knocking at the door he said, 'Diirawic, please open the door for me.' The little girl who was awake answered, chanting:

'Achol is asleep,
Adau is asleep,
Nyankiir is asleep,
Diirawic is asleep,
The girls are asleep!'

The lion heard her and said, 'Little girl, what is the matter with you, staying up so late?'

She answered him, saying, 'My dear man, it is thirst. I am suffering from a dreadful thirst.'

'Why?' asked the lion. 'Don't the girls fetch water from the river?'

'Yes,' answered the little girl, 'they do. But since I was born, I do not drink water from a pot or a gourd. I drink only from a container made of reeds.'

'And don't they bring you water in such a container?' asked the lion.

'No,' she said. 'They only bring water in pots and gourds, even though there is a container of reeds in the house.'

'Where is that container?' asked the lion.

'It is outside there on the platform!' she answered.

So he took it and left to fetch water for her.

The container of reeds would not hold water. The lion spent much time trying to fix it with clay. But when he filled it, the water washed the clay away. The lion kept on trying until dawn. Then he returned with the container of reeds and put it back where it was. He then rushed back to the bush before the girls got up.

This went on for many nights. The little girl slept only during

109

the daytime. The girls rebuked her for this, saying, 'Why do you sleep in the daytime? Can't you sleep at night? Where do you go at night?'

She did not tell them anything. But she worried. She lost so much weight that she became very bony.

One day Diirawic spoke to her sister and said, 'Nyanaguek, my mother's daughter, what is making you so lean? I told you to remain at home. This is too much for a child your age! Is it your mother you are missing? I will not allow you to make the other girls miserable. If necessary, daughter of my mother, I will kill you.'

But Diirawic's sister would not reveal the truth. The girls went on rebuking her but she would not tell them what she knew.

One day, she broke down and cried, and then said, 'My dear sister, Diirawic, I eat, as you see. In fact, I get plenty of food, so much that I do not finish what I receive. But even if I did not receive enough food, I have an enduring heart. Perhaps I am able to endure more than any one of you here. What I am suffering from is something none of you has seen. Every night a lion gives me great trouble. It is just that I am a person who does not speak. That animal you thought to be a dog is a lion. I remain awake at night to protect us all and then sleep in the daytime. He comes and knocks at the door. Then he asks for you by name to open the door. I sing back to him and tell him that you are all asleep. When he wonders why I am awake, I tell him it is because I am thirsty. I explain that I only drink out of a container made of reeds and that the girls bring water only in pots and gourds. Then he goes to fetch water for me. And seeing that he cannot stop the water from flowing out of the container, he returns towards dawn and disappears, only to be back the following night. So that is what is destroying me, my dear sister. You blame me in vain.'

'I have one thing to tell you,' said Diirawic. 'Just be calm and when he comes, do not answer. I will remain awake with you.'

They agreed. Diirawic took a large spear that they had inherited from their ancestors and remained awake, close to the door. The lion came at his usual hour. He came to the door, but somehow he became afraid and jumped away without knocking. He had a feeling that something was going on.

So he left and stayed away for some time. Then he returned to the door towards dawn. He said, 'Diirawic, open the door for me!' There was only silence. He repeated his request. Still there was only silence. He said, 'Well! The little girl who always answered me is at last dead!'

He started to break through the door, and when he succeeded in pushing his head in, Diirawic attacked him with the large spear, forcing him back into the courtyard.

'Please, Diirawic,' he pleaded, 'do not kill me.'

'Why not?' asked Diirawic. 'What brought you here?'

'I only came in search of a sleeping place!'

'Well, I am killing you for that,' said Diirawic.

'Please allow me to be your brother,' the lion continued to plead. 'I will never attempt to hurt anyone again. I will go away if you don't want me here. Please!'

So Diirawic let him go. He went. But before he had gone a long way, he returned and said to the girls then gathered outside, 'I am going, but I will be back in two days with all my horned cattle.'

Then he disappeared. After two days, he came back with all his horned cattle, as he had promised. Then he addressed the girls, saying, 'Here I have come. It is true that I am a lion. I want you to kill that big bull in the herd. Use its meat for taming me. If I live with you untamed, I might become wild at night and attack you. And that would be bad. So kill the bull and tame me by teasing me with the meat.'

They agreed. So they fell on him and beat him so much that his fur made a storm on his back as it fell off.

They killed the bull and roasted the meat. They would bring a fat piece of meat close to his mouth, then pull it away. A puppy dog would jump out of the saliva which dripped from the lion's mouth. They would give the puppy a fatal blow on the head. Then they would beat the lion again. Another piece of fat meat would be held close to his mouth, then pulled away, and another puppy would jump out of the falling saliva. They would give it a blow on the head and beat the lion some more. Four puppies emerged, and all four were killed.

Yet the lion's mouth streamed with a wild saliva. So they took a large quantity of steaming hot broth and poured it down his throat, clearing it of all the remaining saliva. His mouth remained wide open and sore. He could no longer eat anything. He was fed only milk, poured down his throat. He was then released. For four months, he was nursed as a sick person. His throat continued to hurt for all this time. Then he recovered.

The girls remained for another year. It was now five years since they had left home.

The lion asked the girls why they had left their home. The girls asked him to address his questions to Diirawic, as she was their leader. So he turned to Diirawic and asked the same question.

'My brother wanted to make me his wife,' explained Diirawic. 'I killed him for that. I did not want to remain in a place where I had killed my own brother. So I left. I did not care about my life. I expected such dangers as finding you. If you had eaten me, it would have been no more than I expected.'

'Well, I have now become a brother to you all,' said the lion. 'As an older brother, I think I should take you all back home. My cattle have since multiplied. They are yours. If you find that your land has lost its herds, these will replace them. Otherwise they will increase the cattle already there, because I have become a member of your family. Since your only brother is dead, let me be in the place of Teeng, your brother. Cool your heart and return home.'

He pleaded with Diirawic for about three months. Finally she agreed, but cried a great deal. When the girls saw her cry, they all cried. They cried and cried because their leader, Diirawic, had cried.

The lion slaughtered a bull to dry their tears. They ate the meat. Then he said to them, 'Let us wait for three more days, and then leave!'

They slaughtered many bulls in sacrifice to bless the territory they crossed as they returned, throwing meat away everywhere they passed. As they did so, they prayed, 'This is for the animals and the birds that have helped keep us healthy for all this time without death or illness in our midst. May God direct you to share in this meat.'

They had put one bull into their big house and locked the house praying, 'Our dear house, we give you this bull. And you bull, if you should break the rope and get out of the house, that will be a sign of grace from the hut. If you should remain inside, then we bequeath you this hut as we leave.' And they left.

All this time the people at home were in mourning. Diirawic's father never shaved his head. He left the ungroomed hair of mourning on his head and did not care about his appearance. Her mother, too, was in the same condition. She covered herself with ashes so that she looked grey. The rest of the parents mourned, but everyone mourned especially for Diirawic. They did not care as much for their own daughters as they did for Diirawic.

The many men who had wanted to marry Diirawic also neglected themselves in mourning. Young men and girls wore only two beads. But older people and children wore no beads at all.

All the girls came and tethered their herds a distance from the village. They all looked beautiful. Those who had been immature had grown into maturity. The older ones had now reached the peak of youth and beauty. They had blossomed and had also become wiser and adept with words.

The little boy who was Diirawic's youngest brother had now grown up. Diirawic resembled her mother, who had been an extremely beautiful girl. Even in her old age, she still retained her beauty and her resemblance to her daughter still showed.

The little boy had never really known his sister, as he was too young when the girls left. But when he saw Diirawic in the newly arrived cattle camp, he saw a clear resemblance to his mother. He knew that his two sisters and the other girls of the camp had disappeared. So he came and said, 'Mother, I saw a girl in the cattle camp who looks like she could be my sister, even though I do not remember my sisters.'

113

'Child, don't you feel shame? How can you recognise people who left soon after you were born? How can you recall people long dead? This is evil magic! This is the work of an evil spirit!' She started to cry, and all the women joined her in crying.

Age-sets came running from different camps to show her sympathy. They all cried, even as they tried to console her with words.

Then came Diirawic with the girls and said, 'My dear woman, permit us to shave off your mourning hair. And all of you, let us shave off your mourning hair!'

Surprised by her words, they said, 'What has happened that we should shave off our mourning hair?'

Then Diirawic asked them why they were in mourning. The old woman started to cry as Diirawic spoke, and said, 'My dear girl, I lost a girl like you. She died five years ago, and five years is a long time. If she had died only two or even three years ago, I might have dared to say you are my daughter. As it is, I can't. But seeing you, my dear daughter, has cooled my heart.'

Diirawic spoke again, saying, 'Dear Mother, every child is a daughter. As I stand in front of you, I feel as though I were your daughter. So please listen to what I say as though I were your own daughter. We have all heard of you and your famed name. We have come from a very far-off place because of you. Please allow us to shave your head. I offer five cows as a token of my request.'

'Daughter,' said the woman, 'I shall honour your request, but not because of the cows – I have no use for cattle. Night and day, I think of nothing but my lost Diirawic. Even this child you see means nothing to me compared to my lost child, Diirawic. What grieves me is that God has refused to answer my prayers. I have called upon our clan spirits and I have called upon my ancestors, and they do not listen. This I resent. I will listen to your words, my daughter. The fact that God has brought you along and put these words into your mouth is enough to convince me.'

So she was shaved. Diirawic gave the woman beautiful leather skirts made from skins of animals they killed on the way. They were not from the hides of cattle, sheep or goats. She decorated

114

the edges of the skirts with beautiful beads and made bead designs of cattle figures on the skirts. On the bottom of the skirts she left the beautiful natural furs of the animals.

The woman cried and Diirawic pleaded with her to wear them. She and the girls went and brought milk from their own cattle and made a feast. Diirawic's father welcomed the end of mourning. But her mother continued to cry as she saw all the festivities.

So Diirawic came to her and said, 'Mother, cool your heart. I am Diirawic.'

Then she shrieked with cries of joy. Everyone began to cry – old women, small girls, everyone. Even blind women dragged themselves out of their huts, feeling their way with sticks, and cried. Some people died as they cried. Drums were taken out and for seven days, people danced with joy. Men came from distant villages, each with seven bulls to sacrifice for Diirawic. The other girls were almost abandoned. All were concerned with Diirawic.

People danced and danced. They said, 'Diirawic, if God has brought you, then nothing is bad. That is what we wanted.'

Then Diirawic said, 'I have come back. But I have come with this man to take the place of my brother Teeng.'

'Very well,' agreed the people. 'Now there is nothing to worry about.'

There were two other Teengs. Both were sons of chiefs. Each one came forward, asking to marry Diirawic. It was decided that they should compete. Two large kraals were to be made. Each man was to fill his kraal with cattle. The kraals were built. The men began to fill them with cattle. One Teeng failed to fill his kraal. The other Teeng succeeded so well that some cattle even remained outside.

Diirawic said, 'I will not marry anyone until my new brother is given four girls to be his wives. Only then shall I accept the man my people want.'

People listened to her words. Then they asked her how the man became her brother. So she told the whole story from its beginning to its end.

The people agreed with her and picked four of the finest girls for her new brother. Diirawic then accepted the man who had won the competition. She was given to her husband and she continued to treat the lion-man as her full brother. She gave birth first to a son and then to a daughter. She bore twelve children. But when the thirteenth child was born, he had the characteristics of a lion. Her lion-brother had brought his family to her village and was living there when the child was born. The fields of Diirawic and her brother were next to each other. Their children played together. As they played, the small lion-child, then still a baby, would put on leather skirts and sing. When Diirawic returned, the children told her, but she dismissed what they said. 'You are liars. How can such a small child do these things?'

They would explain to her that he pinched them and dug his nails into their skins and would suck blood from the wounds. Their mother simply dismissed their complaints as lies.

But the lion-brother began to wonder about the child. He said, 'Does a newly born human being behave the way this child behaves?' Diirawic tried to dispel his doubts.

But one day her brother hid and saw the child dancing and singing in a way that convinced him that the child was a lion and not a human being. So he went to his sister and said, 'What you bore was a lion! What shall we do?'

The woman said, 'What do you mean? He is my child and should be treated as such.'

'I think we should kill him,' said the lion-brother.

'That is impossible,' she said. 'How can I allow my child to be killed? He will get used to human ways and will cease to be aggressive.'

'No,' continued the lion. 'Let us kill him by poison if you want to be gentle with him.'

'What are you talking about?' retorted his sister. 'Have you forgotten that you yourself were a lion and were then tamed into a human being? Is it true that old people lose their memory?'

The boy grew up with the children. But when he reached the age of herding, he would go and bleed the children by turn and suck blood from their bodies. He would tell them not to speak,

116

and that if they said anything to their elders, he would kill them and eat them. The children would come home with wounds, and when asked, would say their wounds were from thorny trees.

But the lion did not believe them. He would tell them to stop lying and tell the truth, but they would not.

One day he went ahead of them and hid on top of the tree under which they usually spent the day. He saw the lion-child bleed the children and suck their blood. Right there, he speared him. The child died.

He then turned to the children and asked why they had hidden the truth for so long. The children explained how they had been threatened by the lion-child. Then he went and explained to his sister, Diirawic, what he had done.

The Mirror
(*Japanese*)

HERE is a pretty Japanese tale of a small farmer who bought his young wife a mirror. She was surprised and delighted to know that it reflected her face, and cherished her mirror above all her possessions. She gave birth to one daughter, and died young; and the farmer put the mirror away in a press, where it lay for long years.

The daughter grew up the very image of her mother; and one day, when she was almost a woman, her father took her aside, and told her of her mother, and of the mirror which had reflected her beauty. The girl was devoured with curiosity, unearthed the mirror from the old press, and looked into it.

'Father!' she cried, 'See! Here is mother's face!'

It was her own face she saw; but her father said nothing.

The tears were streaming down his cheeks, and the words would not come.

The Frog Maiden
(Burmese)

N old couple was childless, and the husband and the wife longed for a child. So when the wife found that she was with child, they were overjoyed; but to their great disappointment, the wife gave birth not to a human child, but to a little she-frog. However, as the little frog spoke and behaved as a human child, not only the parents but also the neighbours came to love her and called her affectionately 'Little Miss Frog'.

Some years later the woman died, and the man decided to marry again. The woman he chose was a widow with two ugly daughters and they were very jealous of Little Miss Frog's popularity with the neighbours. All three took a delight in ill-treating Little Miss Frog.

One day the youngest of the king's four sons announced that he would perform the hair-washing ceremony on a certain date and he invited all young ladies to join in the ceremony, as he would choose at the end of the ceremony one of them to be his princess.

On the morning of the appointed day the two ugly sisters dressed themselves in fine raiment, and with great hopes of being chosen by the prince they started for the palace. Little Miss Frog ran after them, and pleaded, 'Sisters, please let me come with you.'

The sisters laughed and said mockingly, 'What, the little frog wants to come? The invitation is to young ladies and not to young frogs.' Little Miss Frog walked along with them towards the palace, pleading for permission to come. But the sisters were adamant, and so at the palace gates she was left behind. However, she spoke so sweetly to the guards that they allowed her to go in. Little Miss Frog found hundreds of young ladies

119

gathered round the pool full of lilies in the palace grounds; and she took her place among them and waited for the prince.

The prince now appeared, and washed his hair in the pool. The ladies also let down their hair and joined in the ceremony. At the end of the ceremony, the prince declared that as the ladies were all beautiful, he did not know whom to choose and so he would throw a posy of jasmines into the air; and the lady on whose head the posy fell would be his princess. The prince then threw the posy into the air, and all the ladies present looked up expectantly. The posy, however, fell on Little Miss Frog's head, to the great annoyance of the ladies, especially the two stepsisters. The prince also was disappointed, but he felt that he should keep his word. So Little Miss Frog was married to the prince, and she became Little Princess Frog.

Some time later, the old king called his four sons to him and said, 'My sons, I am now too old to rule the country, and I want to retire to the forest and become a hermit. So I must appoint one of you as my successor. As I love you all alike, I will give you a task to perform, and he who performs it successfully shall be king in my place. The task is, bring me a golden deer at sunrise on the seventh day from now.'

The youngest prince went home to Little Princess Frog and told her about the task. 'What, only a golden deer!' exclaimed Princess Frog. 'Eat as usual, my prince, and on the appointed day I will give you a golden deer.'

So the youngest prince stayed at home, while the three elder princes went into the forest in search of the deer.

On the seventh day before sunrise, Little Princess Frog woke up her husband and said, 'Go to the palace, prince, and here is your golden deer.'

The young prince looked, then rubbed his eyes, and looked again. There was no mistake about it; the deer which Little Princess Frog was holding by a lead was really of pure gold. So he went to the palace, and to the great annoyance of the elder princes who brought ordinary deers, he was declared to be the heir by the king. The elder princes, however, pleaded for a second chance, and the king reluctantly agreed.

'Then perform this second task,' said the king. 'On the seventh day from now at sunrise, you must bring me the rice that never becomes stale, and the meat that is ever fresh.'

The youngest prince went home and told Princess Frog about the new task. 'Don't you worry, sweet prince,' said Princess Frog. 'Eat as usual, sleep as usual, and on the appointed day I will give you the rice and meat.'

So the youngest prince stayed at home, while the three elder princes went in search of the rice and meat.

On the seventh day at sunrise, Little Princess Frog woke up her husband and said, 'My Lord, go to the palace now, and here is your rice and meat.'

The youngest prince took the rice and meat, and went to the palace, and to the great annoyance of the elder princes who brought only well-cooked rice and meat, he was again declared to be the heir. But the two elder princes again pleaded for one more chance, and the king said, 'This is positively the last task. On the seventh day from now at sunrise, bring me the most beautiful woman on this earth.'

'Ho, ho!' said the three elder princes to themselves in great joy. 'Our wives are very beautiful, and we will bring them. One of us is sure to be declared heir, and our good-for-nothing brother will be nowhere this time.'

The youngest prince overheard their remark, and felt sad, for his wife was a frog and ugly. When he reached home, he said to his wife, 'Dear Princess, I must go and look for the most beautiful woman on this earth. My brothers will bring their wives, for they are really beautiful, but I will find someone who is more beautiful.'

'Don't you fret, my prince,' replied Princess Frog. 'Eat as usual, sleep as usual, and you can take me to the palace on the appointed day; surely I shall be declared to be the most beautiful woman.'

The youngest prince looked at the princess in surprise; but he did not want to hurt her feelings, and he said gently, 'All right, Princess, I will take you with me on the appointed day.'

On the seventh day at dawn, Little Princess Frog woke up the prince and said, 'My Lord, I must make myself beautiful. So please wait outside and call me when it is nearly time to go.' The prince left the room as requested. After some moments, the prince shouted from outside, 'Princess, it is time for us to go.'

'Please wait, my Lord,' replied the princess, 'I am just powdering my face.'

After some moments the prince shouted, 'Princess, we must go now.'

'All right, my Lord,' replied the princess, 'please open the door for me.'

The prince thought to himself, 'Perhaps, just as she was able to obtain the golden deer and the wonderful rice and meat, she is able to make herself beautiful', and he expectantly opened the door, but he was disappointed to see Little Princess Frog still a frog and as ugly as ever. However, so as not to hurt her feelings, the prince said nothing and took her along to the palace. When the prince entered the audience chamber with his Frog Princess the three elder princes with their wives were already there. The king looked at the prince in surprise and said, 'Where is your beautiful maiden?'

'I will answer for the prince, my king,' said the Frog Princess. 'I am his beautiful maiden.' She then took off her frog skin and stood a beautiful maiden dressed in silk and satin. The king declared her to be the most beautiful maiden in the world, and selected the prince as his successor on the throne.

The prince asked his princess never to put on the ugly frog skin again, and the Frog Princess, to accede to his request, threw the skin into the fire.

The Sleeping Prince
(Surinamese)

FATHER had a daughter, but the child loved nothing so much as the field of grass which her father had planted. Only that she loved. Every morning her nurse took her to look at the grass. One morning when they went, the horses were feeding on the grass. Then they fought, and fought, and blood fell on the grass. The girl said, 'My nurse, look how the horses are eating my grass till they fight. But look how nice the red is on the earth.'

At once a voice answered her, it said, 'Look how nice the red is on top of the earth. Well, if you were to see the Sleeping Prince! But the one who said the thing must come before eight days are up, and she will see the Sleeping Prince. And she will see a fan, and she should fan the prince until the prince shall awaken. Then she should kiss the prince. And she will see a bottle of water, and she shall sprinkle all the sticks which she sees.'

But, when she went she took her clothes, and she had a black doll and a broken razor. Then she took them and carried them there, too. Then she saw the prince, and she took the fan and began to fan the prince. She fanned so till . . . an old woman sat by at the side. She was a witch. Then she asked her, she said, if she was not tired of fanning? But she said, 'No, no.'

Not long after, the old woman came back, and she asked her, she said, 'Don't you want to go and urinate?' And so at once she got up to go and urinate.

The old woman took up the fan and began to fan. And so, before the girl came back, the prince awakened, and the old woman kissed the prince. And so the old woman had to marry the prince, because the law was that the one who kissed the prince should be the one to marry him.

But when they were already married, then the woman made

123

her look after the fowls. She was very sad, because in her father's country she was a princess, and here she had to look after the fowls. They built a nice little house for her to live in. Then at night when she returned from her work, she put on her fine clothes, and she played a singing box. But when she finished playing, then she took up the black doll and the razor, and she asked it, she said, 'My black doll, my black doll, tell me if that is justice, or I will cut off your neck.' Then she put them back and she went to sleep.

But a soldier passed one night. Then he heard how sweetly the singing box played. He hid at the side of the house, and he heard everything the girl asked the black doll. And so he went and told the king that the girl who looked after the chickens did thus.

The selfsame night the king went to listen. Just as the woman asked the black doll if that was justice, the king knocked on the door that she open the door at once. As the door opened the king saw the woman and at once he fainted, because he did not know that this woman was a princess. She was wearing her fine clothes. And when the king came to himself, he called the woman and said he would call a big audience, and she must explain what made her ask that of the black doll.

When they came to the audience, she said before all the important people, 'Yes, in my father's country I was a princess, and here I must look after the fowls.' And she related everything that had happened between her and the old woman, and she had acted towards her, to cause her (the witch) to marry the prince. And so they found her in the right, and they killed the old woman.

From her bones they made a stepladder to climb to the top of her bed. And from the skin of the old woman she made a carpet to spread on the ground. And from the head she made a wash-basin in which to wash her face.

And so she came to marry the prince later. It was her destiny.

The Orphan
(African, Malawi)

LONG time ago a certain man married. His wife gave birth to a baby girl whom they named Diminga. When Diminga's mother died, her father married again, and his new wife bore him several more children.

Although her husband asked her to care for Diminga, the stepmother cursed the child and would not treat her as her own. She would not bathe her, she fed her only husks, and made her sleep in a kraal. So Diminga looked a dirty miserable little girl, a skeleton dressed in rags. All she longed for was to die so that she might join her real mother.

One night Diminga dreamed that her mother was calling her: 'Diminga! Diminga my child! You need not starve,' said the voice. 'Tomorrow at noon, when you are grazing the cattle, take your big cow Chincheya and tell her to do what I have asked.'

The next day Diminga took her cattle into the fields as usual. When midday came and her hunger was at its worst, she remembered her dream. She went to Chincheya, patted her back, and said, 'Chincheya. Do what my mother told you.'

No sooner had she said this than many plates of food appeared before her. There was rice, beef, chicken, tea and much more. Diminga ate until she was full – and still there was food left over. She made the surplus disappear, and returned home that day so satisfied that she surprised her stepmother by refusing to eat the husks which were offered for her supper. 'Have them yourself,' she said.

Now this happened many times as each day Chincheya produced food for Diminga when they were alone in the fields. As Diminga grew fatter, her stepmother grew more suspicious, asking, 'Why are you growing fat even though you refuse to eat at home? What do you eat?'

But Diminga would not tell her secret and at last the stepmother insisted that her own daughter must accompany Diminga when she grazed her cattle the next day. Diminga was reluctant to take the girl, but she had no choice. When the time came for the midday meal, she told her stepsister to say nothing of what she was about to see.

The girl watched as Diminga took Chincheya aside and spoke to her. She was amazed when suddenly there was food everywhere. Her mouth watered; she tasted all the dishes, then she hid a bit of each under her fingernails before Diminga made the remains vanish.

That night after Diminga had gone to sleep, the girl told her mother to fetch plates, and when these were brought she heaped upon them all the food that she had hidden, saying, 'This food comes from that cow, Chincheya. Abundant and delicious food appears when Diminga speaks to her.'

The old woman was thunderstruck. She gobbled up the food and set about making plans to get all the rest that was still inside the cow. A few days later, she told her husband that she was feeling unwell. Now, for this reason a traditional dance was held and during this dance the stepmother seemed to fall into a trance. She cried out, 'The spirits demand the sacrifice of the cow Chincheya.'

Diminga was furious. She refused to allow the killing. Her stepmother pleaded with her husband, 'Should I die because of your daughter's infatuation with a cow?'

And her husband pleaded with his daughter, but Diminga was determined that Chincheya should not be killed. Then as she slept, one night she heard her mother's voice again. It said, 'My daughter Diminga, let them slaughter Chincheya. But do not eat the meat yourself. Take the stomach. Bury it on an island. You will see what will happen.'

So Diminga allowed the sacrifice to take place. The stepmother was sadly disappointed to find not even a single grain of rice inside the cow, indeed the meat itself was tasteless. Diminga wept at Chincheya's death; but she followed her mother's instructions and planted the cow's stomach on an island.

Where the stomach was planted a golden tree grew. Its leaves were pound notes and its fruits were coins: pennies, shillings, sixpences and florins. The tree glittered and dazzled the eyes of anyone who dared to look at it.

One day a ship passed the island. When the owner saw the golden tree he ordered his men to go ashore and collect the money. They shook the tree and tried to pick off the money, but they could not move it. The owner asked the local chief to shake the tree, then each of his villagers in turn to do the same. Still no one was successful in harvesting the money.

Then the ship's owner, who was a European, asked the chief, 'Is there anyone who has not tried to shake the tree? Go and search your village in case you have left anyone behind.'

The search took place, and the one remaining person who had not tried to shake the tree was found – a ragged dirty girl with sad eyes. It was Diminga. Everyone laughed when she was taken to the tree. 'Can this miserable girl succeed when we have failed!'

'Let her try,' said the European.

The tree swayed as Diminga approached. As she touched it, the tree began to shake, and when she held it, coins and notes showered to the ground in great piles, enough to fill several bags.

Instant marriage was arranged between Diminga and the European, and they went to live at his house. When she had bathed, dressed in new clothes and perfumed herself, Diminga was unrecognisably beautiful. And she was happy with her new life.

After some time Diminga visited her home, taking with her servants, carrying cases of clothes, food and money for her family. They welcomed her warmly, especially when they saw her gifts. And her father was glad that his daughter's troubles were now finished.

But her stepmother was full of envy and began planning once more to get the better of Diminga. Thus it happened that, when Diminga was sitting with her family, her one-eyed stepsister came to her with a needle in her hands, saying, 'Let me find lice in your hair, sister.'

'I have no lice,' said Diminga.

But her stepmother insisted and the girl began her search. Then suddenly, she drove the needle into Diminga's head. Diminga jerked, and was transformed into a bird, which flew away.

The old woman dressed her daughter in Diminga's clothes and veiled her face. She told Diminga's servants that their mistress was sick. They took 'Diminga' home, and told their master of his wife's illness. Whenever he tried to remove the veil, his 'wife' said, 'You must leave it for I am not well.'

One day his servant Guao went to the river to wash clothes and saw a small, bright beautiful bird perched on a tree. It began to sing:

Guao, Guao, Guao
Is Manuel at home
With one eyed-wife
This terrible one-eyed wife?

Guao listened, enchanted by the music and his curiosity was aroused. Each day he saw the little bird and heard the song, then finally he took his master to witness the strange event. The master trapped the bird and took it home, where he made a pet of it. Whenever he touched the bird's head, he noticed, it trembled. He looked closely and saw a needle. When he pulled out the needle the bird was transformed into a beautiful girl – Diminga, his wife.

When Diminga told him of her sufferings her husband ran and unveiled the 'sick wife' – and shot her. He ordered his servants to cut the body into pieces, which were dried then mixed with rice and put into bags. The bags of food were sent to Diminga's stepmother with the message, 'Diminga has arrived safely and sends you this gift.'

The old woman was satisfied to hear the news and shared the food amongst her family. It was only when she looked into the last bag of meat that she realised that she had been truly punished. Inside the bag was a human head, with its one eye fixed upon her in a terrible gaze.

Part Four

MOTHERS AND DAUGHTERS

Achol and Her Wild Mother
(Sudan, Dinka)

CHOL, Lanchichor (The Blind Beast) and Adhalchingeeny (The Exceedingly Brave One) were living with their mother. Their mother would go to fetch firewood. She gathered many pieces of wood and then put her hands behind her back and said, 'O dear, who will help me lift this heavy load?'

A lion came passing by and said, 'If I help you lift the load, what will you give me?'

'I will give you one hand,' she said.

She gave him a hand; he helped her lift the load and she went home. Her daughter, Achol, said, 'Mother, why is your hand like that?'

'My daughter, it is nothing,' she answered.

Then she left again to fetch firewood. She gathered many pieces of wood and then put her hand behind her back and said, 'O dear, who will now help me lift this heavy load?'

The lion came and said, 'If I help you lift the load, what will you give me?'

'I will give you my other hand!' And she gave him the other hand. He lifted the load on to her head and she went home without a hand.

Her daughter saw her and said, 'Mother, what has happened to your hands? You should not go to fetch firewood again! You must stop!'

But she insisted that there was nothing wrong and went to fetch firewood. Again she collected many pieces of firewood, put her arms behind her back and said, 'Who will now help me lift this heavy load?'

Again the lion came and said, 'If I help you lift the load, what will you give me?'

She said, 'I will give you one foot!'

She gave him her foot; he helped her, and she went home.

Her daughter said, 'Mother, this time, I insist that you do not go for the firewood! Why is all this happening? Why are your hands and your foot like this?'

'My daughter, it is nothing to worry about,' she said. 'It is my nature.'

She went back to the forest another time and collected many pieces of firewood. Then she put her arms behind her back and said, 'Who will now help me lift this load?'

The lion came and said, 'What will you now give me?'

She said, 'I will give you my other foot!'

So she gave him the other foot; he helped her, and she went home.

This time she became wild and turned into a lioness. She would not eat cooked meat; she would only have raw meat.

Achol's brothers went to the cattle camp with their mother's relatives. So only Achol remained at home with her mother. When her mother turned wild, she went into the forest, leaving Achol alone. She would only return for a short time in the evening to look for food. Achol would prepare something for her and put it on the platform in the courtyard. Her mother would come at night and sing in a dialogue with Achol.

'Achol, Achol, where is your father?'
'My father is still in the cattle camp!'
'And where is Lanchichor?'
'Lanchichor is still in the cattle camp!'
'And where is Adhalchingeeny?'
'Adhalchingeeny is still in the cattle camp!'
'And where is the food?'
'Mother, scrape the insides of our ancient gourds.'

She would eat and leave. The following night, she would return and sing. Achol would reply; her mother would eat and return to the forest. This went on for a long time.

Meanwhile, Lanchichor came from the cattle camp to visit his mother and sister. When he arrived home, he found his mother absent. He also found a large pot over the cooking fire. He wondered about these things and asked Achol, 'Where is Mother gone, and why are you cooking in such a big pot?'

She replied, 'I am cooking in this big pot because our mother has turned wild and is in the forest, but she comes at night for food.'

'Take that pot off the fire,' he said.

'I cannot,' she replied. 'I must cook for her.'

He let her. She cooked and put the food on the platform before they went to bed. Their mother came at night and sang. Achol replied as usual. Her mother ate and left. Achol's brother got very frightened. He emptied his bowels and left the next morning.

When he was asked in the cattle camp about the people at home, he was too embarrassed to tell the truth; so he said they were well.

Then Achol's father decided to come home to visit his wife and his daughter. He found the big pot on the fire and his wife away. When he asked Achol, she explained everything to him. He also told her to take the pot off the fire, but she would not. She put the food on the platform, and they went to bed. Achol's father told her to let him take care of the situation. Achol agreed. Her mother came and sang as usual. Achol replied. Then her mother ate. But her father was so frightened that he returned to the camp.

Then came Adhalchingeeny (The Exceedingly Brave One) and brought with him a very strong rope. He came and found Achol cooking with the large pot, and when Achol explained to him their mother's condition, he told her to take the pot off the fire, but she would not give in. He let her proceed with her usual plan. He placed the rope near the food in a way that would trap his mother when she took the food. He tied the other end to his foot.

Their mother came and sang as usual. Achol replied. As their mother went towards the food, Adhalchingeeny pulled the rope, gagged her and tied her to a pole. He then went and beat her with part of the heavy rope. He beat her and beat her and beat her. Then he gave her a piece of raw meat, and when she ate it, he beat her again. He beat her and beat her and beat her. Then he gave her two pieces of meat, one raw and one roasted. She refused the raw one and took the roasted one, saying, 'My son, I

have now become human, so please stop beating me.'
They then reunited and lived happily.

Tunjur, Tunjur
(Palestinian Arab)

TELLER: Testify that God is One!
AUDIENCE: There is no god but God.

HERE was once a woman who could not get pregnant and have children. Once upon a day she had an urge; she wanted babies. 'O Lord!' she cried out, 'why of all women am I like this? Would that I could get pregnant and have a baby, and may Allah grant me a girl even if she is only a cooking pot!'

One day she became pregnant. A day came and a day went, and behold! she was ready to deliver. She went into labour and delivered, giving birth to a cooking pot. What was the poor woman to do? She washed it, cleaning it well, put the lid on it, and placed it on the shelf.

One day the pot started to talk. 'Mother,' she said, 'take me down from this shelf!'

'Alas, daughter!' replied the mother, 'where am I going to put you?'

'What do you care?' said the daughter. 'Just bring me down, and I will make you rich for generations to come.'

The mother brought her down. 'Now put my lid on,' said the pot, 'and leave me outside the door.' Putting the lid on, the mother took her outside the door.

The pot started to roll, singing as she went, 'Tunjur, tunjur, clink, clink, O my mama!' She rolled until she came to a place where people usually gather. In a while people were passing by. A man came and found the pot all settled in its place. 'Eh!' he exclaimed, 'who has put this pot in the middle of the path? I'll be damned! What a beautiful pot! It's probably made of silver.' He looked it over well. 'Hey, people!' he called, 'whose pot is this? Who put it here?' No one claimed it. 'By Allah,' he said, 'I'm going to take it home with me.'

On his way home, he went by the honey vendor. He had the

139

pot filled with honey and brought it home to his wife. 'Look, wife,' he said, 'how beautiful is this pot!' The whole family was greatly pleased with it.

In two or three days they had guests, and they wanted to offer them some honey. The woman of the house brought the pot down from the shelf. Push and pull on the lid, but the pot would not open! She called her husband over. Pull and push, but open it he could not. His guests pitched in. Lifting the pot and dropping it, the man tried to break it open with hammer and chisel. He tried everything, but it was no use.

They sent for the blacksmith, and he tried and tried, to no avail. What was the man to do?

'Damn your owners!' he cursed the pot, 'Did you think you were going to make us wealthy?' And, taking it up, he threw it out the window.

When they turned their back and could no longer see it, she started to roll, saying as she went.

'Tunjur, tunjur, O my mama.
In my mouth I brought the honey.
Clink, clink, O my mama.
In my mouth I brought the honey.'

'Bring me up the stairs!' she said to her mother when she reached home.

'Yee!' exclaimed the mother. 'I thought you had disappeared, that someone had taken you.'

'Pick me up!' said the daughter.

Picking her up, my little darlings, the mother took the lid off and found the pot full of honey. Oh! How pleased she was!

'Empty me!' said the pot.

The mother emptied the honey into a jar, and put the pot back on the shelf.

'Mother,' said the daughter the next day, 'take me down!'

The mother brought her down from the shelf.

'Mother, put me outside the door!'

The mother placed her outside the door, and she started rolling – tunjur, tunjur, clink, clink – until she reached a place where people were gathered, and then she stopped. A man passing by found her.

'Eh!' he thought, 'what kind of a pot is this?' He looked it over. How beautiful he found it! 'To whom does this belong?' he asked. 'Hey, people! Who are the owners of this pot?' He waited, but no one said, 'It's mine.' Then he said, 'By Allah, I'm going to take it.'

He took it, and on his way home stopped by the butcher and had it filled with meat. Bringing it home to his wife, he said, 'Look, wife, how beautiful is this pot I've found! By Allah, I found it so pleasing I bought meat and filled it and brought it home.'

'Yee!' they all cheered, 'how lucky we are! What a beautiful pot!' They put it away.

Towards evening they wanted to cook the meat. Push and pull on the pot, it would not open! What was the woman to do? She called her husband over and her children. Lift, drop, strike – no use. They took it to the blacksmith, but with no result.

The husband became angry. 'God damn your owners!' he cursed it. 'What in the world are you?' And he threw it as far as his arm would reach.

As soon as he turned his back, she started rolling, and singing:

'Tunjur, tunjur. O my mama,
In my mouth I brought the meat.
Tunjur, tunjur, O my mama,
In my mouth I brought the meat.'

She kept repeating that till she reached home.

'Lift me up!' she said to her mother. The mother lifted her up, took the meat, washed the pot, and put it away on the shelf.

'Bring me out of the house!' said the daughter the next day. The mother brought her out, and she said, 'Tunjur, tunjur, clink, clink' as she was rolling until she reached a spot close by the king's house, where she came to a stop. In the morning, it is said, the son of the king was on his way out, and behold! there was the pot settled in its place.

'Eh! What's this? Whose pot is it?' No one answered. 'By Allah,' he said, 'I'm going to take it.' He took it inside and called his wife over.

'Wife,' he said, 'take this pot! I brought it home for you. It's the most beautiful pot!'

The wife took the pot. 'Yee! How beautiful it is! By Allah, I'm going to put my jewellery in it.' Taking the pot with her, she gathered all her jewellery, even that which she was wearing, and put it in the pot. She also brought all their gold and money and stuffed them in the pot till it was full to the brim, then she covered it and put it away in the wardrobe.

Two or three days went by, and it was time for the wedding of her brother. She put on her velvet dress and brought the pot out so that she could wear her jewellery. Push and pull, but the pot would not open. She called to her husband, and he could not open it either. All the people who were there tried to open it, lifting and dropping. They took it to the blacksmith, and he tried but could not open it.

The husband felt defeated, 'God damn your owners!' he cursed it, 'what use are you to us?' Taking it up, he threw it out the window. Of course he was not all that anxious to let it go, so he went to catch it from the side of the house. No sooner did he turn around than she started to run:

'Tunjur, tunjur, O my mama,
In my mouth I brought the treasure.
Tunjur, tunjur, O my mama,
In my mouth I brought this treasure.'

'Lift me up!' she said to her mother when she reached home. Lifting her up, the mother removed the lid.

'Yee! May your reputation be blackened!' she cried out. 'Wherever did you get this? What in the world is it?' The mother was now rich. She became very, very happy.

'It's enough now,' she said to her daughter, taking away the treasure. 'You shouldn't go out any more. People will recognise you.'

'No, no!' begged the daughter. 'Let me go out just one last time.'

The next day, my darlings, she went out, saying 'Tunjur, tunjur, O my mama.' The man who found her the first time saw her again.

'Eh! What in the world is this thing?' he exclaimed. 'It must have some magic in it, since it's always tricking people. God damn its owners! By Allah the Great, I'm going to sit and shit in it.' He went ahead, my darlings, and shat right in it. Closing the lid on him,' she rolled along:

'Tunjur, tunjur, O my mama
In my mouth I brought the caca.
Tunjur, tunjur, O my mama,
In my mouth I brought the caca.'

'Lift me up!' she said to her mother when she reached home. The mother lifted her up.

'You naughty thing, you!' said the mother. 'I told you not to go out again, that people would recognise you. Don't you think it's enough now?'

The mother then washed the pot with soap, put perfume on it, and placed it on the shelf.

This is my story, I've told it, and in your hands I leave it.

The Little Old Woman with
Five Cows
(Yakut)

NE morning a little old woman got up and went to the field containing her five cows. She took from the earth a herb with five sprouts and, without breaking either root or branch, carried it home and wrapped it in a blanket and placed it on her pillow.

Then she went out again and sat down to milk her cows. Suddenly she heard tambourine bells jingle and scissors fall, on account of which noise she upset the milk. Having run home and looked, she found that the plant was uninjured. Again she issued forth to milk the cows, and again thought she heard the tambourine bells jingle and scissors fall, and once more she spilt her milk. Returning to the house, she looked into the bedchamber. There sat a maiden with eyes of chalcedony and lips of dark stone, with a face of light-coloured stone and with eyebrows like two dark sables stretching their forefeet towards each other; her body was visible through her dress; her bones were visible through her body; her nerves spreading this way and that, like mercury, were visible through her bones. The plant had become this maiden of indescribable beauty.

Soon afterwards Kharjit-Bergen, son of the meritorious Khan Kara, went into the dark forest. He saw a grey squirrel sitting on a curved twig, near the house of the little old woman with five cows, and he began to shoot, but as the light was bad, for the sun was already setting, he did not at once succeed in his purpose. At this time one of his arrows fell into the chimney.

'Old woman! take the arrow and bring it me!' he cried, but received no answer. His cheeks and forehead grew flushed and he became angry; a wave of arrogance sprang from the back of his neck, and he rushed into the house.

When he entered and saw the maiden he lost consciousness. But he revived and fell in love. Then he went out and, jumping on his horse, raced home at full gallop. 'Parents!' said he, 'there is such a beautiful maiden at the house of a little old woman with five cows! Get hold of this maiden and give her to me!'

The father sent nine servants on horseback, and they galloped at full speed to the house of the little old woman with five cows. All the servants became unconscious when they beheld the maiden's beauty. However, they recovered, and all went away except the best one of them.

'Little old woman!' said he, 'give this girl to the son of the meritorious Khan Khara!'

'I will give her,' was the answer.

They spoke to the maiden. 'I will go,' she announced.

'Now, as the bridegroom's wedding gift,' said the old woman, 'drive up cattle, and fill my open fields with horses and horned stock!'

Immediately the request was uttered and before the agreement was concluded the man gave an order to collect and drive up the animals as the bridegroom's gift.

'Take the maiden and depart!' said the little old woman, when the stock of horses and cattle had been given as arranged.

The maiden was quickly adorned, and a finely speckled horse that spoke like a human being was led up to her skilfully. They put on it a silver halter, saddled it with a silver saddle, which was placed over an upper silver saddle-cloth and a lower silver saddle-cloth, and they attached a little silver whip. Then the son-in-law led the bride from the mother's side by the whip, mounted his horse and took the bride home.

They went along the road, and the young man said, 'In the depth of the forest there is a trap for foxes; I will go there. Proceed along this road! It divides into two paths. On the road leading to the east is hanging a sable skin. But on the road leading to the west there should be the skin of a male bear with the paws and head and with white fur at the neck. Go on the path where the sable skin is hanging.' He pointed out the road and went away.

The girl made her way to the fork in the road, but on coming to it forgot the directions. Going along the path where the bear

145

skin was hanging, she reached a small iron hut. Suddenly out of the hut came a devil's daughter, dressed in an iron garment above the knee. She had only one leg, and that was twisted; a single bent hand projected from below her breast, and her single furious eye was situated in the middle of her forehead. Having shot forth a fifty-foot iron tongue on to her breast, she pulled the girl from the horse, dropped her to the ground and tore all the skin from her face and threw it on her own face. She dragged off all the girl's finery and put it on herself. Then mounting, the devil's daughter rode away.

The husband met the devil's daughter when she arrived at the house of the meritorious Khan Khara. Nine youths came to take her horse by the halter; eight maidens did likewise. It is said that the bride wrongly fastened her horse to the willow tree where the old widow from Semyaksin used to tether her spotted ox. The greater part of those who thus received the bride became sorely depressed and the remainder were disenchanted; sorrow fell on them.

All who met the bride abominated her. Even the red weasels ran away from her, thus showing she was repugnant to them. Grass had been strewn on the pathway up to her hut, and on this grass she was led by the hand. Having entered, she replenished the fire with the tops of three young larch trees. Then they concealed her behind a curtain, while they themselves also drank and played and laughed and made merry.

But the marriage feast came to an end, and there was a return to ordinary life. The little old woman with five cows, on going into open country to seek her cows, found that the plant with five sprouts was growing better than usual. She dug it up with its roots and, carrying it home, wrapped it up and placed it on her pillow. Then she went back and began to milk the cows, but the tambourine with the bells began to tinkle, and the scissors fell with a noise. Going back to the house, the old woman found the lovely maiden seated and looking more lovely than ever.

'Mother,' she said, 'my husband took me away from here. My dear husband said, "I must go away on some business," but before he went he said, "Walk along the path where the sable's skin is hanging, and do not go where the bear's skin is hanging." I forgot and went along the second path to a little iron house. A devil's daughter tore the skin from my face and put it on her own face; she dragged off all my fine things and put them on; and next this devil's daughter mounted my horse and set out. She threw away skin and bones and a grey dog seized my lungs and heart with his teeth and carried them to open country. I grew here as a plant, for it was decreed that I should not die altogether. Perhaps it has been settled that later I shall bear children. The devil's daughter has affected my fate, for she has married my husband and contaminated his flesh and blood; she has absorbed his flesh and blood. When shall I see him?'

The meritorious Khan Khara came to the field belonging to the little old woman with five cows. The speckled white horse, who was endowed with human speech, knew that his mistress had revived, and he began to speak.

He complained to Khan Khara thus: 'The devil's daughter has killed my mistress, torn all the skin from her face and covered her own face with it; she has dragged away my mistress's finery and clothed herself in it. The devil's daughter has gone to live with Khan Khara's son and become his bride. But my mistress has revived and now lives. If your son does not take this fair girl as his bride, then I will complain to the white Lord God on his seat of white stone, by the lake that has silver waves and golden floating ice, and blocks of silver and black ice; and I will shatter your house and your fire, and will leave you no means of living. A divine man must not take a devil's daughter. Fasten this devil's-daughter bride to the legs of a wild horse. Let a stream of rushing water fall on your son and cleanse him during thirty days; and let the worms and reptiles suck away his contaminated blood. Afterwards draw him from the water and expose him to the wind on the top of a tree for thirty nights, so that breezes from the north and from the south may penetrate his heart and liver, and purify his contaminated flesh and blood. When he is cleansed let him persuade and retake his wife!'

The khan heard and understood the horse's words. It is said he threw aside tears from both eyes; then he galloped home. On seeing him the bride changed countenance.

'Son!' said Khan Khara, 'whence and from whom did you take your wife?'

'She is the daughter of the little old woman with five cows.'

147

'What was the appearance of the horse on which you brought her? What kind of woman did you bring? Do you know her origin?'

To these questions the son answered, 'Beyond the third heaven, in the upper region which has the white stone seat is the white God; his younger brother collected migratory birds and united them into one society. Seven maidens, his daughters in the form of seven cranes, came to earth and feasted and entered a round field and danced; and an instructress descended to them. She took the best of the seven cranes and said, "Your mission is to go out to people; to be a Yakut on this middle land; you must not dislike this impure middle land! You are appointed worthy of the son of the meritorious Khan Khara and are to wear a skin made of eight sables. On account of him you will become human and bear children, and bring them up." After speaking she cut off the end of the crane's wings. The maiden wept. "Turn into a mare's tail-grass, and grow!" said the instructress; "A little old woman with five cows will find the herb and turn it into a maiden and give her in marriage to Khan Khara's son." I took her according to this direction and as she was described to me; but I accepted a strange being; in reality, as appears to me, I took nothing!'

After his son's reply the khan said, 'Having seen and heard, I have come. The speckled horse with the human voice has complained to me. When you bore away your wife you spoke to her of a forked road. You said, "On the eastern path there is hanging a sable's skin and on the western path a bear's skin." You said, "Do not go on the path with the bear's skin, but go along the path showing a sable skin!" But she forgot, and passed along the path which had a bear's skin. She reached the iron house and then a devil's daughter jumped out to meet her, dragged her from her horse and threw her down, tore the whole of the skin from her face and placed it on her own face. The devil's daughter dressed herself in the girl's finery and silver ornaments and rode hither as a bride. She fastened the horse to the old willow; it is already a mark. "Attach the devil's daughter to the feet of a wild stallion!" said the horse to me, "and wash your son in a swift stream for a whole month of thirty nights; let worms and reptiles suck away his contaminated body and blood.

Carry him away and expose him to the breeze on the top of a tree during a month of thirty nights. Let the breezes search him from the north and from the south; let it blow through his heart and liver!" said the horse to me. "Let him go and persuade his wife and take her! But away with this woman! Do not show her! She will devour people and cattle. If you do not get rid of her," said the horse, "I will complain to the white God."

On hearing this the son became much ashamed, and a workman called Boloruk seized the bride, who was sitting behind a curtain, and, dragging her by the foot, fastened her on the legs of a wild horse. The horse kicked the devil's daughter to pieces and to death. Her body and blood were attacked on the ground by worms and reptiles, and became worms and reptiles moving about till the present time. After being placed in a stream of rushing water the khan's son was placed on a tree, so that the spring breezes coming from the north and from the south blew through him. Thus his contaminated body and blood were purified and, when he was brought home, dried up and scarcely breathing, only his skin and bones remained.

He rode to the region of the wedding gift as before and, having picketed his horse, dismounted at his mother-in-law's house. The little old woman who owned the five cows fluttered out joyfully; she rejoiced as if the dead had come to life and the lost had been found. From the picketing spot to the tent she strewed green grass and spread on the front bed a white horse-skin with hoofs. She killed a milch cow and a large-breasted mare and made a wedding feast.

The girl approached her husband with tears. 'Why have you come to me?' she asked. 'You spilt my dark blood, you cut my skin deeply. You gave me up as food for dogs and ducks. You gave me to the daughter of an eight-legged devil. After that, how can you seek a wife here? Girls are more numerous than perch, and women than grayling; my heart is wounded and my mind is agitated! I will not come!'

'I did not send you to the daughter of an eight-legged devil and when I went away on an important matter I pointed out your path. I did not knowingly direct you to a perilous place and I did not know what would happen when I said to you "Go and meet your fate!" The lady-instructress and protectress, the creatress, chose you and appointed you for me; therefore you revived and are alive,' he said; 'and whatever may happen, good or ill, I shall unfailingly take you!'

The little old woman with five cows wiped aways tears from both eyes and sat down between these two children. 'How is it that, having met, you do not rejoice when you have returned to life after death, and been found after having been lost? Neither of you must oppose my will!'

The maiden gave her word, but said 'Agreed!' unwillingly. Then the young man sprang up and danced and jumped and embraced and kissed and drew in his breath. The couple played the best games and burst into loud laughter and talked unceasingly. Outside they fastened the speckled horse that spoke like a human being, laid on him the silver saddle-cloth, saddled him with the silver saddle, bridled him with the silver bridle, hung on him the silver saddle bags and attached to him the little silver whip.

When the maiden had been dressed and all was complete on her she was sent off. She and her husband knew as they went along that it was winter by the fine snow that was falling; they knew it was summer by the rain; they knew it was autumn by the fog.

The servants from the nine houses of Khan Khara, the house servants from eight houses and the room attendants from seven houses, and nine lords' sons who came out like nine cranes thought, 'How will the bride arrive? Will she march out or will she saunter? And will sables arise from her footsteps?'

Thinking thus, they prepared arrows so vigorously that the skin came off their fingers; they attended so closely to their work that their sight became dull. Seven grown-up daughters like seven cranes, born at one time, twisted threads so that the skin came from their knees, and said, 'If, when the bride comes, she blows her nose loudly, dear little kings will be plentiful.'

The son arrived with his bride, and two maidens took their horses by the bridle at the picket rope. The son and his bride dismounted and she blew her nose; therefore dear little kings would come! Instantly the women began to weave garments. Sables ran along the place from which the bride stepped forward, and some of the young men hastened into the dark forest to shoot them.

From the foot of the picketing post to the tent the way had been spread with green grass. On arriving, the bride kindled the fire with three branches of larch. Then they hid her behind a curtain. They stretched a strap in nine portions and tied to it ninety white speckled foals. On the right side of the house they thrust into the ground nine posts and fastened to them nine white foals and put on the foals nine friendly sorcerers who drank kumyss. On the left side of the house they set up eight posts.

Wedding festivities were begun in honour of the bride's entry into the home. Warriors collected and experts came together. It is said that nine ancestral spirits came from a higher place and twelve ancestral spirits rose from the ground. It is said that nine tribes came from under the ground and, using whips of dry wood, trotted badly. Those having iron stirrups crowded together and those having copper stirrups went unsteadily.

All had collected from the foreign tribes and from the tents of the nomad villages; there were singers, there were dancers, there were storytellers; there were those who jumped on one foot and there were leapers; there were crowds possessing five-kopeck pieces, there were saunterers. Then the dwellers-on-high flew upwards; those dwelling in the lower regions sank into the earth; and inhabitants of the middle region, the earth, separated and walked away. The litter remained till the third day; but before the morrow most of the fragments had been collected, all animals had been enclosed and children were sporting in the place. Their descendants are said to be alive today.

Achol and Her Adoptive Lioness-Mother

(Sudan, Dinka)

CHIENG gave birth to two children, Maper and Achol. They had three paternal half-brothers. Achol was betrothed to a man called Kwol. The family moved to the lion territory. As Achol was still small, her brother carried her.

Their half-brothers were jealous of Achol's good fortune in being betrothed so young. They agreed on a plan to abandon Achol and her brother Maper in the wilderness. One evening, they secretly put some medicine in their milk. Achol and Maper fell into a heavy sleep. That night, a gourd full of milk was placed near them, and the cattle camp moved on, leaving them behind.

Achol was the first to wake up the next morning. When she saw that they had been left behind, she cried and woke her brother up. 'Maper, son of my mother, the camp has gone and we have been left behind!'

Maper woke up, looked around and said, 'So our own brothers have left us! Never mind, drink your milk.'

They drank some milk and then moved into a ditch made by an elephant. This provided them with shelter and protection. There they slept.

Along came a lioness looking for remains in the camp. When she saw the ditch, she looked into it and saw the children. They cried, 'O, Father, we are dead – we are eaten!'

The lioness spoke and said, 'My children, do not cry. I will not eat you. Are you children of human beings?'

'Yes,' they said.

'Why are you here?' she asked.

'We were abandoned by our half-brothers,' said Maper.

'Come along with me,' said the lioness. 'I will look after you as my own children; I have no children of my own.'

152

They agreed and went with her. On the way, Maper escaped and returned home. Achol remained with the lioness. They went to the lioness's house, and she looked after Achol and raised her until she became a big girl.

In the mean time, Achol's relatives were mourning her loss. The half-brothers denied having played a foul trick. But Maper explained that he and his sister were left behind and found by a lioness, from whom he had escaped.

Some years later, the camp again moved to the lion territory. By this time Maper had become a grown man. One day as he and his age-mates were herding, they came to the home of the lioness. Maper did not recognise the village. The lioness had gone to hunt. Achol was there. But Maper did not recognise her.

One of the age-mates spoke to Achol, saying 'Girl, will you please give us water to drink?'

Achol said, 'This is not a house where people ask for water. I see you are human beings; this place is dangerous for you!'

'We are very thirsty,' they explained. 'Please, let us drink.'

She brought them water, and they drank. Then they left. Achol's mother, the lioness, returned, carrying an animal she had killed. She threw the animal down and sang:

'Achol, Achol,
Come out of the hut,
My daughter whom I raised in plenty
When people were gathering wild grain.
My daughter was never vexed;
Daughter, come out, I am here.
My little one who was left behind,
My little one whom I found unhurt,
My little one whom I raised,
Achol, my beloved one,
Come, meet me my daughter.'

They met and embraced, and then cooked for themselves and ate. Achol's mother told her, 'Daughter, if human beings come, do not run away from them; be nice to them. That is how you will get married.'

Maper was attracted to Achol, and that same evening he returned with a friend to court her. Achol's mother gave her a separate hut in which to entertain her age-mates. So when Maper came with his friend and asked to be accommodated, she let them into that hut. She made their beds on one side of the hut, while she herself slept on the other side.

At night, Maper's desire for Achol increased and he wanted to move over to her side of the hut. But whenever he tried to move, a lizard on the wall spoke, saying, 'The man is about to violate his own sister!' So he stopped. Then he tried to move again, and a rafter on the ceiling spoke and said, 'The man is about to violate his sister!' When he tried again, the grass said the same.

Maper's friend woke up and said, 'Who is speaking? What are they saying?' Maper said, 'I do not know and I do not understand what they mean by "sister".'

So they asked the girl to tell them more about who she was. Achol then told them the story of how she and her brother had been abandoned and how the lioness had found them.

'Really?' said Maper with excitement.

'Yes,' said Achol.

'Then, let us leave for home. You are my sister.'

Achol embraced him and cried and cried. When she became calm she told Maper and his friend that she could not leave the lioness, for the lioness had taken very good care of her. But they persuaded her to leave with them. Their camp moved on the next morning to avoid meeting the lioness.

That morning, the lioness left very early to hunt. When she returned in the evening, she sang to Achol as usual, but Achol did not reply. She repeated the song several times, and Achol did not answer. She went inside the hut and found that Achol was gone. She cried and cried and cried: 'Where has my daughter gone? Has a lion eaten her or have the human beings taken her away from me?'

Then she ran, following the cattle camp. She ran and ran and ran.

The cattle camp arrived at the village, and Achol was hidden.

The lioness continued to run and run and run until she reached the village. She stopped outside the village and began to sing her usual song.

As soon as Achol heard her voice, she jumped out of her hiding place. They ran towards one another and embraced.

154

Achol's father took out a bull and slaughtered it in hospitality for the lioness. The lioness said she would not go back to the forest but would rather stay among the human beings with her daughter, Achol.

Achol was married and was given to her husband. Her mother, the lioness, moved with her to her marital home. And they all lived happily together.

Part Five

MARRIED WOMEN

Story of a Bird Woman
(Siberian tribal, Chukchi)

LAD went to a lake in the open country. There he saw many birds, of which some were geese and some were gulls, but both geese and gulls left their garments on the shore. The youth seized their clothing, whereupon all the geese and gulls said, 'Restore it.'

He gave back the stolen things of all the goose-girls, but kept the clothes of one gull-maiden and took her for himself. She bore him two children, real human children. When the women went to collect leaves the gull-wife went with them into the fields, but as she gathered grasses badly, her mother-in-law scolded her. All the birds were flying away, and the wife, who pined to return to her own land, went with her children behind the tent as the geese passed by.

'How would it be,' she said, 'for me to carry away my children?' The geese plucked their wings and stuck feathers on the children's sleeves, and the wife and her children flew away together.

When the husband came he could not find his wife, for she was gone. He could learn nothing about her, so he said to his mother, 'Make me ten pairs of very good boots.' Then he departed to the birds' country and saw an eagle who said to him, 'Go to the seashore; there you will find an old man cutting down wood; he is making firewood. He is of a monstrous aspect behind, so do not draw near to him from that direction; he would swallow you. Approach him face to face.'

The old man said, 'Whence have you come, and whither are you going?'

The lad answered, 'I married a gull-maiden, who bore me two children, but she has now disappeared with them. I am looking for her.'

159

'How will you travel?'

'I have ten pairs of boots,' was the reply.

The old man said, 'I will make you a canoe.' He made a beautiful canoe, with a cover like a snuff-box. The young man took his place in it, and the old one said, 'If you desire to go to the right, say to the canoe, "Wok, wok", and move your right foot. A little later, if you wish to go to the left, you will say, "Wok, wok!" and move your left foot.'

The canoe was swift as a bird. The old man continued, 'When you reach the shore and wish to land, say "Kay!" and push the cover with your hand!'

The young man approached the shore, pressed the cover, and the canoe grounded. He saw many bird-children at play on the ground. It was bird-land. He found his children and they recognised their father. 'Father has come!'

He said, 'Tell your mother I have arrived.'

They soon returned, and with them came the wife's brother, who approached the young man and said, 'Your wife has been taken as the wife of our chief, a great sea-bird.'

The man entered his wife's house. The chief bird kissed her on the cheek, and said to the young man, 'Why have you come? I will not restore your wife to you.'

The brother-in-law sat down in the tent. The husband and the great bird grappled with one another, and the young man, seizing his opponent by the neck, thrust him out. The chief bird departed to his country and was loud in complaint, whereupon many birds flew hither, and many gulls of various kinds.

While the young man was sleeping with his wife she called out, 'Countless warriors have come, wake up quickly!'

But he remained asleep and, as there were cries and noise around the house, she grew alarmed. Soon the birds drew feathers and poised them like arrows, but the young man went out and, seizing a stick, waved it in various directions; he struck one bird's wing, another's neck and another's back. Then all the birds fled, but on the morrow there came twice as many; they seemed as numerous as a swarm of gnats. But the young man filled a flat vessel with water and sprinkled the birds with it. Afterwards they could not fly, being frozen to the spot, and no more came.

The young man now bore his wife and children home to his own people. Taking his seat in the canoe, he covered it over as before, and coming to the shore, found the little old man.

'Well?' said the latter.

'I have brought them!' was the reply.

'Then depart! Here are your boots, take them and set off.'

When, in time, they forsook the canoe, they found the eagle in the old place. They were exhausted. The eagle said, 'Put on my clothing.' The young man attired himself in the eagle's clothing and flew home. The eagle had said to him, 'You will assume my attire, but do not take it into the house; leave it a little way off in a field!'

So the young man left the garment on the ground, and it flew back to the eagle. They arrived home. The youth now pushed some fallen wood with his foot, and it became a great herd. He drove the herd before him, then anointed his wife with blood and married her. Ceasing to be a bird, she became human and dressed herself as a woman.

Father and Mother Both 'Fast'
(USA, Hillbilly)

H, yes. Well a fella stayed with a girl, and by and by he went to his father and he said, 'Father, I'm going to marry that girl.' He says, 'John, let me tell you – I'se fast when I was young, and that girl's your sister.'

Well, he felt bad and he left her. By and by, he picked up another one, and he stayed with her for a while, and he went to his father and he said, 'Father, I'm going to marry that girl.' He said, 'Johnny, I was fast when I was young – that girl's your sister.'

Felt awful bad, and so one day he's setting up by the stove with his head hung down, and his mother said, 'What's the trouble, John?' 'No nothing.' She says, 'There's something, and I want to know what it is. Why did you leave that girl, the first one you stayed with, and you left your second one?' 'Well,' he said, 'Father told me he was fast when he was young, and they's both my sisters.' Says, 'Johnny, I want to tell you something, I was fast when I'se young, and your father ain't your father at all.'

Reason to Beat Your Wife
(*Egyptian*)

WO friends met. The first said to the second, 'How are you, So-and-so? We have not met for a long time. Those were the days. How are things going for you now?'

The second answered, 'Well, by God, I got married, and my wife is the "daughter of good people". Just as one wishes a wife to be.'

The first asked, 'Have you beaten her yet or not?'

'No, by God, there is no reason to beat her. She does everything as I wish.'

'She has to get at least one beating, just so that she may know who the master of the house is!'

'By God, yes! You are right.'

A week passed, and they met again. The first asked the second, 'Hey, what did you do? Did you beat her?'

'No! I just can't find a reason!'

'I will give you a reason. Buy fish, plenty of it, and take it to her and say, "Cook it, because we will have a guest for dinner", and leave the house. When you go home later, whatever she has cooked, say that you wanted it some other way!'

The man said, 'Fine.' He bought some catfish and went home. At the door, he shoved the fish at his wife and said, 'Cook it, for we will have guests', and he flew outside.

The woman said to herself, 'My girl, what are you going to do with all this fish? He didn't tell you how to fix it.' She thought and thought and finally said, 'I will fry some, bake some, and make some in a casserole with onions and tomatoes.'

She cleaned the house and prepared everything. As dinner time approached, her infant son made a mess on the floor right next to the table where they sit cross-legged on the floor to eat. As she went to get something to clean it, she heard her husband

163

and his friend knocking at the door. She ran to the door, and in order not to leave the mess like that, she covered it with a dish which happened to be in her hand.

They walked in and sat down on the floor at the table and said to her, 'Bring the food, mother of So-and-so.'

First she took out the fried fish. He said, 'Fried! I want it baked!' Immediately she took out the baked fish. He shouted, 'Not baked; I mean in a casserole!' Immediately she took out the casserole. He became frustrated and confused. He said, 'I want – I want –'

She asked, 'What?'

He replied in bafflement, 'I want shit!'

She immediately said, lifting the dish off the floor, 'Here it is!'

The Three Lovers
(USA, New Mexico)

NCE there was a woman who lived in a city and was married to a man named José Pomuceno. This man owned sheep. He was obliged to look after his business in the country. And whenever he would go out of the city, his wife never missed a chance to betray him. So it was that things got so bad that she had three lovers.

It so happened that one night when the husband wasn't at home the three were going to come the same night. That's the way this woman had things arranged when the first one came. Then the second one arrived. He knocked at the door. The wife said to the first one who was there, 'My husband.'

'Where shall I hide?'

'Hide in that wardrobe.'

The man hid in the wardrobe. The other man entered. A little while later the third one arrived and knocked at the door. The woman says to the second one, 'My husband.'

'No,' he says. 'If it is your husband, let him kill me. I'll do as I please. I am sure that it isn't your husband. You are giving several of us the run-around.'

When the woman saw that he didn't believe that it could be her husband, she tried to drive the other one off, telling him to go away, that everything was off, that he should return some other time.

Then this fellow said to her from outside, 'Since you can't do anything else, why don't you at least give me a kiss?'

'Yes' the one who is with her tells her. 'It's all right. Tell him to come to the window.'

The one outside comes to the window and the other one holds up his rump for him there, and the fellow outside kisses it.

When the latter saw that he had kissed the other's posterior,

165

he felt rather bad and tried to get even some way; so he again
called to him that he liked it, and for him to come back again.
The second time that he appeared at the window he didn't try to
kiss as he had done the first time, but struck a match and set fire
to him.

When the one inside felt the flame, he came away from there
yelling and leaping through the room, 'Fire! Fire! Fire!'

Then the one who was shut up in the wardrobe answered,
'Throw your furniture outside, lady.'

So ends the story of the wife of José Pomuceno.

The Seven Leavenings

(Palestinian Arab)

T HERE was once in times past an old woman who lived in a hut all by herself. She had no one at all. One day when the weather was beautiful she said, 'Ah, yes! By Allah, today it's sunny and beautiful, and I'm going to take the air by the seashore. But let me first knead this dough.'

When she had finished kneading the dough, having added the yeast, she put on her best clothes, saying, 'By Allah, I just have to go and take the air by the seashore.' Arriving at the seashore, she sat down to rest, and lo! there was a boat, and it was already filling with people.

'Hey, uncle!' she said to the man, the owner of the boat. 'Where in Allah's safekeeping might you be going?'

'By Allah, we're heading for Beirut.'

'All right, brother. Take me with you.'

'Leave me alone, old woman,' he said. 'The boat's already full, and there's no place for you.'

'Fine,' she said. 'Go. But if you don't take me with you, may your boat get stuck and sink!'

No one paid her any attention, and they set off. But their boat had not gone twenty metres when it started to sink. 'Eh!' they exclaimed, 'It looks as if that old woman's curse has been heard.' Turning back, they called the old woman over and took her with them.

In Beirut, she did not know anybody or anything. It was just before sunset. The passengers went ashore, and she too came down and sat a while, leaning against a wall. What else could she have done? People were passing by, coming and going, and it was getting very late. In a while a man passed by. Everyone was already at home, and here was this woman sitting against the wall.

167

'What are you doing here, sister?' he asked.

'By Allah, brother,' she answered, 'I'm not doing anything. I'm a stranger in town, with no one to turn to. I kneaded my dough and leavened it, and came out for pleasure until it rises, when I'll have to go back.'

'Fine,' he said. 'Come home with me then.'

He took her home with him. There was no one there except him and his wife. They brought food, laughed and played – you should have seen them enjoying themselves. After they had finished, lo! the man brought a bundle of sticks this big and set to it – Where's the side that hurts most? – until he had broken them on his wife's sides.

'Why are you doing this, grandson?' the old woman asked, approaching in order to block his way.

'Get back!' he said. 'You don't know what her sin is. Better stay out of the way!' He kept beating his wife until he had broken the whole bundle.

'You poor woman!' exclaimed the old lady when the man had stopped. 'What's your sin, you sad one?'

'By Allah,' replied the wife, 'I've done nothing, and it hadn't even occurred to me. He says it's because I can't get pregnant and have children.'

'Is that all?' asked the old woman. 'This one's easy. Listen, and let me tell you. Tomorrow, when he comes to beat you, tell him you're pregnant.'

The next day, as usual, the husband came home, bringing with him the needed household goods and a bundle of sticks. After dinner, he came to beat his wife, but he had not hit her with the first stick when she cried out, 'Hold your hand! I'm pregnant!'

'Is it true?'

'Yes, by Allah!'

From that day on, he stopped beating her. She was pampered, her husband not letting her get up to do any of the housework. Whatever she desired was brought to her side.

Every day after that the wife came to the old woman and said, 'What am I going to do, grandmother? What if he should find out?'

'No matter,' the old woman would answer. 'Sleep easy. The burning coals of evening turn to ashes in the morning.' Daily the old woman stuffed the wife's belly with rags to make it look bigger and said, 'Just keep on telling him you're pregnant, and leave it to me. The evening's embers are the morning's ashes.'

Now, this man happened to be the sultan, and people heard what was said: 'The sultan's wife is pregnant! The sultan's wife is pregnant!' When her time to deliver had come, the wife went to the baker and said, 'I want you to bake me a doll in the shape of a baby boy.'

'All right,' he agreed, and baked her a doll which she wrapped and brought home without her husband seeing her. Then people said, 'The sultan's wife is in labour, she's ready to deliver.'

The old woman came forth. 'Back in my country, I'm a midwife,' she said. 'She got pregnant as a result of my efforts, and I should be the one to deliver her. I don't want anyone but me to be around.'

'Fine,' people agreed. In a while, word went out: 'She gave birth! She gave birth!'

'And what did she give birth to?'

'She gave birth to a boy.'

Wrapping the doll up, the wife placed it in the crib. People were saying, 'She gave birth to a boy!' They went up to the sultan and said she had given birth to a boy. The crier made his rounds, announcing to the townspeople that it was forbidden to eat or drink except at the sultan's house for the next week.

Now, the old woman made it known that no one was permitted to see the baby until seven days had passed. On the seventh day it was announced that the sultan's wife and the baby were going to the public baths. Meanwhile, every day the wife asked the old woman, 'What am I going to do, grandmother? What if my husband should find out?' And the old woman would reply, 'Rest easy, my dear! The evening's coals are the morning's ashes.'

On the seventh day the baths were reserved for the sultan's wife. Taking fresh clothes with them, the women went, accompanied by a servant. The sultan's wife went into the bath, and the women set the servant in front of the doll, saying to her, 'Take care of the boy! Watch out that some dog doesn't stray in and snatch him away!'

In a while the servant's attention wandered, and a dog came, grabbed the doll, and ran away with it. After him ran the servant, shouting, 'Shame on you! Leave the son of my master alone!' But the dog just kept running, munching on the doll.

It is said that there was a man in that city who was suffering from extreme depression. He had been that way for seven years, and no one could cure him. Now, the moment he saw a dog running with a servant fast behind him shouting, 'Leave the son of my master alone!' he started to laugh. And he laughed and laughed till his heartsickness melted away and he was well again. Rushing out, he asked her, 'What's your story? I see you running behind a dog who has snatched away a doll, and you're shouting at him to leave the son of your master alone. What's going on?'

'Such and such is the story,' she answered.

This man had a sister who had just given birth to twin boys seven days before. Sending for her, he said, 'Sister, won't you put one of your boys at my disposal?'

'Yes,' she said, giving him one of her babies.

The sultan's wife took him and went home. People came to congratulate her. How happy she was!

After some time the old woman said, 'You know, grand-children, I think my dough must have risen, and I want to go home and bake the bread.'

'Why don't you stay?' they begged her. 'You brought blessings with you.' I don't know what else they said, but she answered, 'No. The land is longing for its people. I want to go home.'

They put her on a boat, filling it with gifts, and said, 'Go in Allah's safekeeping!'

When she came home, she put her gifts away and rested for a day or two. Then she checked her dough. 'Yee, by Allah!' she exclaimed. 'My dough hasn't risen yet. I'm going to the seashore for a good time.' At the shore she sat for a while, and lo! there was a boat.

'Where are you going, uncle?'

'By Allah, we're going to Aleppo,' they answered.

'Take me with you.'

'Leave me alone, old woman. The boat's full and there's no room.'

'If you don't take me with you, may your boat get stuck and sink in the sea!'

They set out, but in a while the boat was about to sink. They returned and called the old lady over, taking her with them. Being a stranger, where was she to go? She sat down by a wall, with people coming and going until late in the evening. After everybody had gone home for the night, a man passed by.

'What are you doing here?'

'By Allah, I'm a stranger in town. I don't know anyone, and here I am, sitting by this wall.'

'Is it right you should be sitting here in the street? Come, get up and go home with me.'

Getting up, she went with him. Again, there was only he and his wife. They had no children or anybody else. They ate and enjoyed themselves, and everything was fine, but when time came for sleep he fetched a bundle of sticks and beat his wife until he had broken the sticks on her sides. The second day the same thing happened. On the third day the old woman said, 'By Allah, I want to find out why this man beats his wife like this.'

She asked her, and the wife replied, 'By Allah, there's nothing the matter with me, except that once my husband brought home a bunch of black grapes. I put them on a bone-white platter and brought them in. "Yee!" I said, "How beautiful is the black on the white!" Then he sprang up and said, "So! May so-and-so of yours be damned! You've been keeping a black slave for a lover behind my back!" I protested that I had only meant the grapes, but he wouldn't believe me. Every day he brings a bundle of sticks and beats me.'

'I'll save you,' said the old woman. 'Go and buy some black grapes and put them on a bone-white platter.'

In the evening, after he had had his dinner, the wife brought the grapes and served them. The old woman then jumped in and said, 'Yee! You see, son. By Allah, there's nothing more beautiful than the black on the white!'

'So!' he exclaimed, shaking his head. 'It's not only my wife who says this! You're an old lady and say the same thing. It turns out my wife hasn't done anything, and I've been treating her like this!'

'Don't tell me you've been beating her just for that!' exclaimed the old woman. 'What! Have you lost your mind? Look here! Don't you see how beautiful are these black grapes on this white plate?'

171

It is said they became good friends, and the husband stopped beating his wife. Having stayed with them a few more months, the old woman said, 'The land has been longing for its people. Maybe my dough has risen by now. I want to go home.'

'Stay, old lady!' they said. 'You brought us blessings.'

'No,' she answered. 'I want to go home.'

They prepared a boat for her and filled it with food and other provisions. She gathered herself together and went home. There, in her own house, after she had sat down, rested, and put her things away, she checked the dough. 'By Allah,' she said, 'it has just begun to rise, and I might as well take it to the baker.' She took it to the baker, who baked her bread.

This is my tale, I've told it, and in your hands I leave it.

The Untrue Wife's Song

(USA, North Carolina)

NCE a man an' his wife were ridin' on a ship. One day the man was talkin' to the captain, an' they got to talkin' about women. The captain said he'd never seen a virtuous woman. The man said his wife was virtuous, and the captain bet the ship's cargo against the man's fiddle that he could seduce the man's wife within three hours. The man sent his wife up to the captain's cabin. After waiting for two hours the man became a little uneasy, so he walked by the captain's cabin, an' played on his fiddle an' sang:

For two long hours
You've resisted the captain's powers.
The cargo will soon be ours.

His wife heard him, an' from within she sang back:

Too late, too late, my dear,
He has me around the middle;
Too late, too late, my dear,
You've lost your damned old fiddle.

The Woman Who Married Her Son

(Palestinian Arab)

 NCE upon a time there was a woman. She went out to gather wood, and gave birth to a daughter. She wrapped the baby in a rag, tossed her under a tree, and went on her way. The birds came, built a nest around the baby, and fed her.

The girl grew up. One day she was sitting in a tree next to a pool. How beautiful she was! (Praise the creator of beauty, and the Creator is more beautiful than all!) Her face was like the moon. The son of the sultan came to the pool to water his mare, but the mare drew back, startled. He dismounted to find out what the matter was, and he saw the girl in the tree, lighting up the whole place with her beauty. He took her with him, drew up a marriage contract, and married her.

When the time for pilgrimage came, the son of the sultan decided to go on the hajj. 'Take care of my wife until I return from the hajj,' he said to his mother.

Now the mother was very jealous of her daughter-in-law, and as soon as her son departed she threw his wife out of the house. Going over to the neighbour's house, the wife lived with them, working as a servant. The mother dug a grave in the palace garden and buried a sheep in it. She then dyed her hair black and put on make-up to make herself look young and pretty. She lived in the palace, acting as if she were her son's wife.

When he came back from the hajj, the son was taken in by his mother's disguise and thought her his wife. He asked her about his mother, and she said, 'Your mother died, and she is buried in the palace garden.'

After she slept with her son, the mother became pregnant and started to crave things. 'My good man,' she said to her son, 'bring me a bunch of sour grapes from our neighbour's vine!' The son

174

sent one of the women servants to ask for the grapes. When the servant knocked on the neighbour's door, the wife of the sultan's son opened it.

'O mistress of our mistress,' said the servant, 'you whose palace is next to ours, give me a bunch of sour grapes to satisfy the craving on our side!'

'My mother gave birth to me in the wilderness,' answered the wife, 'and over me birds have built their nests. The sultan's son has taken his mother to wife, and now wants to satisfy her craving at my expense! Come down, O scissors, and cut out her tongue, lest she betray my secret!' The scissors came down and cut out the servant's tongue. She went home mumbling so badly no one could understand what she was saying.

The son of the sultan then sent one of his men servants to fetch the bunch of sour grapes. The servant went, knocked on the door, and said, 'O mistress of our mistress, you whose palace is next to ours, give me a bunch of sour grapes to satisfy the craving on our side!'

'My mother gave birth to me in the wilderness,' answered the wife of the sultan's son, 'and over me birds have built their nests. The sultan's son has taken his mother to wife, and now wants to satisfy her craving at my expense! Come down, O scissors, and cut out his tongue, lest he betray my secret!' The scissors came down and cut out his tongue.

Finally the son of the sultan himself went and knocked on the door. 'O mistress of our mistress,' he said, 'you whose palace is next to ours, give me a bunch of sour grapes to satisfy the craving on our side!'

'My mother gave birth to me in the wilderness, and over me birds have built their nests. The king's son has taken his mother to wife, and now wants to satisfy her craving at my expense! Come down, O scissors, and cut out his tongue. But I can't find it in myself to let it happen!' The scissors came down and hovered around him, but did not cut out his tongue.

The sultan's son understood. He went and dug up the grave in the garden, and behold! there was a sheep in it. When he was certain that his wife was actually his mother, he sent for the crier. 'Let him who loves the Prophet,' the call went out, 'bring a bundle of wood and a burning coal!'

The son of the sultan then lit the fire.
Hail, hail! Finished is our tale.

Duang and His Wild Life
(Sudan, Dinka)

MOU was so beautiful. She was betrothed to a man from the tribe. But she was not yet given to her betrothed. She still lived with her family.

There was a man called Duang in a neighbouring village. Duang's father said to him, 'My son, Duang, it is high time you married.'

'Father,' replied Duang, 'I cannot marry; I have not yet found the girl of my heart.'

'But my son,' argued his father, 'I want you to marry while I am alive. I may not live long enough to attend your marriage.'

'I will look, Father,' said Duang, 'but I will marry only when I find the girl of my heart.'

'Very well, my son,' said his father with understanding.

They lived together until the father died. Duang did not marry. Then his mother died. He did not marry.

These deaths made him abandon himself in mourning; so he no longer took care of his appearance. His mourning hair grew long and wild. He never shaved or groomed his hair. He was a very rich man. His cattle-byres were full of cattle, sheep and goats.

One day he left for a trip to a nearby tribe. On the way he heard the drums beating loud. He followed the sounds of the drums and found people dancing. So he stood and watched the dance.

In the dance was the girl called Amou. When she saw him standing, she left the dance and went near him. She greeted him. They stood talking. When the relatives of the man who was betrothed to Amou saw her, they became disturbed. 'Why should Amou leave the dance to greet a man who was merely watching? And then she dared to stand and talk with him! Who

177

is the man, anyway?'

They called her and asked her. She answered, 'I don't see anything wrong! I saw the man looking as though he were a stranger who needed help. So I went to greet him in case he wanted something. There is nothing more to it.'

They dismissed the matter, although they were not convinced. Amou did not go back to the dance. She went and talked to the man again. She invited him to her family's home. So they left the dance and went. She seated him and gave him water. She cooked for him and served him.

The man spent two days in her house and then left and returned home. He went and called his relatives and told them that he had found the girl of his heart. They took cattle and returned to Amou's village.

The man who had betrothed Amou had paid thirty cows. Amou's relatives sent them back and accepted Duang's cattle. The marriage was completed, and Amou was given to her husband.

She went with him and gave birth to a daughter, called Kiliingdit. Then she had a son. She and her husband lived alone with their children. Then she conceived her third child. While she was pregnant, her husband was in the cattle camp. But when she gave birth, he came home to visit her and stay with them for the first few days after her delivery.

After she delivered, she felt a very strong craving for meat. She was still newly delivered. She said to her husband, 'I am dying of craving for meat. I cannot even eat.'

Her husband said to her, 'If it is my cattle you have your eyes on, I will not slaughter an animal merely because of your craving! What sort of a craving is this which requires the killing of livestock? I will not slaughter anything.'

That ended the discussion. But she still suffered and could not eat or work. She would just sit there.

Her husband became impatient and embittered by her craving. He slaughtered a lamb openly so that she and the others could see it. Then he went and killed a puppy dog secretly. He roasted both the lamb and the puppy in smouldering smudge.

When they were ready he took the dog meat to his wife in her women's quarters. He grabbed his children by the hands and took them away with him to the male quarters. His wife protested, 'Why are you taking the children away? Aren't they eating with me?'

He said, 'I thought you said you were dying of craving. I think it would be better for you and the children if you ate separately. They will share with me.'

He seated them next to him, and they ate together. She never doubted what he said, even though she felt insulted. That he would poison her was out of the question. So she ate her meat.

As soon as she ate her fill, her mouth started to drip with saliva. In a short while, she became rabid. Then she ran away, leaving her little baby behind.

Her husband took the boy to the cattle camp and left only the girl at home. She suffered very much taking care of her baby brother. Fearing that her mother might return rabid, she took the remainder of her mother's dog meat, dried it, and stored it. She would cook a portion of it and place it on a platform outside the hut together with some other food she had prepared.

For a while, her mother did not come. Then one night, she came. She stood outside the fence of the house and sang:

'Kiliingdit, Kiliingdit,
Where has your father gone?'

Kiliingdit answered:

'My father has gone to Juachnyiel,
Mother, your meat is on the platform,
Your food is on the platform,
The things with which you were poisoned.
Mother, shall we join you in the forest?
What sort of home is this without you?'

Her mother would take the food and share it with the lions. This went on for some time.

In the mean time, the woman's brothers had not heard of her giving birth. One of them, called Bol because he was born after twins, said to the others, 'Brothers, I think we should visit our sister. Maybe she has given birth and is now in some difficulties taking care of herself and the house.'

The little girl continued to labour hard looking after the baby and preparing food for the mother and themselves. She also had to protect herself and the baby so their mother would not find them and, having become a lioness, eat them.

She came again another night and sang. Kiliingdit replied as usual. Her mother ate and left.

In the mean time, Bol took his gourds full of milk and left for his sister's home. He arrived in the daytime. When he saw the village so quiet, he feared that something might have gone wrong. 'Is our sister really at home?' he said to himself. 'Perhaps what I was afraid of in my heart has occurred. Perhaps our sister died in childbirth and her husband with the children have gone away and abandoned the house!'

Another part of him said, 'Don't be foolish! What has killed her? She is a newly delivered mother and is confined inside the hut.'

'I see the little girl,' he said to himself, 'but I do not see her mother.' As soon as the little girl saw him, she raced towards him, crying.

'Where is your mother, Kiliingdit?' he asked her in haste.

She told him the story of how her mother turned wild, beginning with her mother's craving for meat and her father's poisoning her with dog meat.

'When she comes in the evening,' she explained, 'her companions are the wives of lions.'

'Will she come tonight?' asked her uncle.

'She comes every night,' answered Kiliingdit. 'But, Uncle, when she comes, please do not reveal yourself to her. She is no longer your sister. She is a lioness. If you reveal yourself to her, she will kill you and the loss will be ours. We shall then remain without anyone to take care of us.'

'Very well,' he said.

That night, she came again. She sang her usual song. Kiliingdit sang her response.

As she approached the platform to pick up her food, she said, 'Kiliingdit, my daughter, why does the house smell like this? Has a human being come? Has your father returned?'

'Mother, my father has not returned. What would bring him back? Only my little brother and I are here. And were we not human beings when you left us? If you want to eat us, then do so. You will save me from all the troubles I am going through. I have suffered beyond endurance.'

'My darling Kiliingdit,' she said, 'how can I possibly eat you? I know I have become a beast of a mother, but I have not lost my heart for you, my daughter. Is not the fact that you cook for me evidence of our continuing bond? I cannot eat you!'

When Bol heard his sister's voice, he insisted on going out to meet her, but his niece pleaded with him, saying, 'Don't be deceived by her voice. She is a beast and not your sister. She will eat you!'

So he stayed; she ate and left to join the wives of the lions.

The next morning, Bol returned to the cattle camp to tell his brothers that their sister had become a lioness. Bewildered by the news, they took their spears and came to their sister's home. They took a bull with them. They walked and walked and then arrived.

They went and sat down. The little girl went ahead and prepared the food for her mother in the usual way. Then they all went to sleep. The little girl went into the hut with her baby brother, as usual, but the men slept outside, hiding in wait for their sister.

She came at night and sang as usual. Kiliingdit responded. She picked up her food and ate with the wives of the lions. Then she brought the dishes back. As she put them back, she said, 'Kiliingdit!'

'Yes, Mother,' answered Kiliingdit.

'My dear daughter,' she continued, 'why does the house feel so heavy? Has your father returned?'

'Mother,' said Kiliingdit, 'my father has not returned. When he abandoned me with this little baby, was it his intention to return to us?'

'Kiliingdit,' argued the mother, 'if your father has returned, why do you hide it from me, dear daughter? Are you such a small child that you cannot understand my suffering?'

'Mother,' Kiliingdit said again, 'I mean what I say, my father has not come. It is I alone with the little baby. If you want to eat us, then eat us.'

As the mother turned to go, her brothers jumped on her and caught her. She struggled in their hands for quite a long time, but could not break away. They tied her to a tree. The next morning, they slaughtered the bull they had brought. Then they beat her and beat her. They would tease her with raw meat by bringing it close to her mouth and pulling it away from her. Then they would continue to beat her. As she was teased with meat, saliva fell from her mouth and formed little puppies. They continued to tease her and beat her until three puppies had emerged from her saliva. Then she refused raw meat. She was given roast meat from the bull and she ate it. The brothers beat her some more until she shed all the hairs that had grown on her body.

Then she opened her eyes, looked at them closely, sat down and said, 'Please hand me my little baby.'

The baby was brought. He could no longer suck his mother's breasts.

When the mother had fully recovered, her brothers said, 'We shall take you to our cattle camp. You will not go to the cattle camp of such a man again!'

But she insisted on going to her husband's cattle camp, saying, 'I must go back to him. I cannot abandon him.'

Her brothers could not understand her. They wanted to attack her husband and kill him, but she argued against that. When she saw that they did not understand her, she told them that she wanted to take care of him in her own way. She was not going back to him out of love but to take revenge. So they left her and she went to her husband.

When she got to the cattle camp, he was very pleased to have her back. She did not show any grievance at all. She stayed with him, and he was very happy with her.

One day she filled a gourd with sour milk. She pounded grain and made porridge. Then she served him, saying, 'This is my first feast since I left you. I hope you give me the pleasure of finding it your heartiest meal.'

First he drank the milk. Then came the porridge with ghee and sour milk mixed into it. He ate. Then she offered him some more milk to drink on top of the porridge. When he tried to refuse, she pleaded with him. The man ate and ate and ate, until he burst and died.

A Stroke of Luck

(Hungarian)

E went ploughing. He was a poor man. The plough cut a furrow and turned up a lot of money. When he set eyes on it, he began to speculate about what to say to his wife. He feared that she might blurt it out to the neighbours, and they would be served a summons to appear before the magistrate.

He went and bought a hare and a fish.

When she brought him his midday meal, he said to her after he had dined, 'Let's fry a fish.'

She said, 'What do you think! How could we catch a fish here in the field?'

'Come on, woman, I've just seen a couple of them, when I was ploughing around the blackthorn shrub.' He led her to the blackthorn shrub.

Says the woman, 'Look, old man, there's a fish.'

'Haven't I told you so?' And he flung the ox goad at the shrub so that the fish turned out at once.

Then he said, 'Let's catch a hare.'

'Don't be kidding me. You haven't got a gun.'

'Never mind. I'll knock it off with the ox goad.'

They were going along when she cried out, 'Look! there's a hare on the tree yonder there.'

The man flung his goad at the tree and the hare fell down.

They were working till the day drew to a close, and in the evening they made their way home. When they went past the church, they heard an ass braying.

The man said to the woman, 'You know what the ass is braying? He is saying, "The priest says in his sermon that soon a comet will appear and that will be the end of the world!"'

They went on. When they passed the city hall, the ass uttered another loud bray. The man said, 'The ass says that "The

184

magistrate and the town clerk have just been caught embezzling public funds." '

As time wore on they were making good use of their money.

The neighbours kept asking them, 'Where did that lot of money come from?'

Then she said to one of the neighbour women, 'I wouldn't mind telling you, but you mustn't pass it on to anyone.' And she told her that they had found the money. Their neighbour reported it to the magistrate, and they were summoned to appear before him. And when he was questioned about the money, the man denied it. By no means did they find any money. Not a penny had been found by them.

The magistrate then said, 'Your wife will tell me.'

'What's the use asking her. She's just a silly woman,' he said.

The woman flew into a temper and began to shout at him. 'Don't you dare say that again. Didn't we find the money when we caught the fish under the blackthorn bush?'

'Now Your Honour may hear for yourself. Catching a fish in a bush. What next!'

'Can't you remember how you shot down a hare from the tree with the ox goad?'

'Well, haven't I told Your Honour? It's no use asking that fool of a woman.'

'A fool you are yourself. Have you forgotten that on our way home we heard an ass braying when we passed the church, and you said that the priest was preaching that a comet would appear and that would be the end of the world.'

'Now wasn't I right, Your Honour? It would be better to leave her alone, or she might give offence with her silly talk.'

The woman flew into a rage and said, 'Don't you remember that when we were passing the city hall and the ass uttered a loud bray you were telling me, "that the magistrate and the town clerk have been just caught out . . ." ' The magistrate jumped to his feet and said to the man, 'Take her home, my good man, she seems to have lost her wits.'

The Beans in the Quart Jar
(USA, Hillbilly)

THE old man had taken sick and thought he's gonna die anyway, so he called his wife in and confessed, he said, 'I been stepping out, and I want to be honest with you, and I want to ask your forgiveness before I go.' And she said, 'All right', and 'I'll forgive you.' She forgive him.

By and by, she was taken sick and she called him in and she said, 'No, look, I stepped out quite a lot, and I want to ask forgiveness.' He said, 'Yes, I'll forgive you.' She said, 'Every time I stepped out I put a bean in a quart jar. And you'll find they're all there on that mantelpiece, except that quart I cooked the other Saturday.'

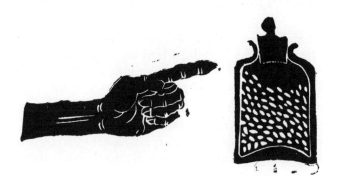

Part Six

USEFUL STORIES

A Fable of a Bird and Her Chicks
(*Yiddish*)

ONCE upon a time a mother bird who had three chicks wanted to cross a river. She put the first one under her wing and started flying across. As she flew she said, 'Tell me, child, when I'm old, will you carry me under your wing the way I'm carrying you now?'

'Of course,' replied the chick. 'What a question!'

'Ah,' said the mother bird, 'you're lying.' With that she let the chick slip, and it fell into the river and drowned.

The mother went back for the second chick, which she took under her wing. Once more as she was flying across the river, she said, 'Tell me, child, when I'm old, will you carry me under your wing the way I'm carrying you now?'

'Of course,' replied the chick. 'What a question!'

'Ah,' said the mother bird, 'you're lying.' With that she let the second chick slip, and it also drowned.

Then the mother went back for the third chick, which she took under her wing. Once more she asked in mid-flight, 'Tell me, child, when I am old, will you carry me under your wing the way I'm carrying you now?'

'No, mother,' replied the third chick. 'How could I? By then I'll have chicks of my own to carry.'

'Ah, my dearest child,' said the mother bird, 'you're the one who tells the truth.' With that she carried the third chick to the other bank of the river.

The Three Aunts

(Norwegian)

NCE upon a time there was a poor man who lived in a hut far away in the wood, and got his living by shooting. He had an only daughter, who was very pretty, and as she had lost her mother when she was a child, and was now half grown up, she said she would go out into the world and earn her bread.

'Well, lassie!' said the father, 'true enough you have learnt nothing here but how to pluck birds and roast them, but still you may as well try to earn your bread.'

So the girl went off to seek a place, and when she had gone a little while, she came to a palace. There she stayed and got a place, and the queen liked her so well that all the other maids got envious of her. So they made up their minds to tell the queen how the lassie said she was good to spin a pound of flax in four-and-twenty hours, for you must know the queen was a great housewife, and thought much of good work.

'Have you said this? Then you shall do it,' said the queen; 'but you may have a little longer time if you choose.'

Now, the poor lassie dared not say she had never spun in all her life, but she only begged for a room to herself. That she got, and the wheel and the flax were brought up to her. There she sat sad and weeping, and knew not how to help herself. She pulled the wheel this way and that, and twisted and turned it about, but she made a poor hand of it, for she had never even seen a spinning-wheel in her life.

But all at once, as she sat there, in came an old woman to her. 'What ails you, child?' she said.

'Ah!' said the lassie, with a deep sigh, 'it's no good to tell you, for you'll never be able to help me.'

'Who knows?' said the old wife. 'Maybe I know how to help

you after all.'

Well, thought the lassie to herself, I may as well tell her, and so she told her how her fellow-servants had given out that she was good to spin a pound of flax in four-and-twenty hours.

'And here am I, wretch that I am, shut up to spin all that heap in a day and a night, when I have never even seen a spinning-wheel in all my born days.'

'Well, never mind, child,' said the old woman. 'If you'll call me Aunt on the happiest day of your life, I'll spin this flax for you, and so you may just go away and lie down to sleep.'

Yes, the lassie was willing enough, and off she went and lay down to sleep.

Next morning when she awoke, there lay all the flax spun on the table, and that so clean and fine, no one had ever seen such even and pretty yarn. The queen was very glad to get such nice yarn, and she set greater store by the lassie than ever. But the rest were still more envious, and agreed to tell the queen how the lassie had said she was good to weave the yarn she had spun in four-and-twenty hours. So the queen said again, as she had said it she must do it; but if she couldn't quite finish it in four-and-twenty hours, she wouldn't be too hard upon her, she might have a little more time. This time, too, the lassie dared not say no, but begged for a room to herself, and then she would try. There she sat again, sobbing and crying, and not knowing which way to turn, when another old woman came in and asked, 'What ails you, child?'

At first the lassie wouldn't say, but at last she told her the whole story of her grief.

'Well, well!' said the old wife, 'never mind. If you'll call me Aunt on the happiest day of your life, I'll weave this yarn for you, and so you may just be off, and lie down to sleep.'

Yes, the lassie was willing enough; so she went away and lay down to sleep. When she awoke, there lay the piece of linen on the table, woven so neat and close, no woof could do better. So the lassie took the piece and ran down to the queen, who was very glad to get such beautiful linen, and set greater store than ever by the lassie. But as for the others, they grew still more bitter against her, and thought of nothing but how to find out something to tell about her.

At last they told the queen the lassie had said she was good to make up the piece of linen into shirts in four-and-twenty hours. Well, all happened as before; the lassie dared not say she couldn't sew; so she was shut up again in a room by herself, and there she sat in tears and grief. But then another old wife came, who said she would sew the shirts for her if she would call her Aunt on the happiest day of her life. The lassie was only too glad to do this, and then she did as the old wife told her, and went and lay down to sleep.

Next morning when she awoke she found the piece of linen made up into shirts, which lay on the table – and such beautiful work no one had ever set eyes on; and more than that, the shirts were all marked and ready for wear. So, when the queen saw the work, she was so glad at the way in which it was sewn, that she clapped her hands, and said, 'Such sewing I never had, nor even saw, in all my born days'; and after that she was as fond of the lassie as of her own children; and she said to her, 'Now, if you like to have the prince for your husband, you shall have him; for you will never need to hire work-women. You can sew, and spin, and weave all yourself.'

So as the lassie was pretty, and the prince was glad to have her, the wedding soon came on. But just as the prince was going to sit down with the bride to the bridal feast, in came an ugly old hag with a long nose – I'm sure it was three ells long.

So up got the bride and made a curtsy, and said, 'Good-day, Auntie.'

'*That* auntie to my bride?' said the prince.

'Yes, she was!'

'Well, then, she'd better sit down with us to the feast,' said the prince; but to tell you the truth, both he and the rest thought she was a loathsome woman to have next you.

But just then in came another ugly old hag. She had a back so humped and broad, she had hard work to get through the door. Up jumped the bride in a trice, and greeted her with 'Good-day, Auntie!'

And the prince asked again if that were his bride's aunt. They both said, yes; so the prince said, if that were so, she too had better sit down with them to the feast.

But they had scarce taken their seats before another ugly old hag came in, with eyes as large as saucers, and so red and bleared, 'twas gruesome to look at her. But up jumped the bride again, with her 'Good-day, Auntie', and her, too, the prince asked to sit down; but I can't say he was very glad, for he thought to himself, 'Heaven shield me from such aunties as my bride has!'

So when he had sat a while, he could not keep his thoughts to himself any longer, but asked 'But how, in all the world can my bride, who is such a lovely lassie, have such loathsome misshapen aunts?'

'I'll soon tell you how it is,' said the first. 'I was just as good-looking when I was her age; but the reason why I've got this long nose is, because I was always kept sitting, and poking, and nodding over my spinning, and so my nose got stretched and stretched, until it got as long as you now see it.'

'And I,' said the second, 'ever since I was young, I have sat and scuttled backwards and forwards over my loom, and that's how my back has got so broad and humped as you now see it.'

'And I,' said the third, 'ever since I was little, I have sat, and stared and sewn, and sewn and stared, night and day; and that's why my eyes have got so ugly and red, and now there's no help for them.'

'So, so!' said the prince, ''twas lucky I came to know this; for if folk can get so ugly and loathsome by all this, then my bride shall neither spin, nor weave, nor sew all her life long.'

Tale of an Old Woman
(Africa, Bondes)

HERE was once an old woman who had no husband and no relations, no money and no food. One day she took her axe and went to the forest to cut a little firewood to sell, so that she could buy something to eat. She went very far, right into the heart of the bush, and she came to a large tree covered with flowers, and the tree was called *Musiwa*. The woman took her axe and began to fell the tree.

The tree said to her, 'Why are you cutting me? What have I done to you?'

The woman said to the tree, 'I am cutting you down to make some firewood to sell, so that I can get some money, so that I can buy food to keep from starving, for I am very poor and have no husband or relations.'

The tree said to her, 'Let me give you some children to be your own children to help you in your work, but you must not beat them, nor are you to scold them. If you scold them you will see the consequences.'

The woman said, 'All right, I won't scold them.' Then the flowers of that tree turned into many boys and girls. The woman took them and brought them home.

Each child had its own work – some tilled, others hunted elephants, and still others fished. There were girls who had the work of cutting firewood, and girls who had the work of collecting vegetables, and girls who pounded flour and cooked it. The old woman didn't have to work any more, for now she was blessed.

Among the girls, there was one smaller than all the rest. The others said to the woman, 'This little girl must not work. When she is hungry and cries for food, give it to her and don't be angry at her for all of this.'

The woman said to them, 'All right, my children, whatever you tell me I will do.'

In this way, they lived together for some time. The woman didn't have to work except to feed the littlest child when it wanted to eat. One day the child said to the woman, 'I am very hungry. Give me some food to eat.'

The woman scolded the child, saying, 'How you pester me, you children of the bush! Get it out of the pot yourself.'

The child cried and cried because it had been scolded by the woman. Some of her brothers and sisters came, and asked her what was the matter. She told them, 'When I said I was hungry and asked for food, our mother said to me, "How I am worried by these bush children."'

Then the boys and girls waited until those who had gone hunting returned, and they told them how the matter stood. So they said to the woman, 'So you said we are children of the bush. We'll just go back to our mother, *Musiwa*, and you can dwell alone.' The woman pleaded with them every way, but they wouldn't stay. They all returned to the tree and became flowers again, as it was before, and all the people laughed at her. She dwelt in poverty till she died, because she did not heed the instruction given to her by the tree.

The Height of Purple Passion
(USA)

HERE was this sailor walking down the street and he met a Lady Wearing Lipstick. And she said to him, 'Do you know what the Height of Purple Passion is?' And he said 'No.' And she said, 'Do you want to find out?' And he said, 'Yes.' So she told him to come to her house at five o'clock *exactly*. So he did, and when he rang the doorbell, birds flew out all around the house. And they went around the house three times and the door opened and they all flew in again. And there was the Lady Wearing Lipstick. And she said, 'Do you still want to know what the Height of Purple Passion is?' And he said he wanted to find out. So she told him to go and take a bath and be very clean. So he did, and he came running back and slipped on the soap and broke his neck. That's the end. He never found out what it was. My girl friend Alice told me this story. It happened to somebody she knows.

Salt, Sauce and Spice, Onion Leaves, Pepper and Drippings
(Africa, Hausa)

 HIS story is about Salt, and Sauce and Spice, and Onion Leaves, and Pepper and Drippings. A story, a story! Let it go, let it come. Salt and Sauce and Spice and Onion Leaves and Pepper and Drippings heard a report of a certain youth who was very handsome, but the son of the evil spirit. They all rose up, turned into beautiful maidens, and then they set off.

As they were going along, Drippings lagged behind the others, who drove her still further off, telling her she stank. But she crouched down and hid until they had gone on, and then she kept following them. When they had reached a certain stream, where they came across an old woman who was bathing, Drippings thought they would rub down her back for her if she asked, but one said, 'May Allah save me that I should lift my hand to touch an old woman's back.' The old woman did not say anything more, and the five passed on.

Soon Drippings came along, encountered the old woman washing, and greeted her. She answered, and said, 'Maiden, where are you going?' Drippings replied, 'I am going to find a certain youth.' And the old woman asked her, too, to rub her back, but unlike the others, Drippings agreed. After she had rubbed her back well for her, the old woman said, 'May Allah bless you.' And she said, too, 'This young man to whom you are all going, do you know his name?' Drippings said, 'No, we do not know his name.' Then the old woman told her, 'He is my son, his name is Daskandarini, but you must not tell the others,' then she fell silent.

Drippings continued to follow far behind the others till they got to the place where the young man dwelled. They were about to go in when he called out to them, 'Go back, and enter one at a time,' which they did.

Salt came forward first and was about to enter, when the voice asked, 'Who is there?' 'It is I,' she replied, 'I, Salt, who make the soup tasty.' He said, 'What is my name?' She said, 'I do not know your name, little boy, I do not know your name.' Then he told her, 'Go back, young lady, go back,' and she did.

Next Sauce came forward. When she was about to enter, she, too, was asked, 'Who are you?' She answered, 'My name is Sauce and I make the soup sweet.' And he said, 'What is my name?' But she did not know, either, and so he said, 'Turn back, little girl, turn back.'

Then Spice rose up and came forward, and she was about to enter when she was asked, 'Who is this, young lady, who is this?' She said, 'It is I who greet you, young man, it is I who greet you.' 'What is your name, young girl, what is your name?' 'My name is Spice, who makes the soup savoury.' 'I have heard your name, young woman, I have heard your name. Speak mine.' She said, 'I do not know your name little boy, I do not know your name.' 'Turn back, young lady, turn back.' So she turned back, and sat down.

Then Onion Leaves came and stuck her head into the room. 'Who is this, young girl, who is this?' asked the voice. 'It is I who salute you young man, it is I who salute you.' 'What is your name, little girl, what is your name?' 'My name is Onion Leaves, who makes the soup smell nicely.' He said, 'I heard your name, little girl. What is my name?' But she didn't know it and so she also had to turn back.

Now Pepper came along. She said, 'Your pardon, young man, your pardon.' She was asked who was there. She said, 'It is I, Pepper, young man, it is I, Pepper, who make the soup hot.' 'I have heard your name, young lady. Tell me my name.' 'I do not know your name, young man, I do not know your name.' He said, 'Turn back, young maid, turn back.'

Now only Drippings was left. When the others asked her if she was going in she said, 'Can I enter the house where such good people as you have gone and been driven away? Would not they the sooner drive out one who stinks?' They said, 'Rise up and go in,' for they wanted Drippings, too, to fail.

So she got up and went in there. When the voice asked her

who she was, she said 'My name is Drippings, little boy, my name is *Batso* which makes the soup smell.' He said, 'I have heard your name. There remains my name to be told.' She said, 'Daskandarini, young man, Daskandarini.' And he said, 'Enter.' A rug was spread for her, clothes were given to her, and slippers of gold. And then of Salt, Sauce, Spice, Onion Leaves and Pepper, who before had despised her, one said, 'I will always sweep for you', another, 'I will pound for you', another, 'I will draw water for you', another, 'I will pound the ingredients of the soup for you', and another, 'I will stir the food for you.' They all became her handmaidens. And the moral of all this is that it is from such common things that our most blessed foods are made. So just as such common stuff may be transformed under the right circumstance, if you see a man is poor, do not despise him. You do not know but that some day he may be better than you. That is all.

Two Sisters and the Boa
(Chinese)

NCE there was an old, Kucong *binbai*, or old woman, who had buried her husband in her youth. Her sole possession was two daughters, the elder, nineteen years old, and the younger, seventeen. One afternoon, she returned home from working in the mountains, feeling thirsty and tired. So she sat down under a mango tree to rest. This mango tree was laden with ripe, golden-yellow fruit hanging down from the branches. A breeze blew from the mountains, carrying the exquisite fragrance of ripe mangoes to her nose, making her mouth water.

Suddenly, the *binbai* heard a swishing sound, 'sha-sha', up in the mango tree, and then thin pieces of bark fell on her. The old woman thought that somebody must be up there, so without even taking a look, she called out, jokingly, 'Who's the young man up in the tree whittling arrows out of mango branches? Whoever you are, if you would honour me by presenting me with a few mangoes, you can have your choice of my two daughters.'

Hardly had the *binbai*'s words escaped her lips, when there came the rustling of leaves, 'hua-hua', and a fully ripe mango fell plop, right on the ground. Feeling delighted and thankful at once, the old woman picked up the mango and began eating it, all the while looking up in the tree. Better for her she had not looked, for she was all agog with what she saw. Coiled all around the mango tree was a boa as thick as a bull's thigh, knocking mangoes free, its tail swishing back and forth. The *binbai* could not care less about picking up any more mangoes, and she scurried down the mountain in leaps and bounds, her bamboo basket on her back.

Wheezing and gasping for breath, the old woman entered her

door. As she saw her two darling daughters coming up to meet her she called to mind what had happened under the mango tree. She couldn't help feeling nervous and confused, as if she were stuck in a briar patch. She walked outside and was met by a strange sight. Though it was already dark, all her chickens were still circling around outside the chicken coop. She tried repeatedly to drive them inside, but they would not go. She went up to the coop and peeped in. Gosh! The very same boa which had been coiled around the mango was right there, lying in the chicken coop! As she was about to run away, the huge, long boa began to speak.

'*Binbai*, just now, you made a promise under the mango tree: whoever picked a mango and gave it to you to eat, could have his choice of one of your two daughters. Now please, keep your promise. Give me one of your girls! If you should go back on your word, don't blame me for getting impolite!'

Seeing that boa in the chicken coop, with its brightly patterned, scaly skin, gleaming eyes, and that long, forked tongue sticking out, the *binbai* shivered from head to foot. She couldn't say yes, but she couldn't say no, either. So all she said was, 'Now don't get mad, boa! be patient, please, Let me talk this over with my girls, so I can tell you what they think.'

The *binbai* went back into the house and recounted all that had happened to her two daughters. 'Oh, my little darlings!' she exclaimed. 'It's not that Mama doesn't love you or dote on you, but I have no choice other than to push you in the burning fire. Now you two sisters have to think it over – who is willing to marry the boa?'

No sooner had the old woman finished speaking than the older daughter started screaming, 'No, no! I won't go! Who could marry such an ugly, dreadful thing?'

The younger sister thought for a while. She saw that her mother's life was threatened, while her older sister was adamant.

'Mama,' she said, 'to prevent the boa from doing you and sister any harm, and so you two can live in peace, I'm willing to marry the boa.' And with that, she cried many a sad, sad tear.

The *binbai* led her second child to the gate of the chicken coop and told the boa he could have her. That very night, the old woman took the snake into her home, and the boa and Second

Daughter were married.

The next morning, when the boa was about to take her second daughter away, mother and child wept in one another's arm. How hard it was to part! Off went the boa, leading the *binbai*'s dear child to the virgin forest, deep in the mountains, where he brought her to a cave. She groped about in the dark, dark cave, following after the boa. On and on they went, never coming to the end. So worried and afraid was Second Daughter, that her teardrops fell like strings of pearls. Rounding a bend in the cave, there was a gleam of light, and suddenly, a resplendent, magnificent palace came in view. There were endless, vermilion walls and yellow tiles without number, long verandas and tiny pavilions, tall buildings and spacious courtyards. Everywhere one could see carved beams, painted rafters, piles of gold, carved jade and wall hangings of red and green silk. Second Daughter was simply dazzled. As she turned around, that terrifying, dreadful boa which had been close by had disappeared. Walking beside her now was a gorgeously dressed young man, looking ever so vigorous and handsome.

'Oh!' she exclaimed, completely outdone. 'How could this be?'

The young man beside her replied, 'Dear Miss! I am the king of the snakes of this region. Not long ago, when I went out to make an inspection tour of the snake tribes, I saw you two sisters. How I admired your wisdom and beauty! I made up my mind right then to have one of you as my wife, and that's how I thought of a way to win your mother's approval. Now, my hopes have come true, Oh, dear Miss! In my palace you'll have gold and silver without end, more cloth than you can ever use, and more rice than you can ever eat. Let us love each other dearly, enjoying a glorious life, to the end of our days!'

As she listened to the snake king's words, Second Sister's heart flooded with warmth. She took hold of his hand, and, smiling sweetly, walked towards the resplendent, magnificent palace.

Second Sister and the snake king lived happily as newly-weds for a time. Then, one day, she took leave of her husband to go back home and visit her mother and sister. She told them all about her rich, full married life with the king of the snakes.

How could the elder daughter not be full of regret? 'Ay!' she thought. 'I'm to blame for being so foolish. If I had promised to marry the boa in the first place, would not I have been the one now enjoying glory, honour and riches in that palace, instead of my younger sister?' So she made up her mind, then and there. 'Right! That's what I'll do. I'll find a way to wed a boa too!'

After the younger sister left to return to the snake king, the elder sister walked deep into the mountains, carrying a basket on her back. To find a boa, she would only go where the grass was tall or the jungles were dense. From dawn to dusk and dusk to dawn, she kept on searching until, at last, after great difficulty, she found a boa under a bush. Its eyes were shut, for the boa was enjoying a good snooze.

First Sister gingerly raked the snake into her basket and left for home in high spirits, the boa on her back. She had only gone halfway when the boa woke up. It stuck out its tongue and licked the back of her neck. Instead of being frightened by what the snake was doing, First Sister secretly felt quite delighted. 'Hey!' she whispered softly. 'Don't be so affectionate just yet! Wait till we get home!'

After getting back home, she laid the boa in her bed, then rushed to make the fire and do the cooking. After supper, First Sister told her mother, 'Mama, I found a boa today too, and I shall marry him tonight. From now on, I can live a rich, comfortable life, just like my baby sister!' And off she went to sleep with her boa.

Not long after the mother went to bed, she heard her daughter's voice, 'Mama, it's up to my thighs!'

The *binbai* did not say a word, thinking all she was hearing was a pair of newly-weds having fun playing around.

After a while, First Sister called out, her voice trembling, 'Mama, it's up to my waist!'

The old woman did not understand what such words could mean, so she did not budge an inch.

Yet more time passed, until this time she heard a mournful voice from the inner room, 'Mama, it's up to my neck now . . .' And then, all was silence.

The *binbai* felt something was not quite right, so she quickly rolled out of bed, lit a pine torch and went to take a look. That dreadful boa had swallowed down her elder daughter, leaving but a lock of her hair!

The old woman felt sad and nervous. She paced back and forth in the room, not knowing what to do to rescue her daughter. In the end, all she could think of doing was to pull down her dear, thatched hut, set it afire, and burn up the boa. In the raging flames a loud 'bang' was heard. As the boa was being burned to death, it burst into many pieces. In a later age, these came to be countless snakes, big and little.

The next morning, the *binbai* picked out of the ashes a few of her daughter's bones that had not been consumed by the fire. She dug a hole in the ground and buried them, holding back her tears.

Afterwards, she declared, 'My elder daughter! This is all because of your greed!' With these words, she went off into the dense jungle, and deep into the mountains, to look for her second daughter and her son-in-law, the king of the snakes.

Spreading the Fingers
(*Surinamese*)

N the early times Ba Yau was a plantation overseer. He had two wives in the city. But as he found provisions on the plantation, he brought them to his wives. But when he brought things, then he said to them, 'When you eat, you must spread your fingers.' But when he said this, the first one did not understand very well what that meant to say. He told the second wife the same thing, and that one understood. What he meant was that when he brought them things, they were not to eat them alone, they were to give others half.

Now the one who did not understand what that said, in the afternoon when she cooked, she ate. Then she went outside, and spread her fingers, and said, 'Ba Yau said when I eat I must spread my fingers.' Ba Yau brought her much bacon and salt fish. She alone ate it. But when Ba Yau brought the things for the other one she shared half with other people, because she had understood what the proverb had said.

Not long afterwards Ba Yau died. But when Ba Yau was dead, nobody brought anything to the wife who had spread her fingers for the air. She sat alone. But to the other one who had shared things with other people, many people brought things. One brought her a cow, one brought her sugar, one brought her coffee. So she received many things from others.

Now one day, the one wife went to the other, and she said, 'Yes, sister, ever since Ba Yau died, I have suffered hunger. No one brought me anything. But look, how is it that so many people have brought things to you?'

Then the other one asked her, 'Well, when Ba Yau had brought you things, what did you do with them?'

She said, 'I alone ate them.'

Then the other one said again, 'When Ba Yau said to you,

"You must spread your fingers", what did you do?'

She said, 'When I ate, I spread my fingers in the air.'

The other one said, 'So . . . Well then, the air must bring you things, because you spread your fingers for the air. As for myself, the same people to whom I gave things, bring me things in return.'

The proverb, when you eat you must spread fingers, means, when you eat, you must eat with people, you must not keep all for yourself. Otherwise, when you have nothing, nobody else is going to give you, because you had not given people what was yours.

Publisher's Note

About a month before she died, Angela Carter was in the Brompton Hospital in London. The manuscript of *The Second Virago Book of Fairy Tales* lay on her bed. 'I'm just finishing this off for the girls', she said. Virago published her first book of non-fiction, *The Sadeian Woman* in 1979. Her loyalty to us was boundless. When we first heard she was ill, we told her not to worry about this collection, we had published *The Virago Book of Fairy Tales*, that was enough. But no, Angela claimed it was *just* the project for an ailing writer to pursue while lying on the couch. And so she worked on the book until a few weeks before her death.

Though all the stories were collected, put in order and grouped under her chosen headings, and Virago was instructed to print the jacket 'beetroot red', Angela Carter was unable to finish the notes beyond 'The Witches Piper' in Part Two. We are extremely grateful to Shahrukh Husain, editor of the forthcoming *The Virago Book of Witches*, who was able to draw on her own extensive knowledge of folklore and fairy tales to complete the remaining 29 notes, including 'Rolando and Brunilde' and 'The Greenish Bird' from Part One. Shahrukh Husain has included the remarks and notes from Angela Carter's own file of notes wherever they were left.

Notes

Part One: STRONG MINDS AND LOW CUNNING

1. The Twelve Wild Ducks

From the collection of Norwegian folk tales made by Peter Christian Asbjørnsen and Jørgan Moe, in George Webb Darsent's handsome Victorian translation, *Popular Tales from the Norse* (Edinburgh, 1903).

The film-maker Alfred Hitchcock thought nothing was more ominous than the look of blood on daisies. Blood on snow catches even more directly at the viscera. The raven, the blood, the snow – these are the elements of the unappeasable northern formulae of desire. In 'The Story of Conall Gulban' in J.F. Campbell's *Popular Tales of the West Highlands* Conall 'would not take a wife forever whose head should be black as the raven, and her face as fair as the snow, and her cheeks as red as blood'.

Campbell crisply suggests the raven must have been eating something, because of all the blood, and offers a variant from Inverness:

> *When he got up in the morning there was young snow, and the raven was upon a spray near him, and a bit of flesh in his beak. The piece of flesh fell and Conall went to lift it, and the raven said to him, that Fair Beauteous Smooth was as white as the snow upon the spray, her cheek as red as the flesh that was in his hand, and her hair as black as the feather that was in his wing.*
> *(Popular Tales of the West Highlands, orally collected with a translation by J.F. Campbell, Vol. III, Paisley, 1892.)*

This carnivorous imagery expresses the depths of a woman's desire for a child in traditional stories. 'Snow-White' in the familiar version collected by the Brothers Grimm starts off the same way. Please note that, according to the editors of Palestinian Arab stories, childless mothers in fairy tales wish for daughters far more frequently than they do for sons.

'The Twelve Wild Ducks', with its savage beginning and theme of sibling devotion, forms the basis of the Danish Hans Christian Andersen's lovely literary story, 'The Wild Swans'. Andersen upgraded the ducks to romantic swans although I feel that if wild ducks were good enough for Ibsen, they should have been good enough for him.

2. *Old Foster*

Collected from Jane Gentry in 1923 in Hot Springs, North Carolina, by Isobel Gordon Carter. Text from *Journal of American Folklore*, 38 (1925), 360–1.

This ancient story of sex murder and serial killing travelled across the Atlantic with the first English settlers of the US in the sixteenth and seventeenth centuries. 'Old Foster' is first cousin to the sinister Mr Fox (see *The Virago Book of Fairy Tales*, edited by Angela Carter, p. 8), and to 'The Robber Bridegroom' of the Brothers Grimm.

3. *Šāhīn*

From *Speak, Bird, Speak Again: Palestinian Arab Folktales*, collected and edited by Ibrahim Muhawi and Sharif Kanaana, and published by the University of California Press.

These stories were collected on tape between 1978 and 1980 in Galilee, since 1948 part of the state of Israel, the West Bank and Gaza. In the Palestinian tradition, women are the custodians of narrative; if men tell stories, they must adopt the narrative style of women. Since storytelling style matures with age, old women have the edge on everybody else. Tales are told on winter nights, when there is little work in the fields, and extended families gather together for mutual entertainment. The oldest woman usually starts. The gatherings are dominated by women; there is a pronounced pro-woman bias to all these Palestinian stories, although the Palestinian family is, as Muhawi and Kanaana explain, 'patrilineal, patrilateral, polygynous, endogamous and patrilocal'.

In their introduction, they note that the pattern of free mate choice by women 'is so consistently at odds with the facts of social life that we must finally conclude that a deeply felt emotional need is being articulated'.

Nevertheless, 'Šāhīn', with its exuberantly self-assertive heroine, was told by a sixty-five-year-old man from Galilee, a ploughman and shepherd all his life. In another variant, the exhausted hero, newly married, says to Šāhīn, 'Believe me you are the man and I am the bride.' And it is nothing but the truth.

4. *The Dog's Snout People*

A story from the Baltic country of Latvia collected in the 1880s and published in a majestic collection called *Siberian and Other Folk-Tales:*

Primitive Literature of the Empire of the Tsars, collected and translated with an introduction and notes by C. Fillingham-Coxwell (London, C.W. Daniel, 1925).

Christian culture was slow to influence the people of heavily forested Latvia, who are said to have retained pagan altars as late as 1835. According to tradition, marriage was obtained by abduction, a risky business. Geographically between, and politically at the mercy of, Germany and Russia for centuries, the Letts, according to Fillingham-Coxwell, regarded the Germans and Russians 'with hatred and despair'. Fillingham-Coxwell also thought the enigmatic 'dog's snout people' themselves might contain memories of aboriginal Lettish inhabitants.

5. The Old Woman Against the Stream

Norwegian, again; from the same Asbjørnsen and Moe collection as 'The Twelve Wild Ducks', in a modern translation by Pat Shaw and Carl Noman (New York, Pantheon Books). Originally published in Oslo by Dreyers Verlag in 1960.

6. The Letter Trick

The people who were taken from West Africa as slaves to the place formerly called Dutch Guiana, now Suriname, took with them an invisible treasure of memory and culture. In the late 1920s, the anthropologists Melville J. Herskovits and Frances S. Herskovits collected a vast number of tales and songs, in the coastal city of Paramaribo. The language of the city was a thick, rich Creole; the Herskovits translated their material into English.

The city of Paramaribo possessed a mixed-race culture – Dutch, Indian, Carib, Arawak, Chinese and Javanese people mingled with those of African descent, but, amongst the latter, a strong African influence remained, expressing itself not only in voodoo beliefs and practices but in such matters as the tying of a headscarf. Descent was traced through the maternal line; the men were often absent as migrant workers.

Storytelling had an important place in this community. Tales were told to entertain the dead as they lay in state. And there was a taboo against telling stories in daytime, because, if you did so, death would come and sit beside you, and you would die, too.

(*Suriname Folk-lore*, collected by Melville J. Herskovits and Frances S. Herskovits [New York, Columbia University Press, 1936], p. 351.)

7. Rolando and Brunilde

This type of industrious spinner or seamstress is often rewarded with an illustrious lover simply for sitting at her window sewing or singing. (See 'The Greenish Bird', this volume p. 37.) Here though, she attracts an evil magician who abducts and thereafter deactivates her. Quite unusually, it is her mother who embarks on the Path of Trials as a sort of trickster-heroine. A fairy-hag is her helper and Rolando her assistant. The tale includes some interesting images of the two old women humping heavy bags over a garden wall and breaking into the castle – activities generally reserved for the young.

8. The Greenish Bird

A Mexican variant of the story most familiar in the beautiful Norwegian form, 'East o' the Sun, West o' the Moon', in Peter Christan Asbjørnsen and Jørgan Moe's collection (see *The Virago Book of Fairy Tales*, p. 122).

Like the last tale, this Mexican one begins with an industrious spinner at a window. Luisa is swiftly won over by her bird-wooer and begins an indeterminate sexual relationship. Like the Greek love god, hero of Apuleius' third-century Latin novella 'Cupid and Psyche' contained in the Golden Ass, the greenish bird is magical, generous and wonderful in bed. Luisa knows nothing about him, which does not particularly bother her. Like Psyche's sisters Luisa's too are jealous, and mar the relationship, causing the severely wounded prince to abandon her with an injunction to come in search of him. The iron shoe clad heroine who visits the sun and the moon in search of her offended lover occurs in Eastern Europe too, most notably attempting to redeem a Pig-prince. The Cap O' Rushes ending to this tale is similar to the Egyptian Cinderella story 'The Princess in the Suit of Leather', *The Virago Book of Fairy Tales*, p. 39), when the Prince, having realised his sweetheart is a servant in his palace, demands that she bring his meals to him. (*Folktales of Mexico*, by Americo Paredes, [Chicago 1970], p. 95.)

9. The Crafty Woman

From the Baltic state of Lithuania, again from C. Fillingham-Coxwell's collection. He quotes a Russian variation, from around Moscow, in which the part of the old woman is played by a young Jew.

Part Two: UP TO SOMETHING – BLACK ARTS AND DIRTY TRICKS

1. Pretty Maid Ibronka

This popular Hungarian story has been narrated in almost every village in the country in fairly similar form. It is also known in Lithuania and Yugoslavia. Hungarian popular belief has a particular dread of a revived corpse but the terrible lover, with his hat 'graced with a crane's feather' and his cloven hoof is reminiscent of the demon lover who returns to claim his faithless mistress in the great Scots ballad, 'The House Carpenter' (in Francis Child's collection *The English and Scottish Popular Ballads*, 3 vols. New York 1957). The demon takes the Scotswoman away on shipboard and destroys her: But Ibronka gets away with it.

This story was narrated by Mihály Fédics, an illiterate day-labourer, in 1938, when he was eighty-six years old. He had gone to the United States at the time of World War I and worked as a labourer there but soon returned to Hungary. He learned his stories during the long winter evenings, in the village houses where people went to spin together. Later, working as a lumberjack, his stories were the principal source of entertainment in the forest camp. 'It was his custom to interrupt his own story, by calling out "Bones" to his listeners, to see whether they had gone to sleep: if the encouraging answer "tiles" came, he went on with the story, but if there was no answer, he knew that his companions had dropped off, and the tale was to be continued the following day' (p. 130 *Folktales of Hungary*).

This information, together with the story, comes from *Folktales from Hungary*, edited by Linda Degh and translated by Judith Halasz (London, Routledge & Kegan Paul, 1965).

Copyright University of Chicago, 1965. In the series 'Folktales of the World', edited by Richard M. Dorson.

2. Enchanter and Enchantress

A witch duel, or transformation contest, tale from tribal Russia. For more about transformation contests see *The Virago Book of Fairy Tales*, p. 235. This story comes from a Finno-Turkish people called the Mordvins, who lived between the rivers Volga and Oka in the heart of Russia when this story was collected in the nineteenth century. The Mordvinian idea of the cosmos was that of the beehive.

Fillingham-Coxwell, p. 568.

3. The Telltale Lilac Bush

As told to Keith Ketchum in 1963 by Mrs Sarah Dadisman of Union, Monroe Country, West Virginia. (From *The Telltale Lilac Bush and Other West Virginian Ghost Tales* collected by Ruth Ann Musick [University of Kentucky Press, 1965], p. 12.)

4. Tatterhood

A Norwegian story from Asbjørnsen and Moe, in George Webb Darsent's translation.

5. The Witchball

An old-fashioned farting story from rural America, as told by seventy-six-year-old V. Ledford, of Clay County, Kentucky. This text is reprinted from *Buying the Wind: Regional Folklore in the United States*, edited and collected by Richard M. Dorson (University of Chicago Press, 1964).

Vance Randolph found another wise woman with access to farting powder in the Ozark mountains in Arkansas; this story may be found in *The Virago Book of Fairy Tales*, p. 73.

6. The Werefox

From *Chinese Ghosts and Goblins*, edited by G. Willoughby-Meade (London, Constable, 1928), p. 123.

7. The Witches' Piper

Narrated by Mihály Bertok, aged sixty-seven, a herdsman of Kishartyan, Nograd County, Hungary, and collected by Linda Degh in 1951.

Once upon a time, the bagpiper provided the music for the Shrove Tuesday dance. Witches would force the piper to play for them and then pay him back with a dirty trick.

8. Vasilissa the Fair

The heroine Vasilissa is as familiar in Russian folklore as the European Ella i.e. Cinderella. (See *The Virago Book of Fairy Tales*, 'Vasilissa the Priest's Daughter', p. 57 and 'The Baba Yaga', p. 151.) The tale contains powerful indicators that the Baba Yaga's origins are probably in the Mother goddess of various mythologies. She refers to the morning, day and night as her 'own' and her mortar and pestle are reminiscent of corn and wheat grinding. In addition, she possesses fire, a basic element. (A more obscure tale tells how she stole fire.) She is stern and harsh in her judgement but just and not devoid of ethics, conforming to the deathly aspect of the Mother goddess. The skulls surrounding her home represent the dead in general, though 'The Witch and her Servants' (*The Yellow Story Book*, ed. Andrew Lang) contains a more specific explanation. When the ubiquitous Iwanich of Russian tales goes to work for a witch, she delivers the following warning:

> *If you look after them both for a year I will give you anything you like to ask; but if, on the other hand, you let any of the animals escape you, your last hour is come, and your head shall be stuck on the last spike of my fence. The other spikes, as you see, are already adorned, and the skulls are all those of different servants I have had who have failed to do what I demanded (p. 161).*

The remaining riddle is that of the invisible pairs of hands. It is clear that the hag is alluding to the secrecy of women's mysteries when she expresses approval that Vasilissa has stopped short of asking the question that would force her to reveal what is inside her house. Her aversion to blessings may well represent the fear of a pagan goddess being driven out by Christianity. Fillingham-Coxwell's note referring to Russian society at the time of collection, says: 'The priest has a difficult, ill-paid and not very exalted position. So superstition and a belief in witchcraft abound, though the efforts of the orthodox church to suppress pagan practices and traditions have not been without a large measure of success' (p. 671 *Siberian and Other Folktales*). A poem entitled 'Russian Folk-Tales' includes the lines:

> *Cannibal witches will scarcely attack or make ready to eat us*
> *Easily, quickly we conquer if enemies dare approach us.*

For details of the Baba Yaga herself, see Angela Carter's note to 'The Baba Yaga' (*The Virago Book of Fairy Tales*, p. 239).

(*Siberian and other Folktales: Primitive Literature of the Empire of the Tsars*, collected, translated and with an introduction by C. Fillingham-Coxwell, London, 1925, p. 680.)

9. The Midwife and the Frog

This story, set in the Magyar Mountains not far from the banks of the Szuscava, was collected by Gyula Orlutory from thirty-three-year-old Mrs Gergely Tamas in 1943. The *gyivak* of this story is glossed in the book as 'a minor devil'.

This tale-type counts as a legend the world over since it continues to be believed. A Middle Eastern variant, in which a midwife delivers a djinn's wife, is always told as if it occurred to an acquaintance of the teller. There the terrified woman accepts a handful of stones which turn to gold when she returns home. A Norse version appears in *Folktales of Norway* edited by Reidar Christiansen (translated by Pat Shaw Iversen, The University of Chicago Press, 1964, p. 105). Numerous variants exist in the British Isles. According to Katharine Briggs, 'the earliest version is from *Gervase of Tilbury* in the 13th C', *Folktales of England*, The University of Chicago Press, 1965. See 'The Fairy Midwife', p. 38 and 'The Midwife', in *The Best-Loved Folktales of the World*, edited by Joanna Cole, Anchor, Doubleday, New York, 1983, p. 280.

(*Folktales from Hungary*, edited by Linda Degh, and translated by Judith Halasz [Chicago, 1965], p. 296.)

Part Three: BEAUTIFUL PEOPLE

1. Fair, Brown and Trembling

This Irish Cinderella was collected by Jeremiah Curtin in 1887 in Galway. The unkind sisters here are Trembling's own. The henwife is the Celtic equivalent of the fairy godmother. Storytellers sometimes preferred to avoid the use of the word 'witch' in Ireland and Scotland. It was too much like 'tempting fate' so they tended to call her a bird-woman or a henwife. Though henwives are usually good (see Duncan Williams's collections, where the henwife is Jack's greatest helper in the Jack tales) they do occasionally let slip a remark that triggers a sequence of malign events (see Frank McKenna, *The Steed of the Bells* [cassette] selected from the archives of the Ulster Folk and Transport Museum). The henwife asks Trembling to stay outside the church rather than going in, perhaps suggesting practices outside the approval of the Church. Magic good, bad or indifferent had the status of the Devil's work in Christianity so magical practices such as the use of the cloak of darkness would have been frowned on. Trembling's husband is the son of the King of the ancient city of Emania in Ulster, called Omania here. He changed his loyalties from Fair to Trembling after seeing her magical regalia. Another story in Curtin's repertoire has the King of Greece marrying an Irish king's eldest daughter then falling in love with the younger, Gil an Og. He curses them both, turning Gil an Og into a 'cat within her castle' and her sister into 'a serpent in the bay'. Gil an Og consults a druid and initiates a series of fights in order to free them both (*Myths and Folktales of Ireland*,

Jeremiah Curtin, reprinted from the 1890 Little, Brown and Co. edition by Dover Publications Inc., Toronto, London, 1975, p. 212).

The golden hair cut adrift occurs as far afield as India (cf. Prince Lionheart, in 'There Was Once a King' (in *Folk Tales of Pakistan*, retold by Sayyid Fayyaz Mahmud, Lok Virsa [Pakistan, undated], p. 117). Strands of Princess Yasmin's golden hair are seen floating downstream by a king, who determines to marry the owner of the hair.

The willingness of the King and Trembling to allow their daughter to marry the cow-herd may have something to do with this statement in Curtin's telling of Kil Arthur: 'In that time there was a law in the world that if a young man came to woo a young woman and her people wouldn't give her to him, the young woman should get her death by law' (Curtin, p. 113).

(*Irish Folk-Tales*, edited by Henry Glassie, Penguin Folklore Library [Harmondsworth, UK, 1985], p. 257.)

2. *Dürrawac and her Incestuous Brother*

This story was told by a twenty-year-old man (who was not a member of editor, Francis Mading Deng's family).

Angela Carter notes that the Dinka are cattle herders and subsistence farmers of the Sudan. Their land – about 10 per cent of the Sudan – is crossed by the Nile and its tributaries, making communications difficult. 'The main goal of a Dinka is to marry and have children' (p. 166).

Adults and children sleep together in huts. One person is asked to tell a story, then people tell stories in succession, notes Angela Carter, then quotes from Francis Mading Deng: 'As the storytelling progresses, people begin to fall asleep one by one. Sometimes they fall asleep, wake up in the middle of a story, and then fall asleep again . . . People who wake up in the middle of a story are usually brought up to date briefly. As time passes and some people begin to sleep and perhaps snore, the storyteller starts to ask from time to time: Are you asleep? . . . As long as there are people still awake, storytelling continues. The last storyteller is quite likely to be the last person awake and so the final story will be left incomplete' (p. 29).

The lions in most Dinka stories are clearly not real lions but represent a wild, untamed side of human nature. Neither are the puppies, who according to a footnote, symbolise wildness and therefore merit such brutal treatment in folk tales. The victim is subdued by severe beating and 'teasing'. The animal's partiality to raw meat indicates his wildness and its selection of cooked meat signifies it has been tamed (see 'Duang and His Wild Wife', p. 177 of the present book).

It is mostly women and young people who tell the stories. Stories tend to be associated with bedtime and are geared towards the children, the primary educators of childhood (p. 198).

It is likely that the sibling incest taboo is powerfully reinforced not only from the community but the most insignificant sources, because of the children's communal sleeping environment. It is for the heroine Diirawac who killed her brother that the village mourns, the elderly allowing their hair to grow matted and the young abandoning their beads to signify disaster. Violation of the incest taboo is considered more unnatural than murder. No single entity in the tale disputes the validity of the taboo.

(*Dinka Folktales: African Stories from the Sudan*, edited by Francis Mading Deng [New York and London, 1974], p. 78.)

3. The Mirror

Though this variant is poignant, even tragic, the motif of the mistaken mirror image is generally found in humorous tales. In one version a man quarrels with his wife after buying a mirror he mistakes for an image of his dead father. A nun mediates. This version of the tale is also found in India, China and Korea.

The Sun goddess of Japanese myth once took exile from the chaotic world in the Heavenly Rock Dwelling and was enticed back when the celestial smith fashioned a mirror of iron and told her that her reflection was a rival goddess. Beguiled by its beauty and brightness, she returned to light up the world.

(*Chinese Ghouls and Goblins*, edited by G. Willoughby-Meade [London, 1928], p. 184.)

4. The Frog Maiden

The start of the tale, with its wicked stepmother and two stepsisters is complemented by further echoes of the Cinderella story when the Frog Maiden arrives to see the prince in a carrot coach with mice for horses. Variations of this story are found all over the world. 'The Three Feathers' (Brothers Grimm), 'The White Cat' (France) and 'The Monkey Princess' (Pakistan) are all standard tales featuring the *Dummling* (simpleton) hero. In her *Introduction to the Interpretation of Fairytales* (Spring Publications Inc., Dallas, USA 1970), Marie Louise von Franz says that 'the bride is either a toad, a frog, a white cat, an ape, a lizard, puppet, rat, a stocking or a hopping nightcap – not even living objects – and sometimes a turtle'. A few lines down she explains that

The main action is concerned with the finding of the right female, upon which

220

depends the inheritance of the female and further, that the hero does not perform any masculine deeds. He is not a hero in the proper sense of the word. He is helped all the time by the feminine element, which solves the whole problem for him . . . The story ends with a marriage – a balanced union of the male and female elements. So the general structure seems to point to a problem in which there is a dominating male attitude, a situation which lacks the feminine element, and the story tells us how the missing feminine is brought up and restored (p. 36).

(*Burmese Folktales*, edited and collected by Maun Htin Aung [Calcutta, 1948], p. 137.)

5. The Sleeping Prince

The motive for the princess's journey is provided by the sight of horses' blood on the grass and her comment about its beauty. This seems a strange sentiment except that the blood and the beauty of it on the grass is probably connected with menstrual initiation and fertility. This is borne out by the invisible voice guiding the princess to go in search of a mate. The voice also mentions sticks and the sprinkling of water – elements that never actually materialise in the story – suggesting a sexual initiation which comes to pass only much later. The gory use to which the princess puts the witch's remnants could again be related to puberty – the pain and trauma of sexual deprivation and isolation represented by the witch are now objects of access to womanhood and sexual fruition, particularly the ladder which leads to her bed.

This tale is found in India too, beginning like the famous British tale 'Cap O'Rushes' with the expulsion of the youngest princess who gives an unacceptable response to her king-father's question. The princess asks the prince for some puppets and he overhears her enacting the incidents of her life. The impostor, her maid, is buried to the waist and trampled by horses.

(*Suriname Folk-lore*, collected by Melville J. Herskovits and Frances S. Herskovits [New York, 1936], p. 381.)

6. The Orphan

The motif of the mother feeding her daughter from beyond the grave occurs the world over. An almost exact parallel with this aspect of the tale is the Grimm Brothers' 'One Eye, Two Eye and Three Eye'. Treasure associated with the tree is also a feature of both, focusing primarily on the heroine's imminent rise in social status. She is not a conjurer though her stepmother proves to have access to spells and enchantment. The heroine's own inner magic emanates from her innocence. The second common motif here is the type found in 'The Goose Girl', where an envious woman deceitfully takes the place of the true bride. See 'The Woman Who Married Her Son' and 'The Sleeping Prince' in this volume. A third standard element in fairy tales is the metamorphosis of women into birds, either at will or by enchantment – for example, 'The White Duck' (European), 'The Crane Wife' (Japanese). See also 'The Bird Woman', included in this collection. A more exciting parallel is found in 'Devil Woman', in *Tales of the Cochiti Indians*, collected by Ruth Benedict (Smithsonian Institution, 1930). Here a demon transforms a new mother into a bird – a dove in this instance – by sticking a pin in her head. The removal of the pin ends the enchantment.

(*Tales of Old Malawi*, retold and edited by E. Singano and A.A. Roscoe [Limbe, Malawi, 1986], p. 69.)

Part Four: MOTHERS AND DAUGHTERS

1. Achol and Her Wild Mother

Another Dinka story featuring a human lion. This one is told by the daughter of Chief Deng Majok, Nyankoc Deng, who was then aged eighteen to twenty. Perhaps Achol's mother's grisly compulsion to gather wood and forfeit her hands and feet to the lion actually represent some other kind of misdemeanour, such as adultery. Angela Carter's notes copied from *Dinka Folktales* would seem to support this: 'lions are what the Dinka fear most' (p. 25) and 'A person who violates fundamental precepts of the Dinka moral code is often identified in the folk tales as an outsider and an animal' (p. 161). She comments: 'this differentiates the animal from the human, the lions of the stories are not really lions. Hence the emphasis on human interaction with lions. As in the other stories, the lioness is fed nightly by her daughter until her son arrives and beats the wildness out of her' (see 'Duang and His Wild Wife' p. 177 in this collection).

(Deng p. 95.)

2. Tunjur, Tunjur

A fifty-five-year-old woman called Fatime, from the village of Arrabe in Galilee told the story of Tunjur, a cooking-pot. Angela Carter's notes quote the description of another teller from *Speak Bird, Speak Again* (p. 31): 'When she came to the part about the man defecating in the cooking pot and the pot closing on him, Im Nabil laughed; then, still laughing she said the pot chopped off the man's equipment.' Angela Carter comments that 'men don't like the stories, partly because some

of the mores of which they are guardians, e.g. the "woman's honour"
thing, are consistently challenged in the tales – in which *heroines
predominate*. She goes on to quote again from *Speak Bird, Speak Again*
(p. 14): 'the ideological basis of the system lies in the father–son bond.
The female is identified as the "other".'

In this story, the daughter – a cooking pot – is quite clearly the
'other', but is sparklingly in step with the cunning and playful heroine
of Šāhīn (see p. 13 note p. 212) in her ability to match every man in wits
and strength. She is a recognisable female trickster of the famous
British Molly Whuppie type (a female Jack-the-Giant-Killer), even to
the extent of going that little bit further than she has to, for the sake of
a bit of fun. The story is well in keeping with the woman's need in
society to articulate her capabilities without being in the custody of the
male infrastructure, so men are entirely peripheral to this story except
as fools.

(Muhawi and Kanaana, p. 55.)

3. The Little Old Woman with Five Cows

A Yakut creation myth tells of a Supreme Being who created a small
and level world, which was scratched up by evil demons and spirits
making the hills and valleys. The evil spirits were regularly appeased
and thanked by Yakut shamans. Today they inhabit the Lena basin and
intermarry with Russians.

The magical maiden in this Yakut tale has her origins in what would
appear to be a foundation myth of sorts. The 'middle land' inhabited
by the human race, here represented by the Yakuts, is clearly in need
of honour or redemption and the maiden is sent down as the saviour,
duly suffering trials, death and resurrection. Unlike 'The Finn King's
Daughter' (Reidar Christiansen, p. 147) and other tales, in which the
reader is informed in a phrase or sentence about the metamorphosis,
this tale contains the horrific and explicit process of transformation.
The demoness herself is, like the *muzayyara*, an Egyptian water-nymph
with iron breasts. (*Folktales of Egypt*, edited and translated by Hasan
M.El-Shamy, University of Chicago, 1938, p. 180). Angela Carter
comments: 'The ancient Indian stories contain many horrible descrip-
tions of Rakshasas' (ogres).

The goddess Kali herself is depicted at her most ferocious, with her
tongue hanging from her mouth like the demoness of this story who
shoots out an iron tongue. Like the troll-woman in 'The Finn King's
Daughter', this demoness is not quite familiar with the social customs of
the society she is attempting to infiltrate. There is a cryptic reference to
the fact that 'she wrongly fastened her horse to the willow tree where

the old widow from Semyaksin used to tether her spotted fox', and this merits the hostility of her husband's clan. The editor of *Siberian and Other Folktales* notes that 'each species of tree has a master of its own except the larch' and it is with a larch branch that the plant maiden kindles the fire when she arrives, suggesting that she is in tune with humans and comes in fulfilment of a greater plan. She also knows of an interesting cleansing ritual vital to get rid of the internal and external pollution of her husband caused by coupling with the demoness. The hanging of the Khan's son from the tree for purification is reminiscent of Christ on the crucifix and other suspended gods such as Attis (Anatolia), Sluy (Wales) and Wotan (Germanic), all of whom returned after a few days.

(C. Fillingham-Coxwell, p. 262.)

4. Achol and her Adoptive Lioness-Mother

In this tale told by a twenty-year-old woman, the incest taboo is once again threatened but maintained through the intervention of non-human creatures. (Cf. 'Diirawac and Her Incestuous Brother' p. 104.) Angela Carter comments: 'Incest taboos are particularly complex and important in polygamous societies. Here for example, Achol and her brother cannot recognize each other, having been separated in early childhood through the deceit of their half brothers.'

Part Five: MARRIED WOMEN

1. Story of a Bird Woman

Angela Carter jotted down some salient quotes from *Siberian and Other Folktales* in her notes. 'Stories of bird-women occur among the Yakuts, the Lapps and the Samoyedes'; 'It is not unknown for a Siberian folktale hero to order a large supply of boots when he undertakes a great feat'; and 'Generally speaking, the Chukchis believe that all nature is animated and that every material object can act, speak and walk by itself.'

The transformations of animal goddesses into human wives is the primary component of this story. Japanese and Chinese folklore abound in these. The journey and magical battle of redemption found here are unusual, though. Generally the husband has to content himself with his children or – possibly – rare encounters with the departed wife. The Welsh classic, 'The Song of Taliesin', includes a series of incidents in which the goddess Ceredwen takes the form of birds, ranging from a mighty eagle to a macabre raven and a lowly hen.

(C. Fillingham-Coxwell, p. 82.)

224

2. Father and Mother Both 'Fast'

The true purpose of this joke, which challenges the incest taboo, is to rebound on the main protagonist. It contains bawdy references to adultery and illegitimacy, as do most cuckolded husband jokes. It was collected from Jim Alley by Richard Dorson.

(*Buying the Wind; Regional Folklore in the United States*, Richard M. Dorson [Chicago, 1964], p. 79.)

3. Reason to Beat Your Wife

This piece of scatological humour comes from a thirty-year-old peasant woman from a village in the Nile delta, who remembered hearing it from her mother when she was ten. Her husband put up some resistance to her offer of telling the story to the (male) editor Hasan El-Shamy and acceded to his appeal only on condition that her voice would not be recorded. He enjoyed the story though, and joked that his wife had put it to good use.

The editor adds:

> *The climactic event in this humorous anecdote belongs under the general motif 'absurd wish'. The overall motif may be contrasted to 'The Taming of the Shrew', which carries the local title of 'Kill Your Cat on Your Wedding Night'.*

In fact it is the notion of a husband establishing his superiority over an already dutiful wife that gets its comeuppance here, so it is appropriate that the tale comes from a woman who got it from an older woman. The tale seems to advocate indulgence of the weaknesses of men and the fact that being dutiful pays off – but it hints at concealed guile with the robust, earthy humour familiar in Arab tales. For the audacious use of shit, see 'Šāhīn' (p. 13) and 'Tanjur, Tanjur' (p. 139 and note pp. 222–223).

(Hasan El-Shamy, p. 217.)

4. The Three Lovers

The paramour at the window in this tale from south-west Mexico receives a similar fate to Chaucer's character in 'The Miller's Tale', after having his rump kissed.

(*Cuentos Españoles de Colorado y de Nuevo Méjico Vol. 1*, original text by Juan B. Rael [Stanford University Press, 1957], p. 105. This text translated by Merle E. Simmons, p. 427.)

5. The Seven Leavenings

Angela Carter notes: 'Fatime again – two tales woven together by the personality of the old woman. The woman moves from father's house to husband's house and at no time has space of her own – but don't dismiss the *power* of the "other" – expressed partly in telling of tales, embroidery, basket-making, pottery, wedding songs, laments.' Then she quotes from *Speak Bird, Speak Easy*: 'for the female, conflict is inherent in the structure of the system'.

A footnote from the editors of that book reads: 'Inability to get pregnant and have children is the most common theme in all the folktales in this collection' (p. 207). Without a doubt this is one of the anxieties expressed by women in tales, particularly since 'a man is more easily forgiven if he hits a wife who doesn't have children' (loc. cit.).

The woman in this story is clearly an old crone with magical instincts, a wily and wise helper of women who speaks in a cryptic language of her own; for example, 'The land is longing for its people, I want to go home.' Perhaps the fact that the bread doesn't leaven means that her work, the deliverance of women from their husbands, is never finished – except of course when it suits the storyteller to bring the tale to its end. Being an old woman, she is particularly suitable as the companion of a younger woman and unlikely to misguide her. This gives her the space to practise the necessary wiles to improve the lot of her protégée. Angela Carter quotes, 'Older women are thought to be asexual; the husband is therefore more ready to believe in his wife's innocence after the old woman confirms her interpretation of "black on white"' (p. 211). The frame/vignette format is standard in the Middle East (cf. the Arabian Nights).

The 'seven' in the title suggests that it is part of a cycle of seven stories narrated in the same formula.

(Muhawi and Kanaana, p. 206.)

6. The Untrue Wife's Song

Another daring woman teaches her husband a lesson in this story collected by Ralph S. Boggs from B.L. Lunsford aged forty-four, of North Carolina. This tale is based on 'Old Hildebrande', a longer tale originating from Europe and with an anti-clerical bias.

(*Journal of American Folklore*, 47, 1934, p. 305.)

7. The Woman Who Married Her Son

This story was told by an eighty-two-year-old woman from the village of Rafidiya, district of Nablus, in Palestine, notes Angela Carter.

The familiar scenario of a wife being replaced by a rival has a twist here, when a mother replaces her daughter-in-law in her son's bed and even becomes pregnant. Muhawi and Kanaana compare her pica (craving) for sour grapes to the western one for pickles. The same theme appears in 'Rom', in Jan Knappert's *Myths and Legends of the Congo*, London, 1979. Rom's mother's action is in part prompted by pity that unknown to him, his sweetheart has abandoned him, so it is the young man himself who commits a grisly suicide, chanting:

I entered the lap I came out of
My strength went back where it came from (p. 27).

Here though, the mother is motivated by selfishness and lust. In part her jealousy is triggered by sharing status with another woman. Angela Carter quotes a Palestinian proverb: 'The household of the father is a playground and that of the husband is an education. A woman always belongs in one household or another.' She jots down some phrases: *sexuality* – utterly disruptive of social fabric, especially female sexuality; sexes segregated; 'honour'.

The tale certainly demonstrates the fear of disruption caused by this example of female sexuality gone rampant. The slur to family honour – guarded by men but lodged in women – is punished with death by burning. Interestingly, though the editors Muhawi and Kanaana attribute the teller's omission of the detail of this punishment to her quickening of pace and brevity towards the end of the story, it is really more likely to be her way of reducing the punitive consequences of female transgression. As for the segregation of sexes – perhaps that is what makes it easier to believe that a son could mistake his mother for his wife, however well disguised she may be. Of course, a mother-in-law could be as young as thirty.

The brutality of the wife's action in casually cutting out the innocent servant's tongue is not particularly unusual in fairy tales or for that matter in history. Here it indicates her commitment to silence. When her time of silence is up she allows the messenger to keep his tongue. The silence of a woman in fairy tales, through either enchantment or commitment, is a standard narrative device to facilitate plot development. This is a legacy from the early Middle Ages, when women in European narratives lost their voices during the period between betrothal and marriage. The silence of heroines appears as a redemption motif in several German fairy tales, where loquacious heroines never became popular. In Europe, the silencing of heroines for fear of evil spells or the threat of everlasting condemnation was linked to concepts of power and retribution for the original sin.

(Muhawi and Kanaana, p. 60.)

227

8. Duang and His Wild Wife

This story was told by Nyanjur Deng, another of Chief Deng Majok's daughters, aged twenty. Angela Carter quotes from *Dinka Folktales*: 'The late Chief of the Nyok extended the practice of diplomatic marriage further than anyone else in the history of the Dinka. He had nearly 200 wives drawn from most of the corners of Dinkaland. The family was closely knit, living in several large villages, and all kinds of dialects were spoken and subcultures represented' (p. 99).

Here Duang considers his wife's pica (craving) to be unreasonable since the Dinka deplore the killing of animals for any reason other than ritual or sacrifice. His deceitful act re-emphasises that from Amou's point of view Duang has behaved as an 'outsider'. Having gone through the civilising ritual (see 'Diirawac and Her Incestuous Brother' p. 104 and 'Achol and Her Wild Mother' p. 135) she avenges herself with his death.

(Deng, p. 97.)

9. A Stroke of Luck

One of a body of jocular tales about the inability of women to keep a secret. In some variants the trusting husband gets into trouble; here he turns it to his advantage.

(Degh, p. 147.)

10. The Beans in the Quart Jar

Another cuckolded husband joke, told by Jim Alley to Richard Dorson (see 'Father and Mother Both "Fast"' p. 162 and 'The Untrue Wife's Song' p. 173).

(Dorson, p. 80.)

Part Six: USEFUL STORIES

1. A Fable of a Bird and Her Chicks

A stern and darkly humorous fable about preparation for the tough and persecutory side of life, this story is representative of Yiddish humour and aphorisms.

From *Yiddish Folktales*, edited by Beatrice Siverman Weinreich with a foreword by Leonard Woolf.

2. The Three Aunts

'Old Habetrot' is the English variant of the Norse tale in which the

helper presents herself to the lazy spinner's husband as an illustration of what might happen to his wife if she is forced to pursue the crafts of spinning and weaving (cf. Vasilissa the Fair p. 78, who actually does spin, weave and stitch the king's shirts to perfection, so is naturally under no pressure to continue). The lazy spinner, though, resists the pressure of her straitened circumstances to tie her to a spinning wheel. Since the only release from her penury lies in marrying an affluent man, guile and subterfuge are necessary escape devices. What is most enjoyable is the conspiracy of women, which not only conceals the heroine's trickery but saves her from a future of drudgery and rebuke. Not so the post-1819 editions of the Grimms' story which demands of the reader, 'You must yourself admit that she was a disgusting woman.'
(Darsent, p. 194.)

3. Tale of an Old Woman

'Muriwa' is the Bondes word for sycamore. An almost identical story occurs in the South Pacific. These stories indicate that the conditions imposed by magical helpers are binding. If they are not duly respected, the creatures withdraw (see 'Story of a Bird Woman', p. 159). In both these stories nothing is left behind as a reminder of the days of grace.
(*African Folktales*, edited by Roger Abrahams [New York, Pantheon Folklore Library, 1983), p. 57.)

4. The Height of Purple Passion

An unsolved mystery riddle ending in anti-climax. The author collected it from a nine-year-old American girl in the presence of her stunned parents. The source of the joke is probably a French literary story that still survives under various names including 'The Bordeaux Diligence', which occurs in a Hitchcock anthology of horror stories from the late sixties.
(*The Rationale of the Dirty Joke*, Vol. II, by C. Legman [London, Panther 1973], p. 121.)

5. Salt, Sauce and Spice, Onion Leaves, Pepper and Drippings

The power of the name is a fundamental premiss of this story. The password – the coveted man's name – is only gained after a specific and vital test has been passed. Unlike the Tom Tit Tot group (stories like 'Rumpelstiltskin') the test is service and generosity of spirit rather than trickery and contest. As in all *Dummling* (simpleton) stories, the most unlikely candidate triumphs.
(Abrahams, p. 299.)

NOTES

6. *Two Sisters and the Boa*

A careless joke with a non-human creature results in a scary mistake (see 'The Midwife and the Frog', p. 87). The tale is otherwise of the Beauty and the Beast type. The point that the wicked sister always seems to miss is that the reward lies not in emulating her sister's actions, but in her generosity of spirit. (Source unknown.)

7. *Spreading the Fingers*

A moral tale from Suriname, reminiscent of an oral Islamic tale in which a pauper shares out the food quota allocated him for his entire life and ensures that he never goes hungry. But his game is with God, who is a willing player in it.

(Melville J. and Frances S. Heskovits, p. 355.)

The End

About the Editor and Illustrator

ANGELA CARTER was born in 1940 and died at the age of 51 in February 1992. 'With Angela Carter's death English literature has lost its high sorceress, its benevolent witch queen, a burlesque artist of genius and antic grace', wrote Salman Rushdie.

Before she died, Angela Carter completed *The Second Virago Book of Fairy Tales* which Virago proudly publish to honour and celebrate the memory of a generous and fine woman. This collection reflects her long-standing passion for the art of the fairy tale. One of Britain's most original writers, she was highly acclaimed for her novels, short stories and journalism. She translated the fairy tales of Charles Perrault and adapted two of her works for film, *The Company of Wolves* and *The Magic Toyshop*. Angela Carter's last novel was the much-lauded *Wise Children*, published in 1991.

CORINNA SARGOOD, one of Angela Carter's oldest friends, is the author and illustrator of *Journey to the Jungle: An Artist in Peru*. Her work includes print-making, illustrating books, film animation, furniture decoration, puppet shows, painting and etching. She illustrated this book while living in Mexico.